A TRACE OF CRIME

(A KERI LOCKE MYSTERY—BOOK 4)

BLAKE PIERCE

ISBN: 978-1-64029-111-9

BOOKS BY BLAKE PIERCE

RILEY PAIGE MYSTERY SERIES
ONCE GONE (Book #1)
ONCE TAKEN (Book #2)
ONCE CRAVED (Book #3)
ONCE LURED (Book #4)
ONCE HUNTED (Book #5)
ONCE PINED (Book #6)
ONCE FORSAKEN (Book #7)
ONCE COLD (Book #8)
ONCE STALKED (Book #9)
ONCE LOST (Book #10)
ONCE BURIED (Book #11)

MACKENZIE WHITE MYSTERY SERIES
BEFORE HE KILLS (Book #1)
BEFORE HE SEES (Book #2)
BEFORE HE COVETS (Book #3)
BEFORE HE TAKES (Book #4)
BEFORE HE NEEDS (Book #5)
BEFORE HE FEELS (Book #6)
BEFORE HE SINS (Book #7)
BEFORE HE HUNTS (Book #8)

AVERY BLACK MYSTERY SERIES
CAUSE TO KILL (Book #1)
CAUSE TO RUN (Book #2)
CAUSE TO HIDE (Book #3)
CAUSE TO FEAR (Book #4)
CAUSE TO SAVE (Book #5)

KERI LOCKE MYSTERY SERIES
A TRACE OF DEATH (Book #1)
A TRACE OF MUDER (Book #2)
A TRACE OF VICE (Book #3)
A TRACE OF CRIME (Book #4)
A TRACE OF HOPE (Book #5)

PROLOGUE

Carolyn Rainey could sense something was wrong. It was hard to explain the feeling. But as she walked along the winding residential street to meet her twelve-year-old daughter, the skin on the back of her neck tingled.

On the surface, nothing was out of the ordinary. Carolyn always left the house around 2:30 to meet up with Jessica. She enjoyed the solitary, if brief, walk. It allowed her to clear her head for the second half of the day.

Playa del Rey Middle School let out at 2:35 and Jessica biked home every day. By the time she got everything from her locker into her backpack, made it to the bike rack, said goodbye to her friends, and got on the road, it was usually around 2:45.

Mother and daughter invariably met up at about the halfway point between the school and house around 2:50. Then they would return home together, Carolyn walking, Jessica biking slowly beside her, occasionally circling her mom playfully.

They would talk about the events of the day: who had a crush on whom, which teacher accidentally used a curse word, what song they were working on in choir. When they got home, there was always a snack waiting, after which Jessica would dive into her homework and Carolyn would get back to her own work. They had their routine and it was always the same, give or take a few minutes.

But Carolyn had been walking for close to a half hour now. It was almost 3 p.m. and she was nearly two-thirds of the way to the school. She should have run into Jessica by now.

Maybe her daughter had needed to go to the bathroom. Or maybe she had gotten caught up in a conversation with Kyle, the cute boy from her English class. But the tingling sensation on her neck told Carolyn that something else had happened.

When she rounded the next corner, she saw that she was right. Jessica's purple bike, covered in stickers from the live-action *Beauty and the Beast* movie and photos of her favorite singers, Selena Gomez and Zara Larsson, was lying on its side, half on the sidewalk, half on the road.

She ran over to it and stared, frozen with fear. Looking around desperately, she caught a glimpse of something in the bushes of the nearest house. She hurried over and pulled at it. A branch snapped and the thing came loose.

She looked at it, almost unable to process what she was seeing. It was Jessica's backpack. Carolyn dropped to her knees, her legs suddenly unsteady. Her heart pounded nearly out of her chest as the realization hit her: her daughter had vanished.

CHAPTER ONE

Detective Keri Locke was frustrated. She sat at her desk in LAPD's West Los Angeles Pacific Division, studying the computer screen in front of her.

All around her, the station was bustling. Two teenagers who had snatched a purse and tried to escape on skateboards were being booked. An elderly man was seated at a nearby desk, explaining to a patient officer how someone took his morning paper every day before he could get outside to collect it. Two chubby guys were handcuffed on benches at opposite ends of the holding area because they'd gotten into a mid-afternoon bar fight and still wanted to go at it. Keri ignored them all.

For the last twenty minutes, she'd been poring over every post in the "strictly platonic" section of the Los Angeles Craigslist. It was the same thing she'd done every day for the last six weeks when her friend, newspaper columnist Margaret "Mags" Merrywether, had given her a tip she hoped would help her find her missing daughter, Evie.

Evie had been abducted over five years ago. But after relentless, mostly fruitless searching, Keri had finally found her, only to have her ripped away again. The memory of seeing Evie being driven away in a black van, turning a corner and disappearing from sight, perhaps forever, was too much. She shook the thought from her head and refocused on what was in front of her. After all, it was a lead. And she desperately needed a lead.

It was in late November when Mags had reached out to a shadowy figure known only as the Black Widower. He was a fixer, legendary for doing the dirty work of the rich and powerful, whether that was assassinating political enemies, making troublesome reporters disappear, or stealing sensitive material.

In this case, Keri suspected that he either had her daughter or at least knew her location. That was because just six weeks ago, Keri had tracked down the man who had abducted Evie all those years ago. He was a professional kidnapper known as the

Collector. Keri had learned that his real name was Brian Wickwire after she killed him in a life-or-death struggle.

Using information she later found in Wickwire's apartment, Keri had been able to piece together Evie's location. She'd gone there just in time to see an older man forcing the girl into a black van. She had called out and even locked eyes with her daughter, now thirteen. She had actually heard Evie say the word "Mommy."

But the man rammed Keri's car with the van and escaped. Dazed and unable to follow, she'd been forced to watch helplessly as her daughter disappeared from her sight a second time. Later that night, she'd been told that the van had been found in an empty parking lot. The older man had been shot in the head execution style. Evie was gone.

For several weeks after, the department had run down every lead, shaken every tree in search of her daughter. But they were all dead ends. And without any evidence to go on, the team eventually had to pursue other cases.

Ultimately it was Mags, who looked like a cover model for *Southern Socialite* magazine but was actually a tough-as-nails investigative reporter, who had provided a new lead. She told Keri that the situation with Evie reminded her of someone she had investigated years ago called the Black Widower. He was notorious for double taps in parking lots late at night. He was known to drive a Lincoln Continental without plates, which had been visible in the parking lot surveillance footage where the black van was found.

And it was Mags who, using a tip from a confidential source and writing anonymously, had reached out to him using the seemingly outdated Craigslist message board. It was apparently how he liked to communicate with potential new clients.

And to her amazement, he'd responded almost immediately. He said that he'd be in touch and would soon ask her to create a new email address so they could communicate confidentially.

Unfortunately, after that initial communication, he'd gone dark. Mags had reached out a second time about three weeks ago but hadn't heard anything back. Keri wanted her to try again but Mags insisted it was a bad idea. Pressuring this guy would only make him go to ground. As frustrating as it was, they had to wait for him to reach out again.

But Keri was worried it would never happen. And as she scoured the "strictly platonic" board for the third time today, she couldn't help think that what had once seemed like such a promising lead might just be another devastating dead end.

She closed the window on her screen and shut her eyes as she took several deep breaths. Trying not to let hopelessness overwhelm her, she allowed her mind to drift wherever it wanted. Sometimes it took her to unexpected, revealing places that helped unlock puzzles she thought were beyond her.

What am I missing? There's always a clue. I just have to recognize it when I see it.

But it didn't work this time. Her brain kept circling around the idea of the Black Widower, untraceable and unknowable.

Of course, at one time she had thought that same thing about the Collector too. And despite that, she had been able to track him down, kill him, and use information in his apartment to discover her daughter's location. If she did it once, she could do it again.

Maybe I need to review the Collector's emails again or go back through his apartment. Maybe I missed something the first time because I didn't know what to look for.

It occurred to her that both men—the Collector and the Black Widower—operated in the same world. They were both professional criminals for hire—one a child abductor, the other a killer. It didn't seem impossible that their paths might have crossed at some point. Maybe the Collector had a record of that somewhere.

And then she realized there was one other piece of connective tissue. They both had links to the same man, a well-heeled downtown lawyer named Jackson Cave.

To most people, Cave was a prominent corporate attorney. But Keri knew him as a shady dealmaker who represented the dregs of society, was secretly involved in everything from sex slave rings to drug trafficking operations to outright murder for hire. Unfortunately, she couldn't prove any of that without revealing some secrets of her own.

But even without proof, she was certain that Cave was involved with both men. And if that was the case, maybe they had interacted. It wasn't much. But it was something to follow up on. And she needed something, anything, to keep her from going crazy.

She was about to go to the evidence room to look through Wickwire's stuff again when her partner, Detective Ray Sands, walked over.

"I ran into Lieutenant Hillman in the break room," he said. "He just got a call and he's assigned us a case. I can give you the details on the drive over. Are you okay to head out? You look like you're in the middle of something."

"Just some research," she answered, locking the screen, "nothing that can't wait. Let's go."

Ray looked at her curiously. She knew he was fully aware that she wasn't being completely straight with him. But he said nothing as she stood up and led the way out of the station.

*

Keri and Ray were members of West Los Angeles Division's Missing Persons Unit. It was generally regarded as the best in all of the LAPD and they were the two major reasons why. They had solved more cases in the last eighteen months than most entire divisions had in double that time.

It was also true that Keri was viewed as a loose cannon who could create as many problems as she solved. In fact, she was currently technically under investigation by Internal Affairs for how the Collector confrontation had gone down. Everyone kept telling her it was only a formality. And yet it hovered over her, like a rain cloud always threatening to open up.

Still, despite the corners they sometime cut, no one could question their results. Ray and Keri were the best of the best, even if they were going through a few personal hiccups these days.

Keri chose not to think about that as Ray walked her through the case details on the drive over to the scene. She couldn't handle focusing on both a missing persons case and her complicated relationship with Ray at the same time. In fact, she had to look out the window to avoid focusing on his strong, dark forearms gripping the steering wheel.

"The potential victim is Jessica Rainey," Ray said. "She's twelve and lives in Playa del Rey. The mom typically meets her on her bike ride home from school. Today she found the bike lying at the edge of the street and her backpack shoved in a bush nearby."

"Do we know anything about the parents?" Keri asked as they barreled down Culver Boulevard in the direction of the seaside community, where she also happened to live. Often parental estrangement was a determining factor. A good half of their missing child cases involved one parent kidnapping the kid.

"Not much yet," Ray said as he weaved through traffic. It was early January and cold out but Keri noticed beads of sweat trickling down Ray's bald head as he drove. He seemed nervous about something. Before she could pursue it, he went on.

"They're married. Mom works at home. She designs 'artisanal' wedding invitations. Dad works in Silicon Beach, for a tech company. They have a younger child, a six-year-old boy. He's in his school's aftercare today. The mom checked and he's there, safe and sound. Hillman told her to leave him there for now, so his day can stay normal for as long as possible."

"Not much to go on," Keri noted. "Is CSU on the way?"

"Yeah, Hillman sent them at the same time as us. They may already be there, hopefully processing the bike and backpack for prints."

Ray zipped past the intersection with Jefferson Boulevard. Keri could almost see her apartment in the distance now. The ocean was only half a mile beyond that. The Rainey home was in a separate, fancier section of the community, on a big hill with multimillion-dollar homes. They were less than five minutes away.

Keri noticed that Ray had become unusually quiet. She could tell he was working up the courage to say something. She couldn't explain why but she dreaded it.

She and Ray Sands had known each other for over seven years, back before Evie had been abducted, when she was a criminology professor at Loyola Marymount University and he was the local detective who'd been volunteered by his boss to talk to her class.

After Evie was taken and Keri's life had fallen apart, he'd been there both as a detective working the case and as a supportive friend. He was there for her during her divorce and her career meltdown. It was Ray who had convinced her to join the force. And when she came to West LA division after two years as a street officer, she became his partner in the Missing Persons Unit.

Somewhere along the line, their relationship had gotten closer. Maybe it was partly all the playful flirting. Maybe it was the fact that they'd each saved the other's life multiple times. Maybe it was partly simple attraction. She'd even noticed that

Ray, a notorious ladies' man, had stopped mentioning other women, even in jest.

Whatever it was, in the last few months, they'd spent a lot of time hanging out at each other's place after work, going to restaurants together, calling each other for non-work conversations. It was like they were a couple in all ways but one. They'd never made that final leap to consummate their connection. Hell, they'd never even kissed.

So why am I dreading what I think he's about to say?

Keri loved spending time with Ray and a part of her wanted to take things to the next level. She felt so close to the man that it was almost weird that nothing had happened. And yet, for reasons she couldn't find words for, she feared taking that next step. And she could feel Ray about to cross the threshold.

"Can I ask you something?" he said as he turned left off Culver onto Pershing Drive, the snaking road that led up to the wealthiest part of Playa del Rey.

"I guess."

No. Please no. You're going to ruin everything.

"I feel closer to you than anyone else in the world," he said softly. "And I get the sense that you feel the same way toward me. Am I right?"

"Yes."

We're almost to the house. Just drive a little faster so I can get out of this car.

"But we haven't done anything about that," he said.

"I guess not," she agreed, unsure what else to say.

"I want to change that."

"Uh-huh."

"So I'm officially asking you out on a date, Keri. I'd like to take you out this weekend. Would you like to go to dinner with me?"

There was a long pause before she responded. When she opened her mouth, she wasn't entirely sure what would come out.

"I don't think so, Ray. Thanks though."

Ray sat in the driver's seat, his eyes straight ahead, his mouth agape, saying nothing.

Keri, also stunned at her own response, stayed silent as well and fought the urge to jump out of the moving car.

CHAPTER TWO

Without another word between them, they turned right off Pershing Drive onto the steep incline of Rees Street and then left onto Ridge Avenue. Keri saw the Crime Scene Unit truck in front of a big house at the top of the hill.

"I see the CSU truck," she said dumbly, just to break the silence.

Ray nodded and pulled up behind it. They got out and headed for the house. Keri fiddled with her gun belt to allow Ray to get ahead of her a bit. She could sense he wasn't in the mood to walk side by side.

As she followed him down the walk to the front door, she once again marveled at the sheer physical specimen he was. Ray was a six-foot-four, 230-pound, bald, forty-one-year-old African-American former professional boxer.

Despite the challenges he'd faced since retiring from the sport, including a divorce, getting a glass eye, and being shot, he still looked like he could step into the ring. He was muscular but not heavy, with a lithe agility unexpected for a man his size. There was a reason he was so popular with women.

A few months ago, she might have wondered why he'd be into her. But lately, despite nearing her thirty-sixth birthday, she'd recaptured some of the youthful zest that had made her pretty popular herself.

She would never be a supermodel. But since she'd resumed Krav Maga and cut down on the drinking, she had lost almost ten pounds. She was back to her pre-divorce fighting weight of 125, which looked pretty darned good on her five-foot-six frame. The bags under her eyes had disappeared and she occasionally wore her dirty blonde hair down instead of in her usual ponytail. She was feeling good about herself these days. So why had she said no to the date?

Deal with your personal issues later, Keri. Focus on your job. Focus on the case.

She forced all extraneous thoughts out of her head and glanced around as they approached the house, trying to get a sense of the Raineys' world.

Playa del Rey wasn't a large neighborhood but the social divisions were quite stark. Down near where Keri lived, in an apartment above a cheap Chinese restaurant, most folks were working class.

The same was true of the small residential streets heading inland off Manchester Avenue. They were almost all populated by the residents of huge condominium and apartment complexes. But closer to the beach, and on the large hill where the Raineys lived, the homes varied from big to massive, and almost all of them had ocean views.

This house was somewhere in between big and massive, not truly a mansion, but as close as one could get without the protective outer wall and the huge pillars. Despite that, it felt like a genuine home.

The grass on the front lawn was a little long and it was littered with toys, including a plastic slide and a tricycle that was currently lying upside down. The path they took to reach the house was covered in colored chalk designs, some clearly the work of a six-year-old. Other sections were more sophisticated, done by a preteen.

Ray rang the bell and stared straight at the peephole, refusing to glance over at Keri. She could feel the frustration and confusion emanating from him and chose to stay quiet. She didn't know what to say anyway.

Keri heard the rapid footsteps of someone running to the door and seconds later it opened to reveal a woman in her late thirties. She was dressed in slacks and a casual but professional top. She had short dark hair and was attractive in a pleasant, open-faced way that even her tear-stained eyes couldn't hide.

"Mrs. Rainey?" Keri asked in her most reassuring voice.

"Yes. Are you the detectives?" she asked pleadingly.

"We are," Keri answered. "I'm Keri Locke and this is my partner, Ray Sands. May we come in?"

"Of course. Please. My husband, Tim, is upstairs gathering pictures of Jess. He'll be down in a minute. Do you know anything yet?"

"Not yet," Ray said. "But I see our crime scene unit has arrived. Where are they?"

"In the garage—they're checking Jess's things for fingerprints. One of them told me I shouldn't have moved them from where I found them. But I was afraid to just leave them on the street. What if they were stolen and we lost any evidence?"

As she spoke, her voice got higher and the words started tumbling out at a frenzied pace. Keri could tell she was barely holding it together.

"It's okay, Mrs. Rainey," she assured her. "CSU will still be able to get any potential prints and you can show us where you found her things later."

Just then they heard footsteps and turned to see a man walking down the stairs holding a stack of photos. Skinny, with a bird's nest of unruly brown hair and thin wire-rimmed glasses, Tim Rainey wore khakis and a button-down shirt. He looked exactly as Keri imagined a tech industry executive would.

"Tim," his wife said, "these are the detectives here to help find Jess."

"Thank you for coming," he said, his voice almost a whisper.

Keri and Ray shook his hand and she noticed that the other hand holding the pictures was shaking slightly. His eyes weren't red like his wife's but his brow was furrowed and his whole face looked pinched. He seemed like a man overwhelmed by the stress of the moment. Keri couldn't blame him. After all, she'd been there.

"Why don't we all sit down and you can tell us what you know," she said, noting that his knees seemed close to buckling.

Carolyn Rainey led them all to the front sitting room where her husband dropped the pictures on a coffee table and slumped heavily onto a couch. She sat beside him and put her hand on his knee, which was bouncing up and down wildly. He got the message and sat still.

"I was walking to meet Jess after school," Carolyn began. "We have the same routine every day. I walk. She rides her bike. We meet up somewhere in between and come back together. We almost always connect around the same spot, give or take a block."

Tim Rainey's knee started bouncing again and she gave him a gentle pat to remind him to collect himself. Once again, he stilled. She continued.

"I started to worry when I got two-thirds of the way to school and hadn't seen her. That's only happened twice before. Once was because she forgot a textbook in her locker and had to go back. The other time she had a bad stomachache. Both times she called me to let me know what was going on."

"I'm sorry to interrupt," Ray said. "But can you give me her cell number? We might be able to trace it."

"I thought of that first thing. In fact, I called her as soon as I saw her stuff. It started ringing right away. I found it under the same bush her backpack was in."

"Do you have it now?" Keri asked. "There might still be valuable data to gather from it."

"The crime scene people are dusting it too."

"That's great," Keri said. "We'll look at it when they're done. Let's go through a few basic questions if you don't mind."

"Of course," Carolyn Rainey said.

"Had Jessica mentioned anything recently about having a falling out with a friend?"

"No. She did change who she had a crush on recently. School just started up again this week after winter break and she said the time off had made her see things differently. But since the first boy never even knew she liked him, I don't think that matters."

"Still, if you could write down both their names, it would be helpful," Ray said. "Did she ever mention seeing any unusual people either at school or on her way there or home?"

The Raineys both shook their heads.

"May I?" Keri asked, pointing to the photos on the table.

Carolyn nodded. Keri picked up the stack and began to go through them. Jessica Rainey was a perfectly normal-looking twelve-year-old girl with a broad smile, her mother's twinkly eyes, and her father's wild brown hair.

"We're going to follow every possible lead," Ray assured them. "But I don't want you to jump to any conclusions just yet. There's still a chance that this is just a misunderstanding of some sort. We haven't had a report of an abducted child in this community in well over two years, so we don't want to make any assumptions at this point."

"I appreciate that," Carolyn Rainey said. "But Jess isn't the sort of girl to just run off to a friend's and leave all her stuff lying by the side of the street. And she would never willingly part with her phone. It's just not her."

Ray didn't reply. Keri knew he had felt obligated to suggest other possibilities. And he was usually far less likely to leap to the abduction theory than Keri. But even he was having trouble coming up with legitimate reasons why Jessica would abandon all her things.

"Is it okay if we take a few of these photos?" she asked, breaking the uncomfortable silence. "We want to circulate them among law enforcement."

"Of course. Take them all if you want," Carolyn said.

"Not all," Tim said, pulling one out of the pile. It was the first time he'd spoken since they all sat down. "I'd like to hold on to this one if you can do without it."

It was a photo of Jessica in the woods wearing hiking gear, with a way-too-big-for-her backpack strapped to her back. Her face was smeared with what looked like war paint and she had a rainbow bandanna tied around her head. She was grinning happily. It wouldn't help much for identification purposes. And even if it had, Keri could tell it was very special to him.

"Keep it. We've got more than enough," she said softly before getting down to business. "Now there are a few things we are going to need from you and all of it in short order. You may want to write this down. In situations like this, time is crucial so we may have to sacrifice your feelings for information. Are you two okay with that?"

They both nodded.

"Good," she said before diving in. "So here's what's going to happen. Mrs. Rainey, we're going to need you to show us the route you took to meet your daughter and her usual route from that point to the school. We're going to want to look through her room, including any computers or tablets she might have. As I mentioned, we'll also look through her phone when CSU is done with it."

"Okay," Mrs. Rainey said, writing it all down as Keri continued.

"We'll need the contact information for every friend you can think of and any kids she might have had issues with during the last year. We'll need the principal's number. We can get teacher and guidance counselor contact information from the school. But if you already have it, that would be great."

"We can get you all that," Carolyn promised them.

"We'll also need the names and numbers of any coaches or tutors she has," Ray added, "as well as those names of both the boys she was crushing on. Detective Locke and I will split up to maximize time."

Keri looked at him. His voice sounded completely normal but she could tell that there was more than simple professional expediency at work.

Don't take it personally. It's a good idea.

"Yes," she agreed. "Why don't Mrs. Rainey and I walk the route to school before it gets too dark out? At this time of year, the sun will be setting in less than an hour. You can give me those contact numbers on the way."

"And Mr. Rainey," Ray said, "you can show me Jessica's room. After that, I recommend you go get your son. What's his name?"

"Nathaniel. Nate."

"Okay, well, CSU will be gone by the time you get back so there won't be so many people around. You're going to want to try to keep things as normal as possible for him. That way, if we need to ask him questions, he won't shut down."

Tim Rainey nodded absently, as if he'd only just remembered he had a son as well. Ray continued.

"When you go, I'll head over to the school to talk to the folks there. We'll also check to see if there's any video that can be helpful. Mrs. Rainey, I'll meet you and Detective Locke at the school and drive you back home."

"Are you going to put out an Amber Alert?" Carolyn Rainey asked, referring to the abduction messages sent out to the general public.

"Not yet," Ray said. "It's very possible that we'll do that soon, but not until we have more information to share. We just don't know enough yet."

"Let's get moving," Keri said. "The more quickly we check off all these boxes, the better picture we'll have of what might have happened."

They all stood up. Carolyn Rainey grabbed her purse and led them to the front door.

"I'll let you know if we learn anything," she said to her husband as she gave him a kiss on the cheek. He nodded, then pulled her in for a long, tight hug.

Keri glanced over at Ray, who was watching the couple. Despite himself, he glanced over at her. She could still see the hurt in his eyes.

"I'll call you when we get to the school," Keri said quietly to Ray. He nodded without replying.

She felt stung by his coldness but she got it. He had opened up and taken a big risk. And she had shut him down without explanation. It was probably good that they had some space for the next little while.

As the two women stepped outside and began to walk away from the house, one thought reverberated in her head.

I   have   screwed   up   massively.

CHAPTER THREE

Ninety minutes later, back at her desk, Keri let out a sigh of deep frustration. Most of the last hour and a half had been fruitless.

They hadn't found anything unusual on the walk to the school and didn't come across any obvious signs of struggle. There were no odd tire marks near the spot where Mrs. Rainey had found Jessica's stuff. Keri had stopped at every house nearby to determine if any residents had street-facing video cameras that might be of use. None did.

When they got to the school, Ray was already there talking to the principal, who promised to send out an email blast to all school parents asking for any information they might have. The security officer had all the surveillance footage from the day queued up so Keri suggested Ray stick around and view it while she got Mrs. Rainey back home and returned to the office to call all the potential leads.

To Carolyn Rainey, it must have simply looked like two partners effectively multi-tasking. And to a degree, it was. But the thought of sitting awkwardly in the passenger seat as Ray drove her back to West LA division was something she wasn't up for right now.

So instead, they got a Lyft back to the Rainey house and Keri continued to the station from there. That's where she'd spent the last half hour calling all Jessica's friends and classmates. No one had anything unusual to share. Three friends all remembered her leaving school on her bike and waving to them as she left the parking lot. Everything seemed fine.

She called both the boys Jessica had crushes on in recent weeks and while both knew who she was, neither seemed to know her well or even be aware of how she felt. Keri wasn't shocked at that. She remembered that at that age, she'd filled up whole notebooks with the names of boys she liked, without ever actually speaking to them.

She spoke to, or left messages with, all of Jessica's teachers, her softball coach, her math tutor, and even the head of the neighborhood watch group. No one she reached knew anything.

She called Ray, who picked up on the first ring.

"Sands."

"I've got nothing here," she said, deciding to focus solely on the matter at hand. "No one saw anything out of the ordinary. Her friends say everything seemed fine when she left school. I'm still waiting for some calls back but I'm not optimistic. You having better luck?"

"Not so far. The video camera range only extends to the end of the school's block in each direction. I can see her saying goodbye to her friends, just as you describe, then biking off. Nothing happens while she's visible. I'm having the guard queue up footage from earlier in the week to see if there was anyone loitering around on prior days. It might be a while."

Unspoken in that last line was the assumption he wouldn't be returning to the station anytime soon. She pretended not to notice.

"I think we should post the Amber Alert," she said. "It's six p.m. now. So it's been three hours since her mom called nine-one-one. We don't have any evidence suggesting this is anything other than an abduction. If she was taken right after school, between two forty-five and three p.m., she could be as far as Palm Springs or San Diego by now. We need to get as many eyes on this as possible."

"Agreed," Ray said. "Can you honcho that so I can keep reviewing this footage?"

"Of course. Are you coming back to the station afterward?"

"I don't know," he answered noncommittally. "Depends on what I find."

"Okay, well, keep me posted," she said.

"Will do," he replied and hung up without saying goodbye.

Keri ordered herself not to focus on the perceived slight and put her attention into preparing the Amber Alert and getting it out. As she was finishing up, she saw her boss, Lieutenant Cole Hillman, walking toward his office.

He was wearing his usual uniform of slacks, sport coat, loose tie, and short-sleeved dress shirt that he couldn't keep tucked in because of his ample girth. He was a little over fifty but the job had aged him so that there were deep lines in his forehead and at the corners of his eyes. His salt-and-pepper hair was more salt than pepper these days.

She thought he was going to come over to her desk and demand a status update but he never even looked in her direction. That was fine with her, as she wanted to check with the CSU folks to see of they'd found any prints.

After she submitted the Amber Alert, Keri walked though station bullpen, which was unusually quiet for this time of night, and down the hall. She knocked on the CSU door and poked her head in without waiting for permission.

"Any luck on the Jessica Rainey case?"

The clerk, a twenty-something girl with dark hair and glasses, looked up from the magazine she'd been reading. Keri didn't recognize her. The CSU clerk job was a grind and had a lot of turnover. She typed the name in the database.

"Nothing from the backpack or bike," the girl said. "They're still checking a few prints from the phone but the way they were talking, it didn't sound promising."

"Can you please have them let Detective Keri Locke know as soon as they're done, regardless of the result? Even if there are no usable prints, I need to check that phone."

"You got it, Detective," she said, burying her nose back in the magazine before Keri had even closed the door.

Standing alone in the quiet hallway, Keri took a deep breath and realized there was nothing else for her to do. Ray was checking the school surveillance footage. She had put out the Amber Alert. The CSU report was pending and she couldn't look at Jessica's phone until they were done with it. She'd either spoken to or was waiting to hear back from everyone she had called.

She leaned against the wall and closed her eyes, allowing her brain to relax for the first time in hours. But as soon as she did, unwelcome thoughts flooded in.

She saw the image of Ray's face, hurt and confused. She saw a black van with her daughter inside rounding a corner into darkness. She saw the eyes of the Collector as she squeezed his neck, draining the life out of the man who'd abducted her daughter over five years ago, even as he was already dying from a head wound. She saw grainy footage of a man known only as the Black Widower as he shot another man in the head, took Evie from the man's van, and shoved her into the trunk of his own car before disappearing forever.

Her eyes snapped open and she saw that she was facing the evidence room. She'd been in there many times in recent weeks, poring over photos from Brian "The Collector" Wickwire's apartment.

The actual evidence was held at Downtown Division because his apartment was in their jurisdiction. They had consented to let the West LA police photographer take pictures of everything as long as it stayed in the evidence room. As she had killed the man, Keri wasn't in a position to argue with them.

But she hadn't gone through the photos in several days and now something about them was eating at her. There was an itch at the edge of her brain that she just couldn't scratch, some kind of connection she knew was hiding just out of the corner of her consciousness. She walked into the room.

The evidence clerk wasn't surprised to see her and slid the sign-in sheet toward her without a word. She checked in, then went straight to the row with the box of photos. She didn't need the reference data as she knew exactly what row and shelf it was. She grabbed the box from the shelf and lugged it to one of the tables in the back.

She sat down, turned on the desk lamp, and spread all the photos out in her front of her. She'd looked at them dozens of times before. Every book Wickwire owned was catalogued and photographed, as was every piece of clothing and each item from his kitchen shelves. This man was believed to be involved in the abduction and sale of as many as fifty children over the years and the detectives from Downtown Division were leaving no stone unturned.

But Keri sensed that what was teasing her wasn't in any of those photos she'd studied previously. It was something she'd only registered in passing before. Something had been jogged in her mind when she stood in the hall minutes before, letting all her painful memories wash over her.

What is it? What's the connection you're trying to make?

And then she saw it. In the background of a picture of the Collector's desk was a series of nature photos. They were all 5 x 7 images lined up in a row. There was a frog on a rock. Beside it was picture of a jackrabbit with its ears pricked up. And next to that was a beaver working on a dam. A woodpecker was in mid-peck. A salmon caught on film as it leapt from a stream. And next to it was the image of a spider on a patch of dirt—a black widow.

Black widow. Black Widower. Is there something to that?

It might have just been a coincidence. Obviously the Downtown detectives didn't think much of the photos as they hadn't even been catalogued as evidence. But Keri knew that the Collector liked to keep coded records.

In fact, that's how she'd found the addresses where Evie and multiple other abductees were being kept. The Collector had hidden them in plain sight, in an alpha-numeric code on a bunch of seemingly innocuous postcards in his desk drawer.

Keri knew that the Collector and the Black Widower shared a connection: they had both been hired at various points by the attorney Jackson Cave.

Did their paths cross at some point, maybe on a job? Was this Wickwire's way of keeping the contact information of a fellow sinner for hire, in case they ever needed to team up?

Keri felt a certainty wash over her, one that usually only came when she'd uncovered a crucial clue in a case. She was certain that if she could access that photo, she would find something useful about it.

The only problem was that it was in Brian Wickwire's apartment, which was still cordoned off by the Downtown police. The last time she'd tried to get in, two weeks ago, there was crime scene tape all around it and two cops stationed in front of the building to deter any looky-loos.

Keri was just beginning to consider how she might navigate that challenge when her phone rang. It was Ray.

"Hey," she said hesitantly.

"Can you come back to the Rainey place right now?" he asked, skipping the pleasantries.

"Of course. What's up?"

"They just got a ransom note."

CHAPTER FOUR

Twenty anxious minutes later, Keri pulled up to the Rainey house. Once again a CSU truck was already out front. She knocked on the front door. Ray opened it almost immediately and she could tell from the look on his face that the situation was grim. She glanced over his shoulder and saw the Raineys sitting together on a couch. She was weeping. He looked shell-shocked.

"I'm glad you're here," Ray said sincerely. "I've only been here five minutes but I'm having a hard time keeping them from going off the rails."

"Is there a clock on the note?" Keri asked quietly as she stepped inside.

"Yeah. The guy wants the transfer to happen tonight at midnight. He's demanding a hundred grand."

"Jeez."

"That's not the worst of it," Ray said. "You need to read the letter. It's…weird."

Keri walked into the room. One CSU investigator was dusting what looked like a FedEx envelope. She looked back at Ray, who nodded.

"Crazy, huh?" he said. "I've never heard of a ransom note come via FedEx before. It was same-day. I already gave the tracking number to Edgerton. He says it was posted from a location in El Segundo. The time stamp was one fifty-eight p.m."

"But that's before Jessica was taken," Keri said.

"Exactly. The abductor must have sent it before he grabbed her—pretty brazen. Suarez is headed over there now to look for any potential footage from the place."

"Sounds good," Keri said as she headed to the living room where the Raineys sat. She was reassured that some of their best people were in the mix. Detective Kevin Edgerton was a tech wizard and Detective Manny Suarez was a dogged, experienced cop. Nothing would slip by them.

"Hi," she said softly and the Raineys both looked up at her. Carolyn's eyes were puffy and red but there were no tears left. Tim was ghostly pale, his face dour and tight.

"Hello, Detective," Carolyn managed to whisper.

"May I take a look at the letter?" she asked, glancing at the sheet of paper on the coffee table. It was already in a clear evidence envelope.

They nodded wordlessly. She moved closer to get a better look. Even before reading the contents, she could tell that the letter hadn't been printed using a computer. It had been typed on a standard 8 x 11 sheet of paper. That immediately concerned her.

Every computer printer had its own identifiable signature, represented through a pattern of dots not recognizable to the undiscerning eye. The dots printed out in a code along with the text of the document and provided the make, model, and even the serial number of the printer used. If the person who typed this letter knew enough to avoid a computer printer, it suggested he probably wasn't an amateur.

The letter itself was equally troubling. It read:

Your child has a dark spirit. The spirit must be pruned so that a healthy child can grow in its place. That will destroy the body of the child but save its soul. So sad but it must be done. The hothouse desire of the creator demands it. I can free this child of the spirit with my holy shears, the mechanism of the Lord. The demons must be uprooted from within her.

However, if you promise to redeem her yourself through bloodletting purification as he has commanded, I will return her to you for the procedure. But you must compensate me for my sacrifice. I demand $100,000 to be made whole. It must be cash, untraceable. Do not involve the authorities, the filthy purveyors of sordid wretchedness upon this world. If you do, I will return the child to the soil from which she came. I will employ the machinery of the Lord to spread her dripping remains among the spoiled weeds of the city. I have provided proof that I am sincere in my claims.

Midnight. Father only. For fathers alone will save this world from impurity.

Chace Park. The bridge by the water.

$100,000. Midnight. Alone.

The flesh of your flesh depends on your supplication.

Keri looked up at Ray. There was so much to process that she chose to set most of it aside for the time being and focus on the clearest elements of the letter.

"What does he mean about providing proof?" she asked him.

"There were several strands of hair in a baggie in the package as well," he answered. "We're having them tested to see if they're a match."

"Okay, there's a lot to pore over in that thing," Keri said, turning to the Raineys. "But for now let's focus on the non-psycho stuff. First off, you made the right choice by reaching out to us. Parents who follow instructions not to contact authorities usually have worse outcomes."

"I didn't want to call you," Tim Rainey admitted. "But Carrie insisted."

"Well, we're glad you did," Keri reiterated, then turned to Ray. "Have you talked to them about the money?"

"We were just about to when you got here," Ray said, then focused his attention on the Raineys. "It's not a bad idea to secure the money, even if we hope not to hand it over. It gives us more options. Have you thought about how you might get it?"

"We have the money," Tim Rainey said, "but not in cash. I called our bank to talk about transferring some securities over. They said that it's hard to do that kind of transaction after hours and impossible on such short notice."

"I've reached out to our fund managers and they say the same thing," Carolyn Rainey added. "They might be able to get it for us by early tomorrow morning, but not by midnight and not in cash."

Keri turned to Ray.

"It is odd that he had the letter arrive so late," she said. "He had to know it would be almost impossible to get the money in time. Why make it so difficult?"

"This guy doesn't sound like he's operating from a full deck," Ray noted. "Maybe he's not up to speed on the timing challenges of financial institutions."

"There is another option," Tim Rainey interrupted.

"What's that?" Ray asked.

"I work for Venergy, the new mobile gaming platform based in Playa Vista. I work directly for Gary Rosterman, the guy who runs the company. He's filthy rich and he likes me. Plus Jessica and his daughter went to the same Montessori school until last year. They're friends. I know he has cash on hand. Maybe he'd front me."

"Call him," Ray said. "But if he agrees, ask him to be discreet."

Rainey nodded aggressively. His dark visage lifted slightly. He seemed heartened by having renewed hope. Or maybe it was just having something on which to focus his attention.

As he dialed the number, Ray turned back to Keri and nodded for them to step away from the Raineys. When they were out of earshot, he whispered, "I think we should take the letter back to the station. We need to have the whole unit on this, get their ideas on what it means; maybe bring in the psychologist. We should check for recent similar cases in the area."

"Agreed," Keri said. "I also want to filter the letter through the federal database to see if it matches anything else. Who knows what we'll find? I've got a really bad feeling about this one."

"More than usual? Why?"

Keri explained her concerns about typing the letter versus using a computer. It resonated with Ray.

"Whether this guy is crazy or crazy like a fox, he seems like a pro," he said.

Tim Rainey ended his call and turned to them.

"Gary said he'll do it," he said. "He said he can have the cash in hand in about three hours."

"That's great," Ray said. "We'll send someone to collect it when it's ready. We don't want a civilian transporting that kind of money if we can avoid it."

"We're going to head back to the station now," Keri told them. Seeing the sudden anxiety in their faces, she quickly added, "We're going to leave two uniformed officers here with you, as a precaution. They can reach us any time."

"But why are you leaving?" Carolyn Rainey asked.

"We want to run the ransom note through our databases and talk to some experts. We're getting our entire Missing Persons Unit involved in your case. But I promise we'll be back in a few hours. We'll lay out the whole plan for the park with you and explain exactly what we're doing. As soon as we leave you, I'm going to call to have surveillance set up there right away. Everything will be in place well in advance of the meet. We've got this."

Carolyn Rainey stood up and gave her a surprisingly powerful hug. She did the same to Ray. Tim Rainey nodded politely at both of them. Keri could tell that his brief respite from his angst had faded and he was back in permanent crisis mode.

She understood his position better than most and knew that trying to talk him down or tell him to try to be calm was a waste of time. His daughter was missing. He was freaking out. He just did it more quietly than most.

As they left, Ray muttered under his breath, "We better find her quick. If we don't, I'm worried her dad is going to have a stroke."

Keri wanted to disagree but couldn't. If she'd gotten a letter like this when Evie was taken, she might have literally lost her mind. But the Raineys had something going for them, even if they didn't know it. They had Keri.

"Then let's find her quick," she said.

CHAPTER FIVE

"I'm telling you, it's just a cover," Detective Frank Brody shouted indignantly. "All that blather about mechanisms and the Lord is just to throw us off. This guy is a con man, pure and simple!"

The station conference room was a mass of noisy, angry voices and it was starting to piss Keri off. She was tempted to yell at everyone to shut up, but painful experience had taught her that some of these people needed to wear themselves out before anything useful could be accomplished.

Brody, an old-school veteran of the unit less than a month from retirement, was convinced the letter was a sham. As usual, he had some kind of sauce on his shirt, which was tucked in but missing a button so that part of his large stomach was exposed. And as usual, Keri thought, he was more interested in being loud than in being right.

"You don't know that!" shouted back Officer Jamie Castillo. "You just want it to be true because that makes the case easier to understand."

Castillo wasn't a detective yet, but because of her competence and enthusiasm, she'd become essentially a junior member of the unit, almost always assigned to their cases. And despite her junior status, she was no shrinking violet.

Right now, her dark eyes were blazing and her black hair, tied back in a ponytail, was bobbing up and down along with her animated responses. Her muscular arms and athletic frame were both tightly coiled in frustration.

"None of us are experts in this sort of thing," Detective Kevin Edgerton insisted. "We need to bring in the police psychologist."

Keri wasn't surprised that Edgerton wanted to go that route. Tall and skinny with perpetually unkempt brown hair, he was a computer genius who knew the ins and outs of everything from a smartphone to the utility grid. But not yet thirty years old, he didn't always trust his instincts when it came to things with less clear-cut solutions. It was his nature to defer to expertise, if it was available.

The problem was that Keri wasn't confident the police psychologist would have any more insight into the letter than the rest of them. Any conclusions he was likely to draw would just be speculation. If that was the case, she trusted her own speculation more than most others'.

Lieutenant Hillman held up his hands in an appeal for calm and quiet. To Keri's surprise, everyone complied.

"I sent a copy of the letter to Dr. Feeney at home. He's looking at it now. We'll probably get feedback soon. In the meantime, any other thoughts? Sands?"

Ray had been sitting quietly, rubbing the top of his bald head, taking it all in. From this angle, Keri could clearly see the reflection of the station lights off the glass left eye that replaced the eye he'd lost boxing. He looked up and she could tell where he stood before he even spoke.

"I'm inclined to agree with Frank. That letter is just so over the top that it's hard to buy. Everything is so overheated. That is, except for the part about wanting the money and where to bring it. That section is completely straightforward; pretty convenient, if you ask me. Still…"

"What?" Hillman asked.

"Well, I'm just not sure whether it makes any difference. We know so little and don't have much time. Regardless of whether he's a psycho or a con artist, there's still a drop with him in a few hours."

"I'm not sure I agree," Keri finally said. She didn't love contradicting her partner publicly under any circumstances and especially not with the way things were between them at the moment. But it wasn't about that right now. It was about the job and finding this girl. Keri had never held her tongue about a case before and she wasn't about to start now, regardless of the personal consequences.

"Look, I don't know for sure if this guy is faking or for real. But I think it does matter which is true. If he's just pretending to be some kind of religious fanatic and this is all just about money, I'd prefer it. Then this is transactional for him, not personal. And that scenario is way more predictable. It means he's more likely to show up. And it's more of a priority for him to keep Jessica alive."

"But you don't buy it," Ray said, proving he knew her as well as she knew him.

"I'm skeptical. I think it's possible that money stuff was so straightforward because he didn't really believe in it and was just saying what he was supposed to in a ransom note. What if that's the fake part and the real part is the crazy stuff? I mean the contrast between those sections is so dramatic as to be ridiculous. The 'overheated' language seems to be where his passion is."

"Seems to be," Brody interrupted. Keri reminded herself to keep a level head. The short-timer was baiting her, hoping he could rile her up to make her argument seem less credible. She nodded politely and continued.

"Yes, Frank, seems to be. I don't pretend to know anything for sure. But all that talk of freeing her from her own evil spirit, of the machinery of the Lord, it's pretty detailed, like he's developed some kind of personal liturgy to reflect his own warped religion—one where he's in control, like he's the Pope of his own demented faith. And if that's true, we've got a much bigger problem."

"How so?" Edgerton asked.

"Because if this is all truly about cleansing spirits and pleasing his deity, then he doesn't really care about the money. It might just be a way to justify the abduction to himself in societal terms. He tells himself it's about the money so he can function in some kind of normal way. But deep down, he knows that's just an excuse, that the real reason he took her is much deeper and darker."

"So Locke," Hillman said, "you're suggesting this guy is having some internal struggle and that the money is just a way for him to hide what he really wants to do to the girl from himself?"

"Maybe."

"That seems like a stretch," he said. "Other than the language he used, what do you have to support the theory?"

"It's not just the language, Lieutenant. The very fact that he offered to return her, to let her own father purify her, suggests that he might be trying to fight this thing, that he's trying to find an 'out,' some way to *not* free her from the demon by killing her."

She stopped talking and looked around at the faces of her co-workers, which were a mix of skepticism and genuine intrigue. Even Hillman seemed to be reconsidering.

"Or he could just be after the money and your mumbo-jumbo is as full of BS as he is," Brody said derisively. His comment seemed to drain the room of goodwill and Keri felt everyone retreating to their safe corners.

"You're a Neanderthal!" Castillo said, disgusted.

"Yeah?" he spat back. "I think you could use a good hair dragging."

"You want to go right now, old man?" Castillo said, taking a step toward him. "I'll knock your beached whale ass back in the ocean."

"Enough!" Hillman shouted. "We've got a twelve-year-old girl to save and we don't have time for this crap. And Brody, another sexist comment like that and I'll dock your pay for the rest of your frickin' career, even if that's only a month, you got me?"

Brody reluctantly shut his mouth. Castillo looked like she wasn't done yet so Keri put her hand on her shoulder and led her away.

"Let it go, Jamie," she muttered under her breath. "The guy's one more burrito away from a heart attack. You don't want to get blamed when he keels over."

Castillo chuckled despite her anger. She was about to reply when Detective Manny Suarez walked into the room. Manny wasn't much to look at, with his longish stubble, his love handles, and his heavy-lidded eyes that reminded Keri of Sleepy the dwarf. But he was a tough, able detective. And most importantly right now, he was returning from the FedEx office where the ransom note had been dropped off. Keri hoped he had good news.

"Give me something good," Hillman said.

Suarez shook his head as he sat down at the conference room table and pulled out one lonely receipt from the manila envelope he was holding. He slammed it on the table.

This is it," he said. "This is the one piece of meaningful evidence I was able to retrieve from the FedEx store. It has the time and date of the purchase, which was made with cash. That's it."

"Wasn't there any security footage you could match to the time of purchase?" Hillman asked.

"There is, but it's mostly useless. The exterior footage from the place shows someone walking in. But that person is wearing a bulky sweatshirt with a hoodie and sunglasses. I'm having it circulated but it won't be much help. It's hard to even tell whether it's a male or female."

"What about inside the FedEx store?" Castillo asked.

Suarez pulled out a second sheet of paper from the envelope and put it on the desk too. It looked like a photo but it was basically white with black around the edges.

"This is a still image from the interior camera," he said. "It looks like he was using a pair of laser refraction sunglasses that blow out anything onscreen. This is what the footage looks like the whole time the person is in there."

"That's hardcore tech," Edgerton noted, impressed. "Usually that sort of thing is only used in high-end robberies."

"What about other cameras?" Ray asked. "Ones he didn't look at directly."

"They were unaffected. But the suspect stood conveniently out of frame of each of them. It's like he knew exactly where every camera would be and steered clear of all but the one he couldn't avoid, right behind the register. And that's the one that's blown out."

"I'm assuming he avoided any other exterior cameras on the way out too?" Keri guessed. "No chance he walked to his car and we can get a make or license plate?"

"No chance," Suarez confirmed. "We have him walking around the corner. But the direction he went leads to an industrial block where none of the businesses have cameras. He could have gone anywhere from there."

"I hate to pile on," Edgerton added, studying the laptop in front of him. "But I've got more bad news. Jessica's backpack and phone were busts. CSU just emailed me that they didn't find any unexpected prints."

Lieutenant Hillman's cell phone rang but he indicated for Edgerton to continue as he stepped out of the room to take the call. Kevin picked up where he'd left off.

"And I've been running a program using her SIM card to look for suspicious activity. It just finished. But there's nothing out of the ordinary. Every single call she made or received in the last three months is from either her family or friends."

Keri and Ray exchanged a silent glance. Even the tension between them couldn't undermine their shared concern that this case was going downhill fast.

Before anyone could respond to Edgerton, Hillman walked back in. Keri could tell from his expression that there was more bad news coming.

"That was Dr. Feeney," he said. "He buys the con man theory too. He thinks this guy's faking the crazy stuff and just wants the money."

Great. Every lead we have has gone nowhere and now the unit consensus is that this guy is just a run of the mill kidnapper.

Keri couldn't explain it, even to herself. But her instincts were telling her that the consensus was dangerously wrong; that this kidnapper was something else entirely. And she feared that if they didn't get on the right track soon, Jessica Rainey would pay the price.

CHAPTER SIX

As the minutes leading up to the drop passed, Keri tried to ignore the pit of anxiety growing in her stomach. Time was running short and Keri felt like they were losing options fast. She actively told herself not to lose hope, to remember that Jessica was out there somewhere, desperately waiting for someone to find her.

Since the FedEx office and Jessica's backpack and phone were dead ends, the team began pursuing less case-specific, and therefore less promising, options.

Edgerton put the case parameters into a federal database to see if there was any record of similar kidnappings. The results would come in soon but culling through them would be time-consuming.

He also input the ransom note in the system on the off chance that the language checked the boxes of any previous letters. That was a long shot. If a letter this strange had been sent to someone before, they felt confident they would have heard about it.

Suarez was looking at a list of registered sex offenders who lived in the area to see if any of them had a record of this kind of crime. Castillo had gone to the park to prep for surveillance. Brody had left the station, claiming he was going to talk to some of his street informants. Keri suspected he'd just gone out to get something else to eat.

She and Ray pored through old case files, looking for any old or unsolved cases that matched Jessica's. It was possible that this was the work of someone back out on the streets after a long prison stretch. If that was the situation, it would predate either of their time on the force and they wouldn't remember the particulars. Neither of them thought the exercise would bear fruit but they weren't sure what else to do.

After over an hour without success they headed out. It was almost 10 p.m. and she and Ray were returning to the Rainey house. It was the same route they'd taken that morning, when everything had been normal, right up until the moment he'd asked her out. Both of them were aware of that fact, but they were too busy to allow that to get in their way at the moment.

As they drove, Ray was on the phone with Detective Garrett Patterson, who was still at the station coordinating the surveillance for the drop location, Chace Park.

Patterson, a quiet, bookish guy in his thirties, was a tech geek like Edgerton. But unlike his younger colleague, Patterson seemed content to focus on the minutiae of cases. He loved activities like poring over phone records and comparing IP addresses, so much so that it had gotten him the nickname Grunt Work, which he didn't mind at all.

Patterson wasn't the kind of detective who was going to make instinctive leaps of deduction. But he could be counted on to set up a thorough perimeter of video and electronic surveillance that would be both effective and undetectable.

"They're prepped," Ray told her as he hung up. "The surveillance team is in place. Manny is headed over to Rainey's boss's place now to accompany him and the money to the remote headquarters in the van at the Waterside shopping center."

"Great," Keri said. "While you were talking, I had an idea. I have a friend I know from when I used to live on the houseboat in the marina. He has a sailboat and I bet he'd take us out so we could observe the drop area from the water. What do you think?"

"I say reach out," Ray said. "The more eyes we can get on the drop area without being noticed, the better."

Keri texted her friend, a crusty old sailor named Butch. He was actually less of a friend than a sometime drinking companion who liked scotch as much as she did. After she lost Evie, her marriage, and her job in quick succession, she'd bought a decrepit old houseboat in the marina and lived there for several years.

Butch was a friendly, retired Navy man who liked to call her "Copper," didn't ask about her past, and was happy to swap professional war stories with her. At the time, that was exactly the kind of companionship she was looking for. But since she'd moved from the marina to her apartment and significantly reduced her alcohol consumption, they hadn't hung out much recently.

Apparently he wasn't holding a grudge as she heard back almost immediately with a text that read: "no problem - see you soon, Copper."

"We're good," she told Ray, then let her mind drift to something that had been eating at her. She didn't realize how long she'd been quiet until Ray broke into her thoughts.

"What is it, Keri?" Ray asked expectantly. "I can tell you're turning some clue over in your head."

Once again Keri marveled at how he seemed capable of reading her mind.

"It's just the drop. Something about it bugs me. Why would this guy, assuming it's a guy, give us the location so early? He must know that if the Raineys contacted us, we'd have hours to do exactly what we're doing—establish a perimeter, install surveillance, gather manpower. Why give us a head start? I understand demanding the money early to give them time to gather it. But if it was me, I'd call at eleven forty-five p.m. to reveal the drop location and say the meet was at midnight."

"Fair question," he agreed. "And it fits with your suspicion that he doesn't really care about the money."

"I don't want to belabor it, but I really don't think he does," she said.

"So what do you think he cares about?" Ray asked.

Keri had been mulling this over in her head and was happy for the opportunity to share it out loud.

"Whoever this guy is, I think he's fixated on Jessica. I feel like he knows her or has at least met her. He's been watching her."

"That fits. Everything suggests he's been planning this for a while."

"Exactly. Those special sunglasses he used at FedEx, knowing where the cameras were there, abducting her at the perfect time when she was out of sight of the school but not yet to her mother, in a part of the neighborhood where no neighbors had exterior security cameras. These are all signs of someone who has been working on this for a long time."

"That makes sense. But the security officer at the school came up empty with staff. I checked again at the station. No teachers had records of anything more than parking tickets."

"What about school janitors or bus drivers?"

"They're employed through outside companies. But everyone who comes in contact with the school has to pass a background check. We can go through the list again. But the guy was pretty thorough."

"Okay then, what about employees at businesses along her bike route or construction workers on a house being built nearby—people who would see her every day and be familiar with her routine and who have a record?"

"Those are good leads we can pursue in the morning. But I'm hoping we nab this guy tonight and none of that is necessary."

They pulled up to the Rainey house and noticed a police car parked far down the block. It had been instructed not to park too close to the house in case the abductor drove by. They walked to the door and knocked. An officer opened it immediately and they stepped inside.

"How are they doing?" Ray asked him quietly.

"The mom has spent most of her time upstairs with the little boy, trying to keep him busy," the officer replied.

"And keep herself busy," Keri added.

"I think so," the officer agreed. "The dad has been mostly quiet. He's spent a lot of time studying the park layout on his laptop. He's been asking us all kinds of questions about our surveillance, most of which we don't have answers to."

"Okay, thanks," Ray said. "Hopefully we can provide a few."

Just as the officer said, Tim Rainey was seated at the kitchen table, with a Google map of Burton Chace Park on his laptop screen.

"Hi, Mr. Rainey," Keri said. "We understand you have a few questions."

Rainey looked up and for a moment, barely seemed to recognize them. Then his eyes focused and he nodded.

"I have a lot actually."

"Go ahead," Ray said.

"Okay. The note said not to contact the authorities. How are you going to keep from being seen?"

"First, we've set up hidden cameras throughout the park," Ray answered. "We'll be able to monitor them remotely from a van in a nearby parking lot. Also, the park is populated by some homeless people and we've dressed up an officer accordingly to fit in. She's been there for hours so as not to draw suspicion from the others. We'll have people at the Windjammers Yacht Club next door, watching from a second-floor room with tinted glass. One of them is a sniper."

Keri saw Tim Rainey's eyes widen but he said nothing as Ray continued.

"We'll have an overhead drone available but won't use it unless absolutely necessary. It's almost silent and can operate up to five hundred feet. But we don't want to take any chances with that. In total, we'll have almost a dozen officers offsite but within sixty seconds of the location to assist you if things go south. That includes Detective Locke and myself. We'll be on a civilian boat in the marina, far enough away to avoid suspicion but close enough to watch events through binoculars. We've thought this through, Mr. Rainey."

"Okay, that's obvious. So what exactly do I need to do?"

"I'm glad you asked," Ray said. "That's what we're here to go over now. Why don't we prep right here, since you already have the map up?"

He and Keri sat down on either side of Rainey and she took over.

"So you're supposed to meet him on the bridge between the pergolas at the back of the park near the water. And that's exactly what you're going to do," Keri said. "The park itself will be officially closed so you can't park in the metered lot. That's probably partly why he's doing this at midnight. Any car in the lot would look suspicious. You'll park in the public lot a block away. We'll give you change. All you have to do is park, pay, and walk toward the drop area. Does all this make sense so far?"

"Yes," Rainey said. "When will I get the ransom money?"

"You're going to pick it up at Waterside shopping center near the park."

"What if the kidnapper is watching?"

"That's okay," Keri assured him. "Your boss will be making the handoff to you, right in front of the Bank of America ATMs. He's being prepped by one of our detectives right now. There will be officers in the area, also out of sight, in case the abductor tries to grab the money then."

"Are you tagging the money with some kind of GPS locator?"

"We are," Ray admitted, jumping in, "and the bag too. But the locators are all very small. The one in the bag will be sewn into the stitching. The tags placed on the money are tiny, clear stickers placed on individual bills. Even if he found the exact bills, the tags are very hard to see."

Keri knew why Ray had answered that question. It was clear from Rainey's sour expression that he wasn't happy about the locators. He didn't say it but they could tell that he was worried they might put Jessica at risk.

Ray had spoken up so he would be the bearer of that unwelcome information. That way, the rapport and trust Keri was developing with the anxious father wouldn't be undermined. Keri nodded her imperceptible thanks to her partner. Rainey didn't seem to notice. She could tell he was agitated by what Ray had said but didn't object. He moved on.

"So what do I do next?' he asked Keri, pointedly looking away from Ray.

"Like I said before, after you get the ransom money, drive to the parking lot a block from Chace Park. Then just get out and walk to the bridge between the pergolas. There will be officers in the area but you won't see them. And it's not your job to worry about any of that. All you have to do is go to the bridge with the money."

"What happens when he arrives?" Rainey wanted to know.

"You're going to ask for your daughter. In theory, he's going to be under the impression that you're alone. So it won't feel right if you just give him the money without a fight. He'd get suspicious. I seriously doubt he'll have brought her with him. He may give you a location. He might tell you he'll text you the location once he's safely away. He might say he'll FedEx the location—"

"You don't think she'll be there?" Rainey interrupted.

"I'd be very surprised. He'd be giving up all his leverage if he had her with him. His best bet to keep you in line is to keep you in fear for Jessica's safety. You need to prepare yourself for the likelihood that she won't be there."

"I understand. What next?"

"After you express your misgivings about giving up the money, give up the money. Don't try to negotiate some other plan with him. Don't try to overpower him. He might be jumpy. He'll probably be armed. We don't want to do anything that will cause a confrontation."

Tim Rainey nodded reluctantly. Keri didn't like his vibe and decided she needed to be more forceful.

"Mr. Rainey. I need your promise that you won't do anything foolish. Our best bet is for him to either tell you where to find your daughter or return to her after the drop. Even if he tells you nothing, don't panic. We will track him. When the time is right, we will apprehend him. If you take matters into your own hands, it could end badly for both you and Jessica. Are we clear on that, sir?"

"Yes. Don't worry. I'm not going to do anything to put Jessica at risk."

"Of course not," Keri said reassuringly despite her doubts. "What you will do is complete the drop, return to your car, and drive back here. We'll deal with everything else as it comes, okay?"

"Will you be putting a microphone on me?" he asked, notably not answering her directly.

"Yes," Ray said, jumping in again, "and a tiny camera as well. Neither will be noticeable, especially at night. But the camera may help us identify him. And the audio will let us know if you're in any danger."

"Will we be able to communicate?"

"No," Ray told him. "I mean, we'll obviously be able to hear you. But giving you an earpiece would be risky. He might see it. And we want you to stay focused on what *you* need to do."

"One more thing," Keri added. "There's a chance he may not show up at all. He could get spooked and back out. He might never have intended to come. Be prepared for that as well."

"Do you think that's what going to happen?" Rainey asked. He clearly had never even considered the possibility.

Keri gave him the most truthful answer she could muster.

"I have absolutely no idea what's going to happen. But we're about to find out."

CHAPTER SEVEN

Keri thought she might be sick. It was almost funny. After all, she'd lived on a floating houseboat for several years. But floating on a sailboat in open channel waters while holding binoculars to her eyes for long stretches was a different proposition.

Butch had offered to drop anchor on the *Pipsqueak* but both Keri and Ray worried that a stationary boat in the water might look suspicious. Of course, a boat aimlessly traipsing back and forth wasn't much better.

After about fifteen minutes of that, Butch suggested they loiter near a dock across the channel from the park, where at least the other boats would make them stand out less. Keri, uncertain that she could hold off the nausea much longer, jumped at the suggestion.

They found an unoccupied spot and lingered there as midnight drew near. The biting winter wind howled outside. Sitting on the small bench near the window, Keri could hear the water lapping loudly against the hull. She embraced it, trying to match her breathing to its rhythm. She felt the knot in her stomach start to loosen and the sweat on her brow subside a bit.

It was 11:57 p.m. Keri put the binoculars to her eyes again and looked across the water at the park. Ray, several feet over, was doing the same.

"See anything?" Butch asked from up above. He was excited to be a part of a police operation and was having a hard time hiding it. This was probably the most eventful thing to happen to him in years.

He was the same crusty guy she remembered, defined by his weather-beaten skin, his shock of unbrushed white hair, and the perpetual smell of liquor on his breath. Under normal circumstances, operating a boat in his condition was a violation. But she was willing to let it slide considering the situation.

"There are some trees partially blocking the view," she whispered back loudly. "And it's hard to see with the glare from the window, even with the lights out down here."

"I can't do anything about the trees," Butch said. "But you know, the windows open part way."

"I didn't know that," she admitted.

"How long did you live on that boat?" Ray asked.

Keri, happily surprised that he was willing to engage in teasing, stuck her tongue out at him before adding, "Apparently not long enough."

A voice came over their comms, interrupting the most natural moment they'd had all day. It was Lieutenant Hillman.

"All units be advised. This is Unit One. The messenger has the cargo, has parked, and is en route to the destination on foot."

Hillman was one of the people stationed on the second floor of the Windjammers Club, which had a good vantage point of much of the park, including the bridge. He was using pre-assigned non-specific terms for everyone involved to avoid sharing too much information over communication lines, which always seemed to be hacked by curious citizens who liked to listen in on police traffic. Rainey was the messenger. The bag of money was the cargo. The bridge was the destination. The kidnapper would be referred to as the subject and Jessica would be the asset.

"This is Unit Four. I can see the destination," Keri said, finally finding an angle with a clear view of the bridge. "There's no one visible in the vicinity."

"This is Unit Two," came the voice of Officer Jamie Castillo, who was playing the role of the homeless woman in the park. "The messenger has just passed my location west of the community building near the cafe. The only other people I see are two homeless individuals. Both of them have been here all afternoon. Both appear to be sleeping."

"Keep an eye on those individuals, Unit Two," Hillman said. "We don't know what the subject looks like. Anything is possible."

"Copy that, Unit One."

"I hope you guys can hear me," a nervous-sounding Tim Rainey whispered loudly into his lavalier microphone. "I'm in the park and headed toward the bridge."

"Ugh," Ray muttered under his breath. "Are we going to get a running commentary from this guy?"

Keri scowled at him.

"He's nervous, Ray. Cut him some slack."

"All units be advised. This is HQ," Manny Suarez said from the van in the shopping center parking lot that served as mobile headquarters. "We have eyes on the entire area and there is no movement at this point besides the messenger, who is fifty yards from the destination."

Keri looked at her watch. 11:59 p.m. In the distance she heard the motor of a boat at the far end of the marina's main channel. Seals, who liked to sunbathe on the docks in the day, were calling out to one another. Other than that, the wind, and the waves, it was silent.

"Movement along Mindanao Way approaching the park," came an unfamiliar, agitated voice.

"Identify your unit," Hillman barked, "and don't use proper names."

"Sorry, sir. This is Unit Three. There is a vehicle approaching the park along…the street leading up to it. It appears to be a motorcycle."

Keri realized who Unit Three was—Officer Roger Gentry. West LA wasn't the largest division of LAPD and they were short on available manpower at this hour, so Hillman had pulled in every unassigned officer and that included Gentry. He was a rookie, on the job less than a year, about as long as Castillo but far less confident or, apparently, capable.

"Does anyone else have eyes?" Hillman asked.

"Can anybody else hear that?" Tim Rainey asked way too loudly, apparently forgetting no one could reply to him. "It sounds like someone's coming."

"This is Unit Two," Castillo said from her makeshift nook near the community center. "I have eyes. It *is* a motorcycle. Can't identify from my location but it's small, a Honda, I think. Only a driver. It has entered the park and is traveling along the south edge of the service road in the general direction of the destination and the messenger."

Keri saw the bike now too, speeding along the service road that skirted the edge of the park near the water. She turned her attention to Tim Rainey, who was standing stiffly in the middle of the bridge, his right hand tightly clutching the bag.

"This is Unit One," Hillman announced. "We have rifle on standby, prepared to assist. Does anyone have an updated visual on the vehicle?"

"This is Unit Four," Ray said. "We have a visual. Solo rider is traveling about fifty miles per hour along the edge of the service road. Vehicle is turning right, that's north, in the general direction of the destination."

"I think it's someone on a motorcycle," Tim Rainey said. "Can anyone tell who it is? Is it the guy? Does he have Jess?"

"Unit Four, this is Unit One," Hillman said, ignoring the chatter from Rainey. "Do you see any weapons? Rifle, stand ready."

"Rifle ready," came the voice of the sniper next to Hillman in the second-floor room of the yacht club.

"This is Unit Four," Ray replied. "I don't see any weapons. But my visual is compromised by darkness and the speed of the vehicle."

"Rifle on my mark," Hillman said.

"On your mark," the sniper replied calmly.

Keri watched as the driver of the bike hit the brakes and did a sudden, dramatic wheelie. When the front wheel hit the road again, the driver forced the bike in a tight donut, circling three times before coming out of it and speeding back in the direction from which it came.

"This is Unit Four," she said quickly. "Stand down. Repeat, recommend Rifle stand down. I think we've got a late-night joyrider on our hands."

"Rifle, stand down," Hillman ordered.

Sure enough, the bike continued back the way it had come, down the service road and through the metered parking lot. She lost sight of it when it got back on Mindanao.

"Who has eyes on the messenger?" Hillman asked urgently.

"This is Unit Four," Keri continued. "The messenger is shaken but unharmed. He's standing there, unsure how to proceed."

"Frankly, I'm unsure too," Hillman admitted. "Let's just keep alert, people. That may have been a decoy."

"Is anyone coming to get me?" Rainey asked, as if in response to Hillman. "Should I just stay here? I'm going to assume I should stay here unless I hear different."

"God, I wish he'd shut up," Ray muttered, putting his hand over his mic so only Keri and Butch could hear him. Keri didn't respond.

After about ten minutes, Keri saw Rainey, still standing in the middle of the bridge, check his phone.

"I hope you can hear me," he said. "I just got a text. It says 'By involving the authorities, you have betrayed my trust. You have sacrificed the opportunity to redeem the child sinner. I must now determine whether to remove the demon myself or forgive your insubordination and allow you one more chance to purify her soul. Her fate was in your hands. Now it is in mine.' He knew you were here. All your elaborate planning was for nothing. And now I have no idea whether he'll even reach out to me again. You might have killed my daughter!"

He screamed the last line, his voice cracking in fury. Keri could hear his voice across the marina even as it came over the comm. She saw him drop to his knees, let go of the bag, put his hands to his face, and begin weeping. His pain felt intimately familiar.

It was the anguished cry of a parent who believed his child was lost to him forever. She recognized it because she had wept the same way when her own daughter had been taken and she could do nothing to stop it.

Keri rushed out of the boat cabin and just made it up on deck in time to vomit over the side into the ocean.

CHAPTER EIGHT

Jessica Rainey wriggled her fingers to keep them from falling asleep again. They were tied behind her back, attached to the pipe she sat leaning against. The ground was asphalt, hard and cold. The one fluorescent light that dangled from the ceiling flickered intermittently, making it impossible to fall asleep.

She wasn't sure how long she'd been in this place but knew it had been long enough for day to turn into night. She could tell because of tiny cracks in the wall that let in the light from the sun. There was no light now.

She hadn't even noticed the cracks initially. When she woke up, all she did was scream and try to yank herself free. She screamed for help. She screamed for her parents. She even screamed for her little brother, Nate, not that he could have helped her.

And she pulled so hard at the restraints on her wrists that when she looked behind her, she could see the drops of blood where they had dug into her skin and dripped onto the ground.

It was around that time that she noticed she wasn't wearing her own clothes. Someone had removed them and replaced them with a sleeveless dress that went to her knees. It was clearly homemade, stitched together unevenly.

Beyond that, it was rough and scratchy, as if it had been made from several burlap sacks. If she wasn't so sore, she'd be totally focused on how itchy she was. She refused to think about how she had actually gotten from one outfit into the other.

After she had worn herself out from screaming and yanking and the adrenaline had faded from her system, she tried to remember what had happened to her. The last thing she could recall was riding her bike up the big hill on Rees Street, when she'd felt a sudden sharp pain in her back. It felt like the electrical shock she sometimes got from touching a metal door handle after walking on a carpet, only a hundred times worse.

And that was it. The next thing she knew she was in this room that was only lit for about six feet around her before it collapsed into darkness. She no idea of its dimensions but she was pretty sure the walls were made of the same asphalt as the floor. When she yelled, it sounded muffled, as if no sound could escape the room.

And her back hurt, not in the way all of the rest of her hurt, which was mostly an ache due to being stuck in the same position for so long. There was one particular spot on her back that felt burned.

In fact, it was the same spot where she'd felt the pain earlier. The more she thought about it, the more Jessica suspected someone had poked her in that spot with something like a cattle prod. She remembered reading about them in her history class's section on Western States.

Ranchers sometimes used them on their cows to get them to go in the direction they wanted. She remembered Mr. Hensarling saying that it gave a cow a jolt but that a cattle prod would do much worse to a human being.

Now that the initial terror and exhaustion had worn off, Jessica realized something else: she was hungry. She hadn't had anything to eat or drink since lunch. And whatever time it was now, she was sure it was late.

But no one had come by to offer food or even check to see if she was still alive. She hadn't heard anything other than her own voice and the occasional rattle of the pipes since she'd arrived.

Have I just been left here to die? Will I ever see my family again? Will I ever even learn who did this to me?

Just then, the light above her burned out completely. Too tired and hoarse to scream, she pressed her back against the pipe as if it could offer her some kind of protection.

After a few seconds, a hum kicked in and a dull blue emergency light came on in the far corner of the room. Her eyes slowly started to adjust to the half-darkness and she noticed something in the same corner where the light emanated from. She squinted, in the vain hope that could somehow help. Eventually the form came into focus and she realized that it had the shape of a human.

"Hello," she called out excitedly. "You in the corner—can you hear me?"

There was no response. She looked a little closer and realized there was something odd about the figure, lying limply on its side. It looked human but somehow different. She was perplexed. And then, in a flash of recognition, she realized what she was looking at. It was a human skeleton.

Jessica Rainey discovered that she could still scream after all.

CHAPTER NINE

Even though she didn't really feel it, Keri pretended to stay calm and collected for the sake of her passenger.

Tim Rainey was so shell-shocked that she had to drive him home in his own car. Ray said he wanted to check on some leads at the station so Manny Suarez followed her and picked her up to drive her back.

On the way, she tried to tell Rainey that there was still hope, that they still had lots of leads to follow. But she could tell he wasn't really listening and stopped trying after a few minutes. When they got to his house, he got out of the car and closed the door behind him without saying a word.

Back at the station, Keri was surprised to find there was very little in the way of investigative activity. That was until she remembered that it was after 1 a.m. and there wasn't much more that could be done until morning.

"How's Rainey doing?" Hillman asked when he saw Keri and Manny walk in.

"Not great," Keri admitted. "He was equal parts pissed and stunned. I'd expect it to tip more toward pissed by morning. Do we know what gave us away? How the hell did this guy know we were there?"

"I'm reviewing the footage from the scene," Edgerton said. "So far, I can't find any errors on our part."

Hillman sighed heavily. He'd seen a lot of these situations and Keri noticed that he wasn't as quick to place blame as usual.

"Folks, we may not have done anything wrong at all. This guy has clearly been planning this for a long time. It's reasonable to think he prepared for this contingency as well."

"It's like Keri mentioned to me earlier," Ray added. "He gave us a lot of lead time on the drop area. It's possible he had already set up cameras in the area or at the Rainey house. If he was testing them to see if they'd call us, it wouldn't have been hard to discover they had."

Keri appreciated that even though he was upset with her, Ray was willing to acknowledge that her misgivings hadn't been misplaced.

"I'm just worried we might not get another chance," Manny said. "He may not want to risk another attempt."

Keri was tempted to remind them about her doubts that the kidnapper ever intended to show up but decided now wasn't the time.

"What happened with the motorcyclist?" she asked instead.

"Nothing," came a voice from the couch in the corner. Keri looked over and saw that it was Frank Brody, sprawled out lazily.

"Can you be a bit more specific?" she asked, trying to keep her tone non-confrontational. She hadn't even realized he had been part of the operation.

"He was just some joyriding teenager. We pulled him over a few blocks away. We checked and he has no record other than two speeding tickets for the same sort of thing. He goes to high school in Venice—no obvious connection to the girl or anything else in the area."

Garrett Patterson, who had remained back at the station to help with coordination, cleared his throat.

"If you got something to say, Patterson, just spit it out," growled Brody. "This isn't a finishing school."

For once Keri agreed with him. Patterson was great at sifting through data but his reticence to go in the field or even speak up in meetings was getting tiresome. Patterson swallowed hard and spoke.

"I was just going to say that we traced the phone that texted Mr. Rainey. It was a burner. Its last GPS location was in the marina, not too far from the park. We think it was dumped in the ocean after it was used."

"What I want to know is how this guy even had Rainey's cell number," Ray wondered. "I checked his phone. His contact list is small and he doesn't make many calls. You can tell that he's very careful, what with working on so much proprietary stuff at that gaming company. He's not just handing out his number to everyone."

"It's a fair question," Hillman said. "But considering how much time this guy's put into his plan, I can't say I'm shocked that he got his hands on it somehow. Here's my question. Is there anything else we can do here tonight or are we just spinning our wheels?"

"The case parameters I put into the federal missing persons database are being collated," Edgerton said. "We'll be able to look for similar cases in a few hours. That's around the time the day shifts for other local police departments on the East Coast and in the Midwest will be getting in. They'll see our alert then. Maybe someone will recognize a pattern and reach out. But other than that, I can't think of anything we should be doing."

"Anyone else?" Hillman asked. When no one spoke up, he continued. "Then everyone go home. Get a few hours' sleep. Be back here bright and early. Hopefully something will have popped by then."

As Keri turned to leave, she glanced up at one of the television monitors in the corner of the bullpen.

"Oh no," she groaned.

Everyone else looked up and saw what had upset her. The screen was showing a local news alert about Jessica Rainey's disappearance. Keri didn't have to hear what the reporter was saying to know this was a frustrating development. The woman was standing in front of the Raineys' house and the banner at the bottom of the screen read: "Local girl taken near her home."

"Get a couple more black-and-whites out there now!" Hillman barked to the desk sergeant. "I want a perimeter around the house and the neighborhood closed off. When the news directors balk, tell them it's an active crime scene. No one but residents are allowed on that block without clearance. Reporters will have to do their stand-ups from down on Pershing. Got it?"

"Got it, Lieutenant," the desk sergeant yelled back.

"And tell the officers on scene that as soon as that live shot ends, they need to escort that TV crew off the block, understood?"

"Understood, Lieutenant."

Hillman looked around and seeing everyone still there, he reminded them, "This doesn't change anything for all of you. Go home. Sleep. Come back early. See you tomorrow."

As if to make his point, he walked straight out of the station without looking back. Ray made a beeline right after him and Keri had to run to try to catch up.

"Hey, Ray, can we talk for a minute?" she asked as they both stepped out the employee entrance into the chilly night. She hoped their little moment of levity on Butch's sailboat had opened the door a crack.

"Listen, Keri. I'm just not up for it right now. I'm exhausted. I'm confused. I don't want to be pissy but can we just keep things professional for now and say goodbye until the morning?"

"Sure," she said, trying to keep her tone from sounding too bruised. "Of course. Sure."

She stopped walking and let him cross the parking lot alone. She stood there silently as he got in his car, pulled out, and left the lot. He never even glanced her way.

Unsure what to do, she walked slowly to her own car, a used Honda Civic Hybrid that had replaced her used Toyota Prius, which was destroyed when the man abducting Evie had smashed into her head-on. She closed the door and rested her head on the steering wheel.

She knew there wasn't anything else she could do for Jessica Rainey in the next few hours. Anything she tried would be the investigative equivalent of grinding metal on metal. But she also knew she was too wired to go home and sleep.

She imagined Tim and Carolyn Rainey lying in bed, eyes wide open, horrifying thoughts pinballing around in their heads. Mr. Rainey would have almost certainly gone out to confront the reporter invading their privacy. That's what she would have done, partly out of anger, partly just to have something to do. She hoped the officers stationed outside their house stopped him. That would only make things worse.

Stuck in their house, they would obsess over every little detail of the day, wondering what they might have done differently, what they might have missed. It was what she did every day. It was why she pored over the surveillance footage of the Black Widower executing the man who had been holding Evie and shoving her in the trunk of his car.

Keri yanked her head up off the wheel so suddenly that she almost pulled a muscle in her neck. She had just had what some folks might call a moment of clarity.

There's one detail I haven't checked out. And now is as good a time as any to do it.

*

Keri parked on Sunset Boulevard, about a block away from Brian Wickwire's Echo Park apartment, and walked the rest of the way. It was still hard to think of him as Brian Wickwire, a man with a name and an apartment and a fridge filled with food.

For so long she'd only thought of him as the Collector, the monster who abducted her daughter from a park right in front of her; the man who'd killed an innocent teenager who tried to stop him.

49

Of course, now he was no longer a threat, after their confrontation around Thanksgiving. It hadn't gone how she'd hoped. She'd wanted a confession and Evie's location. But it became quickly clear that he wasn't going to be sharing that information.

And then, even after they fought and he was dying from a fall that left blood pouring out of his skull, he'd baited her to the point that she found herself choking what little life remained out of him.

She'd gone straight to his apartment afterward and found the clue that led to her temporary, painfully short reunion with Evie and the discovery of dozens of other missing children. Now she was hoping that his apartment might hold one more clue, something about the identity or location of the Black Widower.

Keri knew that there was still a unit from Downtown Division stationed out front of Wickwire's apartment building, which was why she was dressed in a sweatshirt with an oversized hoodie hiding her face. Apart from herself, several ghoulishly curious true crime fans had tried to break into the home of the infamous Collector to steal some kind of memento.

Unlike most of those amateurs, Keri had access to the building design and knew that in addition to the front and rear entrances to the building, there was also a door next to the parking garage gate in the alley. It locked automatically and there was no exterior handle so it was supposedly secure.

But Keri knew that with this door model, an extremely powerful, specially designed magnet could be used to slide the latch back just enough so that it could be opened from the outside. After checking to make sure she was alone in the alley, she did exactly that. It was a trick she'd learned from a thief she'd busted in her days as a patrol officer and this was not the first time it had come in handy.

After gaining entry, she took the stairs from the garage to Wickwire's floor. Peeking out into the hallway, she saw it was empty. Anything else would have been surprising at 2 a.m. on a weeknight. As quietly as she could, she made her way down the hall, checking for any new surveillance cameras that might have been installed since her last visit.

Seeing nothing, she reached his door and quickly jimmied it open, ignoring the police tape plastered across it. Once inside and leaving the lights off, she ignored everything else and moved to the wall behind Wickwire's desk.

The photos of animals in nature were still lined up, just as they had been in the photo she'd seen earlier. And there was the black widow picture she had been so desperately hoping to see.

She stared at it, suddenly nervous to touch it for fear that her suspicions would be dashed and she'd be back at square one, without any leads to follow or clues to study. If this one didn't bear fruit, she didn't know what she'd do.

You don't have time for this kind of navel gazing. Do what you came here to do.

Ignoring the nervous tingles running down her spine, Keri reached out using her gloved hands and delicately removed the photo from the wall. She turned it over to look at the back. It was too dark to see if there was any writing or marking.

Keri looked around and decided to go into the bathroom, which had no exterior windows and couldn't betray her presence if she turned on the light. She walked in, closed the door, and flipped the switch—nothing. The power must have been turned off.

No big deal. That's what cell phone flashlights are for.

She turned hers on and studied the back of the photo frame closely. But there was nothing unusual about it. It was just standard picture frame backing. Keri slid out the backing to see if anything had been written on the back of the photo itself. There was nothing. Frustrated and without any idea what to do next, she fought the urge to rip the photo to shreds. Instead, she slid it back into place.

She was about to turn off her flashlight and return the photo to the wall, when she caught a glimpse of something on the floor near her shoe. It was a slip of paper. She might have missed it completely if she'd turned off the light a fraction of a second earlier.

She picked it up, realizing it must have been placed between the frame backing and the photo itself and fallen out without her noticing. She held the light up to it and saw a phrase written in light pencil: "the truth can be found in the weeds."

While she had no idea what it meant, Keri knew the line had been written by Wickwire. She recognized both his handwriting and the way he refused to capitalize any letters, ever. She snapped a photo of the paper and returned it to the frame.

If anything came of this, she'd want to direct Downtown Division to where they could find the relevant evidence. If she took it with her, it was useless in terms of prosecuting someone down the line, although that seemed like a pipe dream right now.

She put the photo back on the wall and left the apartment complex the same way she'd entered, avoiding human contact the entire time. She hurried up Sunset to her car and had just opened the door, excited to get in and finally pull off the heavy hoodie, when a car pulled up behind her, parked, and turned off the engine.

She glanced back, unsettled. There was a ton of available street parking. Why would someone choose to park directly behind her in the middle of the night? The driver turned off the car's headlights and she immediately knew why. It was the Collector's lawyer, Jackson Cave.

CHAPTER TEN

Keri felt her knees start to buckle and gripped the roof of her car for support. She tried to hide the shock and creeping fear she felt growing inside her.

What is he doing here? How did he know I would be here at this hour? Had he called the Downtown Division cops?

All those questions were swimming simultaneously in her head but she forced herself to look nonchalant, as this was the most expected turn of events she'd encountered today.

Cave got out of his car, a late model Tesla, and closed the door. He was dressed in what Keri imagined was 2 a.m. casual attire for him—slacks with loafers, a turtleneck sweater, and a sport coat. Even at this hour, his slicked-back black hair was immaculate. His perfectly bronzed skin almost glowed under the street lights.

"Surprised to see me?" he asked as he walked toward her with something between a grin and a sneer on his face, exposing his disturbingly white teeth.

"Headed to a croquet match?" Keri countered, nodding at his outfit. She'd learned that when dealing with Jackson Cave, any hint of vulnerability was a liability.

"You're funny," he said, not laughing. He came to a stop about six feet from her. His penetrating blue eyes fixed on her and narrowed. "What a coincidence, you and I meeting. After all, my main residence is in the Hollywood Hills and you live in that rundown Playa del Rey apartment above a Chinese restaurant that stinks for miles. And yet, here we both are, right outside Mr. Wickwire's apartment, in the middle of the night. Strange, don't you think?"

"I couldn't sleep—working a tough case. So I went for a drive, and a walk. What's your excuse, Cave? Scoping out preschools to troll later this morning?"

"You are delicious, Detective," Cave said and this time his smile seemed genuine. "I could spend all night sparring with you. You're much more fun than most of the lawyers I see in court. Alas, time is short. Shall we speak frankly?"

"Always."

53

"I'm not very happy about the death of my client, Mr. Wickwire. He...how can I put this? He brought in a lot of business, if you know what I mean."

"I know exactly what you mean," Keri said flatly.

"Well, I feel like you never got your proper comeuppance for that. My understanding is that Mr. Wickwire might have been choked to death even as he was bleeding from the brain. And yet, despite their investigation, Internal Affairs has yet to see fit to charge you with anything."

"Got to respect the process."

"Yes, that's true. The process is very important, which is why the pace of that investigation may need to be...escalated. I know your Lieutenant Hillman went to bat for you in your hearing. And I understand that Chief Beecher is still gaga over her prized detective, the one who rescued young Ashley Penn, who foiled the cruel machinations of Dr. Jeremy Burlingame, and who saved Sarah Caldwell from a Mexican brothel. But Detective, you're not the only one with connections high up in the LAPD."

"You don't say? Who are you paying off these days, Cave?" Keri asked casually, despite sensing that he was about to drop the hammer he'd been holding back.

"I would never pay anyone, Detective," he replied, mock offended. "And I'm not just saying that because I know you turned on the recorder on your phone the second you realized it was me behind you."

Keri involuntarily looked down at the pocket where her phone rested and mentally kicked herself for it. He continued, either not noticing or not caring.

"What I am saying is that your time has come, Detective Locke. The days of you skating by without consequences for your actions are coming to an end. I've got my eye on you. I think you know that. So whether it's for breaking into Brian Wickwire's apartment, stealing a thumb drive from my office, or murdering a helpless man suffering from a head injury, you will face justice. Things are about to get very bad for you."

Despite feeling the urge to puke, Keri refused to allow even a beat of silence to pass between them for fear of giving him the upper hand.

"You know, if a person didn't know any better, they'd think you were just a little bit scared. Is that what's going on? Is Jacky a scaredy-cat?"

Cave didn't reply, instead giving her his thinnest smile before turning around and returning to his car. He opened the door and was just getting in when he added one last thing.

"Be seeing you," he said before slamming the door, starting the car, and pulling out onto the deserted boulevard.

Keri waited until his taillights had rounded a curve before sitting down herself. Despite a temperature in the low fifties, she was sweating. She pulled off her hoodie, closed the door, and took in several gulps of air. She realized she'd been holding her breath.

She turned off the recorder on her phone and sat silently in the car for a few minutes, allowing her body to regain equilibrium. It was almost too much to process. Jackson Cave had known she was here and had come to confront her.

She didn't bother to worry about how he'd known. He might have had cameras set up, sensors put in the apartment, or found a new way to bug her phone or put a tracker on her car. He'd done both in the past, though she couldn't prove it was him.

What worried her more were his threats. She really had done all those things he'd alleged—breaking into an apartment, stealing data from his office, killing a man who was no longer a threat to her, purely for vengeance.

Can he prove any of that? Does he really have connections high up in the force?

She was almost certain the latter was true. And with his connections, financial resources, and malicious intent, he stood a more than reasonable chance of getting her fired, and potentially incarcerated.

Those things were true. But then she remembered something else that was true.

He's not the only one with cards to play. And he knows it.

Why else would Jackson Cave show up to try and intimidate her in the middle of the night? She'd hit a nerve. He really was scared.

After all, while she had committed crimes of her own, so had he. He was a crucial cog in, if not the leader of, a sex slave ring. He was involved in multiple child abductions and the sale of those children. He consorted with kidnappers and if her suspicions were correct, maybe even an assassin.

She couldn't prove any of that without exposing her own violations of law. But all of it was true. And he knew Keri was on to all of it. He was terrified that she had found something in

Wickwire's apartment that could link him to untold crimes. He was worried that she was sitting on something that could bring him down.

And he had no idea if she'd shared that information with others or put it in a safety deposit box. And until he knew that, he couldn't risk having her killed. He had to destroy her reputation so that any allegation she made against him would seem desperate and pathetic.

He was good at hiding it but Jackson Cave was scared.

Keri thoughts were interrupted by her ringing phone. She glanced at the clock in the car. It was 2:44 a.m. Who would be calling at this hour? She took out the phone. It was Ray. She answered immediately.

"I thought you didn't want to talk until morning. Have a change of heart?" she asked.

"We have a lead," he said, ignoring her question. "One of Jessica's friends woke up in the middle of the night and remembered something. She said Jessica told her about being followed by someone in a black van a few weeks ago."

"Why do all the child abductors have to drive vans?" Keri asked. "I mean, don't they know it's a cliché?"

"Keri, do you want to crack inappropriate jokes or do you want to meet me at the station in twenty minutes so we can go question this girl?"

"Make it thirty and I'm there."

"Why so long?" he asked. "Are you not at your apartment?"

"I'll explain later. See you at the station," she said and hung up before he could ask anything else.

*

Keri drove them from the station to the girl's house. She preferred it because she could focus on the road rather than sitting awkwardly in the passenger seat wondering if it was safe to bring up their conversation from this morning, or technically, yesterday morning.

Ray hadn't asked her about her middle-of-the-night location and it occurred to her that he might think she had been with someone. She wasn't sure how to disavow him of that notion without getting into a topic he clearly didn't want to discuss. It was around the moment when she decided to just let it lie that she heard herself speak.

"I wasn't at some guy's place when you called, if that's what you're thinking."

Unable to pull the words back, she kept her eyes focused on the road and pretended she hadn't said anything at all.

"What?" he asked, dumbfounded.

Change the subject, Keri. Or better yet, just keep your damn mouth shut.

"I'm just saying that if you thought the reason I was evasive on the phone earlier was because I was sleeping with some guy who lived more than twenty minutes away from the station, I wasn't."

"Keri, I don't even know how to respond to that," he answered, surprisingly measured. "I know you're a little punchy but—"

"I just wanted you to know," she said, knowing every word was digging her deeper.

"It's not my business what you do. We're not…you don't owe me…I really don't want to talk about this right now. We're in the middle of a case for chrissakes. Can we just focus on that and deal with this later?"

"Yes," Keri agreed, finally managing to get a handle on herself. "I won't bring it up again. You're right. Lack of sleep is messing with me. Besides, I think we're here."

She pulled up next to house in a less ostentatious but still impressive section of the Playa del Rey at Falmouth Avenue and Cabora Drive. It was almost 3:30 a.m. as they walked up to the front but they could see several lights were on.

Ray knocked quietly in case some people inside were still sleeping. After just a few seconds, a thirty-something man in a robe opened the door. His hair was mussed and his face had hints of stubble but his eyes were wide and clear. He'd obviously been fully awake for a while.

"Detectives Locke and Sands?" he asked.

"Yes," Ray said.

"Please come in. I'm Evan Coombs. My daughter Cate is in the kitchen with my wife. We have twin daughters still sleeping upstairs, so if you can keep your voices down, I'd appreciate it."

"Of course," Keri said as Evan Coombs led them quickly to the back of the house. When they got to the kitchen she saw Mrs. Coombs, also in a robe, putting a few mini-marshmallows in the mug of a blonde girl wearing Wonder Woman pajamas. The girl was absently watching an episode of some animated show on the small TV on the counter. Keri wondered if she'd have recognized the show if Evie was still around.

The mom looked up, saw them, and walked over. Despite the hour and the robe, she looked moderately put together. Her hair was up in a loose bun and she had the forcefully composed expression of someone who'd spent much of the night keeping her child from losing it.

"Hi, I'm Cindy Coombs," she said, extending the hand not holding a coffee cup. "Cate was pretty upset before but she's calmed down. I think she's ready to talk. We told her there's nothing to be scared of. So if you could reinforce that, it would be helpful."

"Of course, Mrs. Coombs," Keri assured her. "We'll be very sensitive. May I go sit next to her?"

"Please. Let me turn off the TV."

Mrs. Coombs walked over to Cate, put a hand on her shoulder, and quietly spoke to her, saying something Keri couldn't hear. Whatever it was, Cate turned immediately away from the set as her mom turned it off. Other than the fearful look on her face, she looked like a perfectly normal, well-adjusted twelve-year old girl.

"Hi, Cate," Keri said. "I'm Detective Locke and this is my partner, Detective Sands. But you can call us Keri and Ray. May we join you?"

Cate nodded hesitantly, her hazel eyes full of apprehension.

"Is that hot chocolate?" Keri asked.

Cate nodded.

"I love the mini-marshmallows," Ray noted, pointing at them. "The problem with the big ones is you have to try to sip around them and stuff spills on you. Has that ever happened to you?"

"Yeah," she said, obviously impressed. "That's why I always go with the minis."

"Smart move," Ray said. "So Cate, is it okay if we ask you a few questions about what you told your folks?"

"Uh-huh."

"Okay, so why don't you just start by telling us what you told your mom and dad, about Jessica and the van."

"Okay," Cate said hesitantly. "Well, I don't remember exactly when it was, definitely before winter break though. But we were having lunch in the picnic area on campus and this van went by. Jessica pointed it out and said that it reminded her of something creepy that had happened the day before with a different van."

"What was that?" Keri asked.

"She said she was biking home and when she turned onto Manitoba, it got behind her and followed her all the way almost to where she usually meets up with her mom. When she pulled into a driveway and stopped, it finally drove away."

"But it wasn't the same van you all saw at lunch?" Ray reconfirmed.

"No. That one was red. She said the one that followed her was black and had gold writing on the side. But it drove by so fast she couldn't read it. It was in cursive."

"Okay, that's really helpful, Cate. Did she say if she got a look at the driver?" Keri asked.

"She just said it was a guy. But she didn't say what he looked like." Her expression suggested she thought she was letting them down.

"This is all great," Ray said reassuringly. "Is there anything else that you can remember? Did she ever mention it again after that?"

"No. She never said anything else. But she seemed really scared when she talked about it that one time."

"And you say it was before winter break," Keri prompted. "Do you remember if it was after Thanksgiving?"

"I think so. Yeah, it was. And it was warm enough to sit outside. Does that help? Can you go back and check the weather from that time?" she asked hopefully.

"We absolutely can," Keri said. "That's an especially great detail to remember. It will really help us narrow it down."

As she spoke, Ray looked over at her and she could tell he had come to the same conclusion she had. They had likely tapped Cate Coombs for all the information she had. She nodded at him.

"Okay, listen, Cate," he said, standing up. "You've been a great help. Jessica is really lucky to have a friend like you. I think we have everything we need for now. But if you remember anything else, please tell your folks and they'll call us. Sound good?"

Cate looked up at Ray, who towered over her. But Keri could tell that she found his size comforting rather than intimidating.

"Is Jess going to be okay?" she asked him.

He bent down next to her and gave her his warmest smile, the one that never failed to melt Keri's heart.

"We're going to work super hard to find her. And when we do, we're going to tell her she owes you a big thank-you hug."

Cate nodded, satisfied if not completely convinced.

As they left the house and headed back to Keri's car, Ray looked at his watch.

"Just after four a.m.," he noted, "you think it's too early to go back to the Raineys and ask them about this?"

Keri looked at him and her expression must have been revealing because he didn't wait for her answer.

"You don't think we'd be waking them up, huh?"

"No, Ray. I guarantee you neither of them has slept a moment tonight. Dreaming is worse."

CHAPTER ELEVEN

Keri was right. After they had passed through the police barriers and parked in front of the house, they spoke to an officer in a car outside who said that Tim Rainey had come out multiple times to talk to him and that the last visit was only twenty minutes earlier.

Rather than knock or ring the bell, Ray texted him saying they were outside and asking if they could come in. The door opened less than fifteen seconds later and from his shortness of breath and panicked look, they could tell he feared the worst.

"We don't have bad news, Mr. Rainey," Keri said immediately. "As far as we know, nothing has changed with Jessica. We're just here to ask a few more questions we think might be helpful."

Rainey seemed to breathe again and motioned them in. He trudged to the kitchen, leaving them to shut the door.

"Is your wife awake?" Ray asked. "We think she might be helpful too."

"She's upstairs in bed with Nate," Rainey said, his voice thin and scratchy from crying and exhaustion. "He wouldn't stop asking for his sister. I'll go get her. There's coffee in the kitchen if you want."

Keri and Ray sat silently at the breakfast table, waiting for the Raineys to come down. Neither wanted to discuss the case for fear of saying something they didn't want overheard. And casual conversation was out of the question for any number of reasons.

After a few minutes, they heard the creak of stairs and soon both Tim and Carolyn Rainey were sitting across the table from them, each staring at them with red, bleary eyes. Keri wasn't sure how to broach the subject, so she just dived in.

"Did Jessica ever mention a van following her, maybe around the second week in December?"

On the way over, she had checked the weather for December and found that there was only one stretch of three days when the temperature had risen to the unseasonably warm high 60s.

"No, I definitely would have remembered that," Carolyn said. "I would have told you right away. Did she say anything to you, Tim?"

He shook his head no.

"Why?" he asked.

Ray answered. "A friend of hers, Cate Coombs, said that Jessica told her a van followed her one day from school to just before where she usually meets up with you, Mrs. Rainey. But apparently it was a one-time thing because she never mentioned it again."

"No, she never said anything," Carolyn Rainey reiterated. "But she might not have. I think she worried that if she said anything like that, I wouldn't let her bike alone anymore, which is true. Did Cate say anything else?"

"She said Jessica told her it was a black van with gold, cursive lettering," Keri said.

The color drained from Carolyn Rainey's face.

"What is it?" Keri asked.

"I think I know the van she's talking about. Back in late October, around Halloween, I had just finished showering and come out into the bedroom when I thought I saw movement through the blinds right outside the window. I screamed and rushed over. When I got there, I couldn't see anyone.

"But when I went downstairs, I saw some guy loading a ladder into a van across the street. It was black and had cursive gold lettering on the side. Our neighbors had some work done on their awning and the van had been parked there all morning. I didn't give it a second thought until then. But when I saw the guy with the ladder, I was suspicious."

"Did you call the police or talk to your neighbor?" Ray asked.

"No. I started to think I might have imagined the whole thing. But I kept an eye out. And the guy stayed there for another hour, doing work on the awning. He didn't act guilty or rush. He just seemed to be doing the work. Then he left and I didn't think about it again until now. Do you think it could be related?"

"Hard to say. What's your neighbor's name?" Ray asked, trying to keep his voice casual.

"Marcy Price."

"I know it's early, but would you mind going over to Marcy's to see if she has the contact info for the construction company?"

"No need. Before all that happened, she gave me a card for them because I was thinking of redoing our back porch in the spring."

She got up and walked over to an old-fashioned Rolodex on the kitchen counter. Within seconds she had found it and handed it over. In gold, cursive lettering, it read Salter Home Improvement.

"Can we hold on to this?" Ray asked.

"Yes," Carolyn Rainey said, obviously letting herself start to hope. "Do you think this could be him?"

"We get lots of false leads," Keri told her, trying to tamp down the enthusiasm. "We'll definitely check it out. But I wouldn't jump to any conclusions at this point."

"I wish you would have told me that last night," Tim Rainey suddenly said, his tone full of bitterness.

Keri bit her tongue, refusing to remind him that she had done exactly that.

"We're going to go check this out," Ray said quickly. "I know it's difficult but try to get a little sleep. Even a few hours might help."

Tim Rainey opened his mouth to respond but his wife put her hand on his and he stopped himself.

"Thank you, Detectives," she said. "Please let us know if you learn anything."

Keri and Ray both nodded, hurrying out before they said something else to upset her husband.

*

Dawn was just on the verge of breaking when Keri and Ray pulled up in front of the home of Enrique Hernandez just off La Brea in Mid-City. According to Martin Salter, owner of Salter Home Improvement, Hernandez had done the work on Marcy Price's awning on October twenty-sixth.

He'd given them Hernandez's address without any fuss, clearly hoping to be helpful and avoid any culpability for whatever his employee might have done. Ray warned him not to call Hernandez to tip him off but it was clearly unnecessary. His voice on the phone suggested the idea had never occurred to him.

Officer Jamie Castillo pulled up next to them a moment later and got out. She wasn't in uniform but she was wearing her gun belt.

63

"So, did you guys call me just because this dude's got a Hispanic surname and you need me to translate?"

"No," Ray said defensively. "We called you because we didn't want to go through the hoops of involving the Mid-City precinct and we wanted some reliable backup. Besides, according to his boss, this guy's English is fine."

"She was teasing you, Ray," Keri noted.

"Yeah, I was teasing you, Ray," Castillo said.

"That's Detective Sands to you, Officer Castillo," he responded gruffly.

"I'm not on the clock," she replied huffily." I can call you Ray-Ray if I want."

"Now he's teasing you, Jamie," Keri said. "Man, am I the only one with a sense of humor around here?"

She saw Ray and Jamie exchange glances that suggested they didn't think her sense of humor was her most notable trait but neither said anything.

"So what's the lowdown?" Castillo asked.

"According to his boss, Hernandez has lived alone since his wife left him last summer and he apparently hasn't been dating. So we think he's by himself in there," Keri said.

"He's had two arrests," Ray added. "Once for peeping, very similar situation to what Carolyn Rainey described. The other was for exposing himself to a woman in a mall. In both cases he pleaded down to probation—never served any time."

"So nothing with kids?" Castillo asked, sounding surprised.

"No, but there's a first time for everything," Ray said.

"I say we smoke him out," Keri suggested. 'We don't have a warrant or a big team so we need to get him outside. If Ray knocks on the door with his chest puffed out and you stand next to him looking surly, he may try to run out the back. I'll be waiting there to take him down. Attempting to evade should be enough to get us an arrest."

"Sounds like a plan," Ray said. "Just please don't try to use yourself as a battering ram with this guy. You've suffered enough damage for one year."

He was referring to the multiple injuries she'd incurred in the last year, including a cracked rib, a broken collarbone, a fractured eye socket, a badly strained neck, more bruises than she could count, and at least two verified concussions.

"I'll do my best, Coach," she said.

"Now she's teasing *you*," Castillo said to Ray, getting into the swing of things.

"Thanks for heads-up, Officer. Shall we get started? It's going to be daylight in a few minutes and the darkness is our friend."

"Let's do it," Keri agreed.

Castillo nodded and they all moved toward the house. Ray and Jamie hung back near the mailbox at the front of the walk while Keri skirted along the side of the house, keeping low enough to avoid being seen out a window. She kept her eyes peeled for any lights but saw none.

There was a wooden fence at the side of the property but it was only five feet high and she was able to scramble over it without much trouble. She stood there silently for a moment, listening for any sound inside.

In her experience, if Hernandez had a dog, this was around the time it would start barking. She heard nothing and proceeded cautiously around the back, undoing her holster and removing her weapon.

The sun was now peeking over the horizon and Keri zipped up her jacket. Dawn was usually the coldest part of the day and this was no exception. The temperature was in the mid-40s and she could see her breath as she inched along the back of the house.

She was reluctant to climb up on the back porch as it was wooden and she didn't know how creaky it might be. She looked around and saw a hose attached to a spigot at one end of the porch and grabbed the end, pulling it gently along the length of the porch before assuming a spot at the other end. In position and certain that Ray was getting antsy, she texted him that she was good to go.

A second later she heard a rap on the front door.

"Police," she heard Ray say in his deepest voice. "We need to speak to Enrique Hernandez. Please come to the front door, sir."

Keri heard stirring inside and then something more like scurrying.

"Please come to the door, Mr. Hernandez," Ray said again, louder and more forcefully.

Keri imagined Hernandez slipping on some shoes and creeping toward the front room, where he could peek through the curtains. Seeing Ray and Jamie, he would have three choices: open the door, demand to see a warrant, or make a run for it.

If he didn't have Jessica in the house or anything to hide, his best bet was to just open the door. If he didn't have Jessica but there was something illegal he wanted to keep hidden, he'd be better off demanding the warrant.

There was almost no circumstance in which it was advisable to run for it, barring holding a preteen girl held against her will inside his home. Then all bets were off. Keri waited anxiously to see which way it would go. It didn't take long to find out.

Within a few seconds, she heard the pitter-patter of heavy footsteps headed in her direction. A moment later, Hernandez shot out the back door. He was a heavy guy, especially for his modest height. He sported an impressive potbelly and wisps of hair clung to his mostly bald head. He had on only boxer shorts and a white tank top that was more holes than shirt.

Despite all that, he was moving fast. Keri barely had time to yank the hose up and clip his left foot as he started down the stairs. He lost his balance and careened forward, landing hard on his stomach and sliding the rest of the way until he came to a stop and the bottom.

Keri rushed around from the side of the porch and moved toward him briskly, her gun aimed directly at him.

"Stay down on the ground," she ordered.

Hernandez glanced up at her and, without a moment's hesitation, turned and started back up the stairs. Part of her wanted to just shoot him. But if he was hiding Jessica somewhere else, they'd need to interrogate him. So instead she chased him back up the stairs and into the house. These were now exigent circumstances and the search warrant could be damned.

The second she stepped through the door, she realized she was at a disadvantage, even with her gun. The sun was coming up outside but it was still dark inside and she didn't know the place. She stopped where she was, squinting in the gray darkness of the room, listening for Hernandez trying to escape.

But she heard nothing. He had only been about ten paces ahead of her when he'd entered the house, which meant he had to be nearby, either hiding or waiting to attack.

She was in the kitchen. There was a small table in a nook to her right. The fridge, stove, and oven were all to her left. The kitchen had two exits besides the back door. One opened into a large living room directly in front of her. The other, to the left next to the fridge, led down a hall that she imagined housed the bedrooms.

There's no way he went down that hall. I was in here before he could have gotten out of sight.

She could hear Ray yelling from outside. He was threatening to break down the door. Castillo was silent and Keri suspected she was making her way around back to enter that way. She didn't know if either of them had heard her order to Hernandez or realized she was already in the house.

They would both be inside soon, but she wasn't sure how soon. And if Hernandez was armed, they could be walking into an ambush, just as she feared *she* might be.

Certain that Hernandez was in the big room in front of her, she moved to the wall abutting it and held still there for a moment, listening for a creaky floorboard, heavy breathing—anything.

She thought she heard something like grunting on the other side of the wall but she couldn't be sure. As she inched closer to the open doorway, she decided her best option was to roll into the room and aim back at the wall she suspected he was leaning against.

She took a moment to gather herself and was about to dive into the living room when she heard a noise behind her. She swiveled her body around just in time to see Hernandez throwing himself at her.

CHAPTER TWELVE

In the fraction of a second before they collided, Keri reminded herself not to overreact.

She saw that his hands were empty so she resisted the urge to shoot. Instead, she lifted her gun so that its butt slammed into Hernandez's forehead as he leapt at her. It smacked square in the middle but that didn't stop his momentum from moving forward. He slammed into her and they both fell back into the main room with him on top of her.

As she fell, Keri let go of her gun so she could use her arms to brace her fall. Luckily Hernandez's living room floor was carpeted and the bulk of his weight landed on her lower half so she was able to lessen the impact as she hit, allowing her elbows and upper arms to take the brunt of it instead of her head.

Without waiting to check if she was injured, Keri looked down at the man collapsed on top of her waist and legs. He appeared dazed from the blow to the head and winded from the fall to the ground. Despite his arms clinging to her, Keri managed to free her right leg and slam it hard into his left shoulder.

His grip immediately relaxed and she was able to wriggle free. She got to her knees and grabbed her gun, which was resting on the carpet dangerously close to Hernandez's left hand. She was just getting to her feet when Ray was finally able to break in the front door. A few seconds later Jamie was in the room too, having entered from the backyard.

"You okay?" Ray asked, his eyes wide with worry.

Keri took a second to make sure. She shook her arms and rolled her shoulders. No damage there. Her lower half had taken most of the impact and she seemed to have survived that as well.

"I'm good," she finally said before looking at Hernandez. "But I'm not so sure about this guy. How about it, Enrique—that shoulder doing okay? You got a bit of a headache?"

Enrique, still out of it, groaned unintelligibly.

"I'll cuff him," Castillo said. "Why don't you take a moment, Keri?"

She was about to when her eye caught a panel jutting out from the wall of the living room. She wandered over and immediately realized how Hernandez had gotten the jump on her. The panel was hinged like a door, essentially allowing a narrow pathway between that room and the bedroom hall. He'd snuck through and come around behind her as her attention was focused on the living room.

She noticed something else about the panel. It was hollow. She turned on her phone flashlight and shined it through the gap. The whole wall between the living room and the bedroom hall wasn't dry walled but hollow as well with a space about fifteen inches wide. She was able to step easily through the gap, although she imagined it might be a challenge for Hernandez.

Could someone be hidden between these walls?

"Found something," she called out. Soon Ray was peering through the gap.

"What do you see?" he shouted. "It's too narrow for me to get through."

She thought about making a crack about how Hernandez seemed to have been able to but didn't think it would be well received so she held back.

"It gets wider the further back I go," she called back to him. And then without warning, she found herself in a small room, about the size of a closet, lit by a tiny lamp on the floor in the corner. But it wasn't the room itself that grabbed her attention. It was what was on the walls.

They were all plastered with dozens of photos of what appeared to be unsuspecting women in various states of undress. Some were taken through blinds, others through glass, and still more through clearly open windows. She recognized Carolyn Rainey in several. Clearly none of the women were aware that they were being photographed.

For a moment Keri felt sure that they had their man. But upon closer inspection, her heart began to sink. She took a few photos of the walls with her phone before snaking her way back through the passage and returning to the living room.

"What did you find?" Ray asked hopefully.

"Give me a second," she said and walked over to couch where Castillo had instructed Hernandez to sit.

"Have you Mirandized him?" she asked the officer.

Castillo nodded. Keri looked at the pitiful man in front of her, sweating profusely despite the cold and being barely clothed.

"Why do you think we're here?" she asked him.

"Because of what I did?" he asked more than said. He had a strong accent but no trouble making himself understood.

"And what was that?" she pressed.

"Taking the girl."

"What girl?"

"The one in Playa; the one whose mother has dark hair—Rainey."

"Are you confessing to taking her?" Castillo demanded, unable to control herself. But it wasn't her interrogation and Keri shot her a look that reminded her of that fact.

"Yes, yes. I took the girl," Hernandez said, almost giddy.

"Then where is she?" Keri asked, studying him closely.

"Can't say," he insisted. "I can only tell you under conditions."

"And what are your conditions?" Keri asked warily. Nothing about this felt right.

"I want to talk to my wife."

"You mean your ex-wife," Ray interjected. "Your boss said she left you because you couldn't stop peeping in women's windows."

"We're only separated," Hernandez insisted. "It's not your business anyway. If you ever want to see the girl alive again, let me talk to my wife. Make her come to see me."

Keri motioned for Castillo to keep an eye on him and she and Ray retreated to the kitchen.

"It's worth a try," Ray said when they were out of earshot.

"Does this seem legit to you?" Keri asked. "Does this seem like the kind of guy who pulled off the abduction and that whole scene at the park last night?"

"Frankly, no," Ray admitted. "But people can be surprising. Maybe this is an act. Or maybe he just stumbled into it. Either way, we've got a guy confessing to a crime. We can't just ignore that."

"Ray, I'm ninety-five percent sure this guy is just confessing so he can get in a room with his ex. He's clearly a pervert. And he may not be all there. But a child abductor—I don't see it."

"What then? What was in that room back there?"

"Pictures—tons of pictures of naked and nearly naked women."

"That's awesome," he said. "I mean, not awesome. But it's compelling evidence, right?"

"I don't think so," Keri said reluctantly as she pulled out her phone to show him the pictures she'd taken.

"Why not?" he asked.

"Because they were all picture of *women*—full-grown adult women. I'd be surprised if there's a female under twenty-five in the lot. It's not a lair back there. It's where he keeps his stash of amateur masturbation material."

She handed over her phone and Ray scrolled silently through the images, processing it all. He was about to reply when his phone rang. He returned hers.

"It's Hillman," he said and picked up. After listening for about twenty seconds, he answered "Yes, sir" and hung up.

"What is it?" Keri asked.

"He said to get over to the Rainey house. They just received another FedEx package."

"What else?" she asked. It was clear he was holding something back.

Ray let out a long sigh before responding.

"In addition to another letter, there was a piece of the clothing Jessica was wearing yesterday in the package. It had blood all over it."

<h1 style="text-align:center">CHAPTER THIRTEEN</h1>

Keri glanced up to realize they were back in Playa del Rey. She'd let Ray drive and gone into some kind of trance on the way over. She wasn't sure what she'd been thinking about on the forty-five-minute trip. She could guess it had something to do with brutalized children and devastated parents but she had no memory of it.

And yet, somehow they were here now. Ray hadn't spoken at all on the way over. During their time as partners, he'd learned that sometimes it was better to leave her alone to chart her way through her thoughts and emotions. He knew she usually made it out the other side. Usually.

There was a time, not so long ago, when moments that intensely reminded Keri of losing her daughter would send her into incapacitating panic attacks. Sometimes she would hyperventilate. Other times she would have trouble breathing at all. A few times, she lost the strength in her legs and collapsed to her knees. On at least one occasion, she'd actually passed out. Luckily she was alone and woke up after just seconds.

But that hadn't happened in months, not since she had made a conscious decision to refuse to let her fear of a horrible outcome trump her determination to reach a positive one. She hoped this extended blackout wasn't a sign that her resolve was slipping.

Once there, it took an extra five minutes to navigate all the police barriers and TV trucks on the streets surrounding the Rainey house. When they finally pulled up on Rindge Avenue, they had to park half a block away because of all the police vehicles.

"What did Castillo do with Hernandez?" Keri asked, realizing she'd been oblivious to everything that happened after Ray mentioned Jessica Rainey's bloody clothes.

"She took him back to the station for booking. Edgerton's going to check the guy's phone GPS. But unless it comes back with something shocking, it looks like he's not our guy. This package was dropped off at the airport FedEx location just after midnight. And the more I think about it, the more your theory about him just being a perv makes sense."

"Yeah," Keri agreed, trying to compel her mind back into investigative mode. "If I had to guess, I'd bet he was just following Jessica home so he could sneak a peek at her mom. He had several photos of her in that room."

They arrived at the door, where they flashed their badges for the officer standing guard out front. He nodded and opened the door. They were about to walk in when Ray put a hand on her shoulder.

"I know this is tough for you. But I have to know—are you good to go now? There's a family in there that needs Keri Locke at full strength."

"Put me in, Coach. I'm up for it," she said with more far more conviction than she felt.

Ray studied her closely and she could tell he wasn't completely persuaded. But they both knew there was nothing to do about it so he simply nodded and motioned for her to lead the way.

When they entered the kitchen, they found much of the team was already there. Lieutenant Hillman and Manny Suarez were off in a corner, looking down at what Keri assumed was the ransom note.

The Raineys were seated at the breakfast table. Carolyn's face was pinched, as if she were trying to keep it together. Tim Rainey had the hollow-eyed look of a man who'd used up all his energy reserves and was nothing but a shell now. He'd been on such an emotional roller coaster that Keri suspected he was mostly just numb.

Edgerton and Brody were sitting at the table with them and Brody was speaking quietly. Keri couldn't hear what he was saying but he was using a tone she'd never heard from him before. He sounded sympathetic, even comforting.

Tim Rainey looked over at them briefly with a stare somewhere between blank and hostile, then returned his attention to Brody. Keri and Ray made their way unobtrusively over to Hillman and Suarez.

"Is that the note?" Ray asked, nodding at the sheet of paper on the counter in a Ziploc bag.

"Yep," Suarez said, sliding it over. "Maybe you'll have more luck with it than we have. It's pretty messed up."

Keri and Ray looked down at the note, which was once again typed out, not printed on a computer. It was much shorter than the first one but equally disturbing.

You do not deserve a second chance. And yet I give you one.

The sinner should be fertilizing the ground at this moment and yet she lives.

You violated the oath of a father by bringing in the unclean pigs.

I am tempted to slaughter the young violator of his law as if she too was a pig.

I have included a small token for you, with a hint of the blood that will be spilled if you fail me again.

This creature must be snuffed out, either by me, or by you.

Provide me $200,000 and it can be you.

Call the number on the clothing.

Keri looked at the small piece of what appeared to be part of a shirt in the baggie next to the letter. It was soaked in blood except for one small section where a phone number had been written in black ink.

"Did Mr. Rainey try the number yet?" Keri asked Hillman, already knowing the answer.

"Right away," he replied. "He got nothing. It didn't even ring. He texted as well and got an error message."

"Edgerton checked," Manny added. "It's not an active number. It never was. It's like he just made it up."

"We at least know the clothing is real though," Hillman said. "The mom identified it as being from the shirt she wore to school yesterday. It's going to take a while to check on the DNA but the blood type is a match."

"I don't get it," Ray said. "He gives a dummy phone number and his note doesn't include any delivery instructions? How are the Raineys supposed to know where and when to take the money?"

They were all quiet for a moment before Keri finally spoke.

"They're not," she said. "I know none of you buy my theory, but I don't think this guy cares about the money. I think he just wants to torture these people."

"But why even mention money at all then?" Manny asked.

"To give them false hope," she replied. "A kidnapper who really wanted the money would be very clear about where to bring it. He wouldn't give an invalid phone number. This is about something else entirely."

"What?" Hillman asked, sounding willing to be convinced.

"I have no idea," she admitted.

"Then what good are you?" a voice demanded from behind her.

Keri spun around to see Tim Rainey staring at her, venom in his eyes.

"Excuse me?" she said, torn between confusion and resentment.

"You have no idea," he said, repeating her words. "But you're supposed to be the genius detective who always finds the missing kid. I've seen you on the news. You're a real hero—"

"Tim, stop," his wife interrupted, putting her hand on his. But he shook it off angrily and continued, now full-on yelling at Keri.

"No! She's the superstar detective, always brings them back safe, except when it comes to finding my daughter—or your own!"

A silence filled the room. Keri felt tears start to form at the back of her eyes but blinked hard to force them back. She felt Ray make an imperceptible move toward her, as if to somehow protect her from the sharpness of Rainey's words.

"Daddy?" a tiny, scared voice said from the corner of the room.

Everyone turned to see little Nate Rainey in the kitchen doorway. He was wearing footy pajamas and holding his dangling Pooh bear by the arm. His brown hair stuck up on one side, where it must have been pressed against a pillow overnight. He was trembling.

"It's okay, Natey," his dad said, immediately standing up, swooping over to his son and scooping him up in his arms. He carried him out of the room without another word and they could hear his footsteps on the stairs as he took the boy back to his room.

With them gone, the room returned to silence. Keri could feel everyone's eyes on her.

"I'm so sorry," Carolyn Rainey said, her voice anguished. "He didn't mean it. He's just so on edge."

"It's okay," Keri said quickly, trying to make things return to normal. But it wasn't okay. Not even close.

*

Jessica awoke with a start.

Despite her awkward position, sitting with her back against a metal pole and her arms handcuffed behind it, she'd managed to drift off. But now there was a loud clanging sound outside the metal door, as if someone was sliding a bar along it. Then there was another bang, as if another lock had been opened.

After a moment, the door slowly creaked open, shining a shaft of light into the otherwise mostly darkened room. Jessica tried to blink the sleep from her eyes. She realized she was holding her breath and reminded herself to inhale.

"Who is it?" she tried to yell. Her voice came out as a raspy croak. There was no response.

A second later someone stepped through the doorway. It was impossible to see anything other than a figure in silhouette. The person was holding something and as the door opened more, she realized it was a small stepladder.

The person walked silently past her, placed the ladder on the floor, and stood on it. Then Jessica realized what he was doing—replacing the burned out light bulb. After a few seconds it was screwed in and light flooded the room. Jessica looked away and closed her eyes, opening them slowly to let them adjust.

"Please let me go," she pleaded. The person said nothing.

She could hear him step down, fold up the ladder, and leave the room. By the time she was able to really see again, he was gone. She looked over in the corner where the skeleton lay and realized that the room wasn't actually any brighter. It was still hard to make out the form. It had just seemed brighter at first because she'd been in darkness for so long.

The shadowy figure returned to the room and she got a good look for the first time. Based on the build, it was a man. He was about five foot ten and around 180 pounds. He wore jeans and a long-sleeved khaki work shirt. He was holding some kind of bucket.

But all of those details fell away when she allowed herself to look at his face—or tried to. He was wearing a circular hat, almost like a safari hat. But hanging from the brim was some kind of tinted netting that made it impossible to see his features. After a second she grasped what it was—a beekeeper's mask. She wasn't sure why, but the realization made her spine run cold.

She looked quickly at the bucket in his hands, wondering if there was a beehive inside it. But when he placed it beside her, she saw that it was filled with some kind of stew. He grabbed something from his back pocket and Jessica flinched in fearful anticipation. But it was only a plastic water bottle. He unscrewed the top and placed the bottle next to the bucket.

He moved behind her and she lost sight of him, unsure what he was doing. Without speaking, he began to adjust her handcuffs. After a moment it became clear what he had done. Her left hand was still attached to the pole but her right hand was now loose and apparently free to drink and to scoop some of the stew from the nearby bucket.

She reached for the bottle, ignoring the mix of pain and numbness the movement caused, and immediately began to chug. Some of it went down the wrong pipe and she coughed for a while, gasping to regain her breath.

Once she had finished the whole thing, she turned her attention to the bucket. Dipping her finger into the mixture, she discovered the stew had been heated but wasn't so hot that she couldn't scoop up chunks in her hand and eat it. She looked up at the man, who was staring down at her silently.

"Why are you doing this?" she asked.

He continued to stare, saying nothing. She wanted to stare him down, to pretend that she wasn't scared. But what was the point? She couldn't see his face. She had no idea what his expression was. And her stomach was growling. Eventually she gave up and pulled the bucket toward her.

The taste was bland but not objectionable. She thought she could identify potatoes, carrots, and maybe even ground beef. She didn't know what time it was or how long it had been since she last ate but she was terribly hungry and it took everything she had to restrain herself from just shoving mounds of the goopy food in her mouth.

The man left the room, leaving the door partly open, and was gone for several minutes. She knew he had returned because she heard some sort of mumbling in the hall. At first she couldn't even identify it as language but as he got closer she was able to make out a few words, like "sin, "punishment," and "redeemer."

As he got closer, she was able to recognize complete sentences. But his low growly voice was hard to understand and the words didn't seem to make any sense at all.

"Purify the body, purify the soul. Till the soil until it runs red. Serve the redeemer by bringing the light of his vengeance into full flower. The dirty have been defiled. The defiled shall return to dirt."

She could see him now. He was backing into the room, dragging something heavy behind him. When it came into view, Jessica saw that it was a large burlap sack, likely the same material that was used to make the dress she wore now.

He dragged the sack over to the corner of the room next to the skeleton. And then, unceremoniously and without any word, he lifted the sack by the bottom. Something dropped out and landed with a thud beside the skeleton before rolling a couple of feet in Jessica's direction.

Even in the dim light, she saw what it was—a girl about her age, maybe a little older. She was wearing a tiny black skirt and a pink tube top. Her face was heavily made up but she had clearly been crying as her mascara ran down her cheeks, making her look like some kind of sad clown.

It wasn't until the man in the beekeeper's mask made the sign of the cross that Jessica fully comprehended the fact that girl wasn't just unconscious—she was dead.

Suddenly, her stomach lurched and she felt the stew rise in her mouth. She tried to reach for the bucket but didn't grab it in time. Vomit spewed everywhere, including all over her. When she was done, she tried to scream but only a little squeak came out.

The man glanced at her briefly. Even though she couldn't see his expression, she could tell he was disgusted by her. He left the room, leaving her to stare at the cold, lifeless body of the teenage girl ten feet from her. Jessica saw that her lips were blue and her skin was chalky white. How had she not realized the girl was dead right away?

The man returned and she saw that he was holding a hose. Even though she knew what was coming, Jessica couldn't help but recoil as the cold spray struck her body. He hit her full blast and the sting of the freezing jet of water took her breath away. After she was drenched, the man sprayed the vomit so that it mostly went down the drain a few feet from her.

The beekeeper finally turned off the water and left, slamming the door behind him. Jessica heard the multiple locks snap shut and the sound of his footsteps drift down the hall. Even after she knew he was gone, she sat there, too scared to speak, shivering silently as water dripped off her soaked, homemade burlap dress.

CHAPTER FOURTEEN

Keri rifled through the list on her desk for what felt like the hundredth time. She sensed the frustration rising in her chest and before she could stop herself, she took her coffee mug and threw it against a nearby filing cabinet. It shattered, sending dozens of ceramic chunks all over the precinct bullpen's floor.

"Sorry," she said to no one in particular, even though she wasn't. It was 8 a.m. and she'd been poring over a list of local sex offenders with zero success.

"Don't worry about it," Ray said and motioned to Roger Gentry, the officer from last night who was scolded by Hillman for using specific location names over the radio at the drop the night before.

"Yes, Detective?" Gentry said, excited to be noticed.

"Yeah, Gentry. I've got an important job for you. Find a broom and dustpan and clean this stuff up."

"Yes, Detective," Gentry said, the enthusiasm gone from his voice.

"You hitting brick walls too?" Ray asked Keri sympathetically.

"Yeah. I've already looked at all the janitors and bus drivers the school contracts with. Not a single hit. I mean, that's good as far as student safety is concerned. But it doesn't help us much. And reviewing these sex offender files feels like a waste of time. If this guy had been arrested before, we'd know about it. He's not the sort who can hide his crazy under a bush."

"Keri, look around," Ray said. "Everyone else has gone home for a nap. The only reason you're still here is because of what Tim Rainey said. You feel like taking a break would be failing Jessica."

"It kind of would, Ray."

"No," he replied. "Running in circles when you're too exhausted to think is failing her. Getting a few hours' sleep so that you can come back at this fresh may actually give her a better shot. Please, go home, even if it's only for a little while. Lie in your bed. Give yourself a little down time. I'll even drive you."

Keri pushed her chair back from the desk and took a deep breath.

He's right. I'm no good to Jessica like this. I need to get away for a bit, get a fresh perspective.

"Fair enough," she said. "I'm going to step away for a bit. Thanks for the ride offer but I think I'm good. I kind of need to be alone anyway."

She got up, grabbed her purse, and started for the exit.

"Keri..." Ray said.

She turned around to look at him and could tell he was wrestling with what to say. Then his expression changed and she knew he'd decided not to go with his original thought.

"Just cut yourself a break, okay?" he pleaded.

"Okay," she said, too tired to argue even though she didn't feel she deserved a break. "I'll see you in a few hours."

She left the station and got in her car. She felt her lids getting heavy and worried she might fall asleep right there. Instead, she grabbed her phone and called someone she'd been meaning to reach out to for hours now.

"Margaret Merrywether here."

Keri smiled at the familiar southern accent of her good friend.

"Mags," she said. "It's Keri. I'm about to do something incredibly stupid and I need your help."

"When and where, darling?" Mags asked without hesitation.

"I need you to help me get in touch with the Black Widower," she said, referencing the assassin-for-hire who had killed the man holding Evie and taken her to an unknown destination.

Mags didn't respond right away and Keri knew she was determining how best to calibrate her answer.

"You know I tried that, dear," Mags said compassionately. "He never responded. What makes you think he will now?"

"Because I think he uses a password to make sure anyone he interacts with is vetted. You didn't have it so he dismissed you. But I think I know what it is."

"What?"

"Weeds," Keri said. "I think he's going to ask a question and the answer will involve the word 'weeds.'"

"How did you learn this?" Mags asked, her curiosity bubbling over.

"Best not get into that, for your own good. But I'm betting that if he responds to me, I won't have much turnaround time."

"Turnaround time to do what?"

"Get Evie."

Once again, there was silence in the other end of the line. Finally, Mags replied.

"Darling, you know I adore you. And I would never underestimate you. I've seen what you're a capable of. You're kind of my hero. But are you sure it's wise to go down this path? You're talking about drawing out a real-life assassin. And even if you get his attention and he doesn't kill you, there's no guarantee that he's going to lead you to your daughter."

"I know that, Mags. But I've got to try."

"Do you?" Mags asked, concerned. "You sound either drunk or exhausted. I'm not judging but either way, you might not be in the best condition to match wits with the Black Widower."

"Maybe not alone," Keri said. "But I'll have the best muckraking journalist on the West Coast with me—Mary Brady."

"Shh. Don't say that out loud," Mags whispered. Mary Brady was the pseudonym she wrote her column under at the alternative newspaper *Weekly L.A.* Mary Brady's true identity was a closely guarded secret, meant to protect Mags against retribution from the often-dangerous targets of her columns.

"Sorry," Keri apologized. "I am a little punchy. I'm in the middle of a tough case and I haven't slept all night. But we've hit a dead end for now and this might be my only window to check up on this thing. So will you help me? Please?"

She knew Mags had a soft spot for her. That, coupled with the excitement of helping out on a case, was too much for her. It only took a second for her to cave.

"Oh fine," she said, trying to sound put out. "How do we do this?"

"Give me the Craigslist handle you have for this guy," Keri said. "I'm going to post to him."

"But what if he traces it and learns who you are?"

"I always have a few burner phones around," Keri said, reaching into her glove compartment to grab one. "I'm going to use one of those."

"Do you even have a Craigslist handle, Keri?"

"I created one the day you told me about how he operates," she admitted.

"What happens if he responds?"

"Then we send in a guy I know for the meet," Keri said. "He already promised to help me out if I ever needed his assistance."

"Who is it?"

"My Krav Maga instructor—his name is Uriel."

"You're going to put a civilian at risk?" Mags asked. She sounded genuinely horrified.

"No, of course not. Uriel can take care of himself. Besides, all he has to do is show up. I'm not even going to ask him to meet with the Black Widower. Like I said, I just want Evie. And I think I know how to find her."

"Then why does your guy have to know Krav Maga?" Mags asked suspiciously.

"In case things go south, I want my patsy to be able to protect himself. It's just a precaution."

"Darling, I'm a little troubled that your term for this gentleman is 'patsy.'"

"Mags, just give me the handle. I know what I'm doing."

Mags finally consented. Keri posted her message. It read:

Looking for a hook up. Heard you could help.

"How long did it take him to respond again?" she asked.

"I don't remember," Mags said. "But it was fast. He must get alerts when someone posts to his handle."

As if in reply, a post came in within seconds.

E-mail me here.

The message was followed by an email address. Keri had set up an anonymous email account for this very purpose and immediately sent him one. She kept it short and sweet.

As you requested.

This time the reply took a few minutes.

What's the truth today?

As she expected, it was a password test. This was where Mags had been stymied. She hadn't been aware of it and no matter how convincing she had been, he wasn't going to respond unless she had the password.

Keri typed her response but held off a moment before sending it.

"How's it going there?" Mags asked nervously over the phone.

"Okay. I'm about to send him the password and I'm worried that if I screw this up and I'm wrong about it, I've lost my one remaining connection to Evie."

"You're just now worrying about that?" Mags asked, incredulous. "I've been worried about that from the second you suggested this idea."

"Yeah, well, I guess it's too late for second guessing," Keri said and hit send. The message read:

The truth can be found in the weeds.

She sat in the front seat of her chilly car for what felt like an eternity. In reality, it was only about twenty seconds. A new response came up onscreen.

How can I help you?

Keri breathed a sigh of relief. Mags heard it.

"What is it?" she asked anxiously. "You have to let me know what's going on, Keri!"

"Sorry. It worked. I'm in."

Keri had been planning her reply to this question for weeks and didn't need time to think about it.

Looking for companionship but my tastes are risky. Heard you could help.

She read the message aloud to Mags before she hit "send."

"What are you doing?" she asked.

"You'll see. Either this will work or it won't."

A reply came in from the Black Widower.

Go on.

Keri did.

The detective's daughter, from the news. I'd like a go at her. Heard you could point me in the right direction.

She was entering perilous territory now. It was possible that the guy might decide this whole conversation wasn't worth the risk and just bug out. A new message popped up.

Where did you hear that?

Now it was time to take the biggest risk so far. Without taking the time to overthink it, she typed her message, reading it aloud to Mags only after she'd sent it, for fear her friend would try to talk her out of it.

An associate of Cave's told me. Said the boss wants to keep her under wraps. But for a finder's fee, he'd spill the beans. I paid up. Can do the same for you.

"Are you crazy?" Mags demanded after she heard what Keri had written. "He's going to run for the hills. Or worse, he'll contact Cave directly to warn him."

"Then I'm no worse off than I was before," Keri said, steel in her voice. "He might do one of those things. But I don't think so. This guy may be a cold-blooded assassin. But I don't think he's an ideologue and I don't think loyalty is a priority for him either."

"What do you mean?" Mags asked.

"He's a facilitator and a businessman. His did a job for Cave—he grabbed my daughter and killed the man who had her. But I doubt he ever promised to keep her location secret. If he can get paid off the same girl twice, why not do it?"

"Maybe because Cave might come after him?" Mags suggested. It was a good point. But it was one Keri had already considered.

"I don't think Cave knows who the Black Widower is any more than I do. This guy operates in the shadows and it's not to his advantage to let any clients know his identity. That allows him the freedom to make this kind of transaction without fearing the consequences."

Mags didn't have a comeback for that one. Keri knew what she was thinking. As someone who used a secret identity in her own work, keeping as many people in the dark as possible was a wise move.

"Keri," Mags said after a moment, "have you reconsidered just pursuing this through the department? With all their resources, wouldn't that be the best route forward?"

"I've tried. That's a dead end. I can prove Cave is into some slimy stuff but not without revealing how I got that information. And I didn't obtain it…completely legally. To be honest, I don't even care about that anymore. If going to jail myself is the price of saving Evie, it's well worth paying."

"So what's the problem then?" Mags asked.

"Proving he's slimy or even a criminal isn't enough. I need some kind of evidence that he's connected to Evie's case for the LAPD to tap his phones or do other surveillance. I *believe* he's involved. I know it in my gut. But I can't prove it. And the department isn't going after a lawyer as powerful as Cave based on my gut. That's why I was hoping to hire my own private detective to tail him."

"You think he might catch Cave going to see Evie?"

"No way," Keri said. "Cave would never do that. Besides I seriously doubt he even knows where she is exactly. If I thought he did, I'd quit the force now and follow him day and night myself. But he's too smart for that. He knows how to insulate himself. He might know a guy who knows a guy who knows where she is. But he wouldn't want too many details himself. This guy knows all the tricks."

They were both quiet for a moment. Keri could tell her friend was mulling over the full magnitude of the predicament.

"Has the Black Widower replied?" she finally asked.

"Not yet," Keri said.

"I think he's running for the hills."

"Margaret Merrywether—I come to you for sophisticated southern wit, not for doubt and recriminations. Let's be positive. Maybe he's just checking on where she is."

"I need a scotch," Mags muttered but otherwise kept quiet.

A new message popped up.

Send $10,000 to this account now. When I have it, I will provide an address.

She read the message to Mags as she replied.

Doing it now.

"Do you have ten grand just sitting around for this sort of thing?" Mags asked.

"I sold my houseboat a few months back. I was going to use the money to hire that private detective I mentioned. But this feels like a more effective use of my resources."

She sent the money from her anonymous PayPal account to his.

"What if he bails with your money and doesn't give you the information?"

"That would be a mistake. Nobody knows this guy. He can't use his charm to win over potential clients. All he has to get work is his reputation. He's known for doing the job he's paid to do. This is a job, maybe the easiest he's ever had. But it's still a job. He can't afford to renege. It's bad for business."

Thirty seconds later, her hunch was confirmed when a new message came in.

6050 Randolph Street, Commerce. Last known location as of 2 days ago. Can't promise she's still there. Good luck and enjoy.

Keri typed a quick "thanks" before switching back to her regular phone and punching the address into a map.

"Where is it?" Mags asked.

"It's a warehouse south of downtown, not far from the LA River," Keri said, her voice deflating.

"What's wrong?" Mags asked. "Do you think he was lying?"

"No. I think he was telling the truth."

"Then what's the problem?" Mags asked, perplexed.

"The last time I saw a warehouse like this, isolated in an industrial area, it was being used as a temporary location for a brothel."

"That doesn't surprise you, does it?" Mags asked, confused.

"No. I always feared that Evie was being forced into prostitution. But I could also let myself think maybe she'd been lucky enough to avoid it somehow. If she's at this place, then I don't even have wishful thinking to fall back on anymore."

CHAPTER FIFTEEN

One hour later, at 9:30 a.m., Keri and Mags, who had insisted on joining her, were sitting in the parking lot of an industrial dry cleaning company across the street from the warehouse. Things had come together shockingly fast.

Keri hadn't wanted Mags to come but got a firsthand look at how relentless her friend must be as an investigative reporter when she tried to warn her away.

"It might not be safe," Keri had said. "And I can't be focused on finding Evie and worrying about you at the same time."

"You don't have to worry about me," Mags had assured her. "I'll stay in the car the whole time. Besides, you're half-comatose as it is. I'm worried you'll fall asleep at the wheel. Let me drive and you can nap on the way."

"I am tired," Keri admitted. "But I still don't think it's a good idea. Who knows what could happen?"

"Listen," Mags had replied in a hard tone Keri was unaccustomed to hearing, "you already told me the address of the warehouse. So I'm going, one way or another. This moving brothel thing feels like a story I should be covering. I won't just ignore it. I can meet you there or we can go together and I can be your chauffeur while you get a few minutes of rest. It's up to you."

"Fine," Keri had grumbled reluctantly.

As it turned out, she didn't get any sleep on the drive over but it was nice to have company and give her brain at least a brief break. As it turned out, it ended up being very brief.

Uriel, her Krav Maga instructor, had cancelled his 9 a.m. beginner class without hesitation in order to help her. He'd driven separately and she'd explained the plan to him en route.

She told him he wasn't to try to be a hero. He was only to pretend to be looking for Evie so he could spend some "quality time" with her. Keri would give him $5,000, also from her houseboat sale. If Evie wasn't there, he was to simply leave.

They might offer him another girl. If they did, he was to decline and say he had his heart set on Evie, give them one of

Keri's burner phone numbers, and ask them to get in touch if she became available later. If Evie was there, he was to say he lost his nerve and couldn't go through with it. If they gave him a hard time or demanded payment for their trouble, he should just pay up, get out, and come to her.

Uriel pulled up at 9:35, parked on the street in front of the warehouse, and got out. He saw Keri across the street and gave her an almost imperceptible nod before heading toward the warehouse.

Uriel Magrev was six foot one and 190 pounds of rippled muscles, which his tight sweater currently showed off. His darkly tanned Israeli skin was the same color as his wavy brown hair. As he walked away from them, Mags let out a low whistle.

"Are you sure he's only your Krav Maga instructor?" she asked. "Because it looks like he could provide instruction in any number of activities."

"Don't make me regret letting you come," Keri said. "The only reason I did is because you offered to drive. I'm so tired I can barely stand up."

"As a journalist," Mags said, her eyebrows raised, "I have to tell you that I noticed you evaded my question."

"No, Mags," Keri said, not as annoyed as she let on. "He's my instructor and my friend. But nothing more."

"That's right. You only have eyes for your partner. How's that going?"

"A story for another time," Keri said.

"Fair enough," Mags said. Keri could tell she was letting that one slide even though she sensed there was more to discuss. "But if you're not interested in Uriel, and if he survives that warehouse, do you mind if I introduce myself to him?"

"Do you not find it inappropriate to be asking me this stuff when my daughter might be inside that brothel?"

"Darling, why do you think I'm doing all this? It's to take your mind off what might be going on in there. I know you well enough to know you'd obsess over this every second if I didn't distract you. Either she's in there or she's not and we'll find out in a few minutes. So in the meantime, is your instructor available?"

Keri smiled despite herself. It was true. If Mags wasn't sitting with her now, getting all aflutter over Uriel, she probably would be going crazy with anxiety. She decided to go with it and stay loose until she had reason to tighten up.

"I believe he's single," Keri said, and, trying not to sound envious but failing, added, "And I suspect he'd be into you too, what with your flaming red hair and porcelain skin and legs that go on for years."

"How nice of you to say," Mags said, playfully batting her eyes. "Maybe I'll ask him out if he leaves that warehouse intact."

"He'll be fine," Keri assured her. "Uriel was in Shayetet 13 for six years before he came here."

"What's that?"

"It's Israeli Special Forces—like their version of Navy SEALS. He could probably kill everyone in that room with his bare hands if he wanted to."

"Oh my," Mags purred, fanning herself ostentatiously.

Keri didn't say it, but the truth was that while she had no doubt Uriel could take care of himself, she was worried. Despite his charm and calm demeanor, Keri sensed that he'd been through a lot in his prior life. He never spoke of it but she could tell he was bottling up some sort of secret pain.

She suspected that it wouldn't take much for his old instincts to kick back in. If he saw Evie, she feared he might ignore her instructions and try to take action. And no matter how good he was with his hands, it just took one bullet to even the odds.

Luckily, he came out of the warehouse after about five minutes, looking unscathed. As he walked to his car, he casually motioned for Keri to come over.

"Stay here," Keri said to Mags as she got out of the car.

"But what about our introduction?"

"Not the time, Mags. This isn't a cotillion."

She thought she heard a hrumph as she ran across the street but paid it no mind.

"How'd it go?" she asked, although she could tell from his expression that he'd come up empty. Part of her was relieved.

"I'm sorry. I didn't see Evie," he told her in his thickly accented but meticulous English. "I know you're disappointed that she's not in there. But it's probably better that she isn't. There are other girls in there, some currently... being used. It was difficult to see that and do nothing."

"I know you wanted help them," Keri said. "But it might actually have put them at greater risk. Thank you for your restraint. Did the pimps say anything about her?"

"They said they didn't know who I was talking about. But I could tell they were lying. And I thought I saw one girl's head perk up when I mentioned her. She was definitely there at some point, probably recently. It doesn't look like they've been set up in there very long."

"Anything else I should know?" Keri asked.

"Yes, if you decide to have a chat with them, I'd focus on the guy in white sweats with the backward Lakers cap. He was clearly in charge and he was the one who denied that she was ever there just a little too much. And one more thing."

"Yes?"

"There are six men total. All of them have nightsticks. They've clearly been using them to keep the girls in line. But only two of them have guns—both pistols. Lakers cap guy is wearing his in the back of his waistband and a fat guy in a gray tank top with a leather coat carries his in a shoulder holster. I got the sense that they didn't trust the other guys to carry— either too young or too volatile."

"Wow, the skills never really leave you, do they?" she said, impressed.

"Sometimes I wish they did, Keri. Why do you think I teach Westside wives instead of doing security? I'm done with that life."

"So there's no way I can convince you to apply to the police academy and join LAPD? We could use you."

"I'm good, thanks," he said, smiling.

"By the way, is that really the main reason you teach the Westside wives? I thought you might just like the company."

"Well, there's that too. Speaking of, maybe you can bring your redheaded friend I saw earlier to the next class. She seems spicy."

"You have no idea," Keri said, turning back to her car and getting why Uriel had said "earlier." Mags was nowhere to be found. "Where did she go?"

"Maybe she had to go to the bathroom," Uriel suggested. "Or maybe's she's just shy."

Keri was about to disavow him of that notion when she saw his wide grin and realized he'd already gathered she wasn't.

"Thanks, Uriel. You should go now, before you get yourself in some real trouble."

"See you at class next week," he said. Then he handed her back her $5,000, gave her a kiss on the cheek, hopped in his car, and pulled out.

Keri returned across the street and pushed on the front door of the dry cleaning company. It was locked. She knocked hard and waited. No response. She wandered around back to see if there was another entrance Mags might have used to find a restroom. It was locked too. The place looked closed. Flummoxed, she texted her.

Where are you?

There was no reply. But almost immediately after she sent it, she heard shouting across the street, near one corner of the warehouse.

"Oh no, Mags," she groaned.

CHAPTER SIXTEEN

Keri grabbed her bulletproof vest and threw it on as she darted across the street and sprinted over to where she heard the raised voices. She ordered herself to stop hyperventilating and maintain control. It seemed to help. As she got closer, she realized that there was only one raised voice. It was young, male, and agitated.

The other voice belonged to Mags. Her tone was calm and measured, betraying none of the fear she must have been feeling. Keri remembered that she wasn't the only one who'd been in sticky situations.

But Mags wasn't armed and two of the guys inside were. Keri briefly thought about calling for backup. But she knew it would take too long. Anything that was going to happen would go down in the next few minutes.

Besides, that would defeat the whole purpose of checking this place out unofficially. If there was a raid of the warehouse, there would be a record of it, one that Jackson Cave could uncover. And if he realized Keri was this close to finding Evie, he might lock her down, or worse.

I have to do this now. And I have to keep it quiet. This is going to require some creativity.

Formulating a plan as she hurried over to the front door, Keri reminded herself that this wasn't just about finding Evie. If it went bad, something might happen to the only real female friend she'd had since Evie was taken. That was unacceptable.

She knocked hard on the main warehouse door. As it was being unlocked, she zipped up her jacket to hide her bulletproof vest and weapon. She also undid her ponytail and let her hair fall forward, so that her fairly recognizable face wasn't visible. If word got out that Keri Locke had been here, Cave would eventually find that out too. She couldn't leave any trace.

The door opened to reveal the fat guy Uriel had mentioned. He hadn't been kidding. The guy was well over 300 pounds and wore a fancy gold necklace that was partially hidden in the folds of his neck skin. Keri noticed that the gun was no longer in his shoulder holster. He was holding it, not pointing it directly at her but not pointing it away either.

"What?" he demanded gruffly.

"I seem to have lost my girlfriend," she said in her most coquettish voice. "We heard that this place might have some young ladies we could play some…special games with. But I went to the little girls' room across the street and I guess she couldn't wait. I could hear her voice in here. Was she causing trouble for you boys?"

The fat guy seemed at a loss as to how to respond. Keri took advantage of his indecision to step inside.

"Thanks, sweetie," she said. "It's really chilly out there."

She took in the warehouse as she pretended to look around for Mags. Three men—boys really—were spread out at various points throughout the place, holding nightsticks at the ready.

The cavernous room was filled with dirty mattresses, most of which were unoccupied. But a few had young girls lying on them. Despite what Uriel had told her, she scanned their faces to see if Evie was among them. She wasn't. But three of those girls were accompanied by adult men who had, until very recently, been having forcible sex with them. Everyone was now staring at her.

Keri had been in a place like this before. Only a few months earlier, while searching for a teenage girl, she'd uncovered another of these pop-up warehouse brothels. She and Ray had taken down the head of that sex ring. She wished she was surprised to learn there were others.

Finally she saw Mags in the corner she'd expected. Next to her were two men. One was another younger boy, probably not more than sixteen. He held a nightstick and stood next to the main man. Uriel had described him well.

He was wearing a thin white sweatsuit with gold lining and had a yellow Los Angeles Lakers cap on backward. He appeared to be in his mid-twenties and had a hard look to him, like he'd seen and done bad things. His gun was still in his waistband for now but he wasn't to be underestimated.

Mags was standing next to him, trying to look casual. It was an almost impossible feat under the circumstances but she was nearly pulling it off. She flashed Keri a tight smile that silently shouted "I have no idea what the hell to do right now."

But Keri did.

"Margaret, I wondered where you ran off to. Your little Mary was worried," she said before turning her attention to

Lakers Cap. "We're supposed to do everything together. That's why they call us M&Ms, boys. Because we melt in…well, you get the idea."

"I was just trying to get a sneak peek at the merchandise, darling," Mags said, catching on quickly and playing along. "But you texted me and I think it startled our friend here."

"So impetuous," Keri said, before turning her attention back to Lakers Cap. "I can't take her anywhere."

Lakers Cap was eyeing her suspiciously and she knew she had to get his guard down quickly or she might never do it. She saw a Chicago Bulls cap lying on a nearby mattress and bent down to pick it up.

"I hope this doesn't offend you as a Lakers fan," she said as she put it on, pulling the brim down to hide her face even more than her hair did. "I don't want to piss off our host. After all, we're here to make love, not war."

She walked toward him as slinkily as she could with a bulletproof vest and a gun under her jacket. Finally Laker Cap spoke.

"What the hell do you think you're doing, bitch?"

Keri barely batted an eye as she kept moving forward.

"Are you saying only gentlemen can have fun with these girls? What about us bitches? Isn't our money good here?"

That seemed to give Laker Cap pause.

"How did you hear about us?" he asked.

"A guy I work with mentioned this place. He knows I'm into…adventure and thought I'd enjoy it. But he never mentioned being treated this way." She nodded at Fat Guy's gun to make her point.

"We got to protect the merchandise, lady," Laker Cap said.

"I understand that. But now that we're all friends, can my lady and I take a look at what you have in stock today?"

"We never had a female customer in here but I guess it don't matter. First we got to search you and make sure you really got the money."

Keri's heart sank. She'd hoped to get out of here without raising suspicion or having a confrontation. But a search would reveal her weapon and her vest, unusual attire for one half of a lesbian couple looking for underage prostitutes. They'd know she was a cop, which would escalate the situation.

"All right, sweetie," she said, trying to channel Mags's southern charm. "But remember, no extra touching. We're not into that sort of thing."

She gave Mags a look that she hoped warned her that things were about to get hairy. Her friend seemed to get it and nodded slightly.

"I'll do you, Red," Laker Cap said to her. "Sammo, you check the little one."

As Laker Cap started to frisk her, Mags giggled, then leaned in and whispered something to him. Keri didn't know what she was saying but it was distracting him, which was good enough.

"Let me take off my jacket for you," she said to Sammo, who was putting his gun back in his shoulder holster as he lumbered toward her.

She turned away from him to unzip her jacket and casually pulled her weapon from her own shoulder holster as she waited for him to touch her from behind. She needed to know where he was in space before she reacted.

Two of the dull-eyed young guys with nightsticks didn't seem to register what she was doing. But the third clearly did. His eyes widened and he looked like he was about to speak. He opened his mouth but couldn't seem to find the words.

Keri watched him, praying for Sammo's rough touch. Luckily, she felt it only a moment later when he put his hands on her waist. She couldn't risk waiting any longer.

She giggled slightly, to draw Sammo's attention up to her face. Glancing back, she saw it had worked. At that moment, she lifted her right leg and slammed the bottom of her shoe back into his right knee.

He grunted and his hands immediately left her waist. She spun around and smashed the butt of her gun into his head as his leg buckled and he crumpled to the ground. Without waiting to see if she'd knocked him out, she gave him a swift kick to the temple to make sure. He lay still. The whole thing had taken less than four seconds.

"Boss!" the more attentive nightstick kid finally shouted.

Keri turned to face Laker Cap, whose back had been to her until now, his attention focused on flirty, wiggly Mags. He processed what was happening quickly and began to reach for the gun from the back of his waistband with one hand as he grabbed Mags's neck with the other.

Keri raised her own gun and pointed it at him.

"I wouldn't do that," she said, her voice staying level, hiding the anxiety she felt. "All we want to do is leave. If you grab that gun, I have to shoot you. If you step away from my lady friend, we just walk out and forget this whole thing happened."

"Who are you?" Laker Cap demanded, his hand still hovering in midair at his side.

"I'm just a girl who grew up in a rough neighborhood and learned to take care of herself. I like to have a good time, Boss. But this isn't any fun. I don't like having guns pointed at me. And I don't like being pawed at. So we're going to leave now."

"I can't let you go bitch. How would that look?"

"How's it going to look if I shoot you and you have to explain to your boss that some chick took you down? That is, if you survive. This way, it's our little secret. No one has to know. I'm sure your boys here can keep it buttoned up, right, boys?"

Out of the corner of her eye she saw them nodding. Laker Cap seemed to be wavering. But then his eyes lit up and she could tell he had an idea.

"How about you drop your gun or I snap your girlfriend's neck?"

CHAPTER SEVENTEEN

Keri felt a bit of bile rise in her throat and swallowed it back down. Her hands shook slightly as she gripped her gun and she hoped Laker Cap couldn't tell from where he stood.

She had been so close to cooling things off but now he'd escalated the situation. She reminded herself that despite his threat, nothing had really changed.

"You don't want to do that, Boss. If you kill my girlfriend, what do you think I'm going to do, crawl up in a ball and start crying? Or shoot you until I'm out of bullets?"

Laker Cap appeared to be considering the scenario. She continued, not wanting to lose the upper hand.

"The only way this ends well for you is if you step away from her, lie down on your stomach, and let her remove your gun from your waistband. Then we go. Margaret here will even leave your gun out front so you can retrieve it once we're gone. You can tell your boss whatever story you like after that. Everybody wins. Otherwise you end up like Sammo over there."

Laker Cap stood silently for a few moments, weighing his options. Finally he replied.

"If that happens, I don't win. I lose face."

Keri's focus turned to Mags, who was clearly trying to get her attention. Up until now, her friend had stayed mostly quiet, allowing the trained detective to handle the situation. But it was clear from her expression that she was about to take matters into her own hands.

Keri wanted to shake her head but Laker Cap was watching her closely and would notice. It didn't matter anyway because a second later, Mags lifted her foot and jammed down the sharp heel of her shoe onto the top of Laker Cap's sneaker.

He gasped in pain and let go of her enough for Mags to yank herself free and step away. Keri started toward him but he quickly regrouped and reached toward his waistband again.

"Don't," Keri ordered, now only ten feet away from him. "You'll be dead before you get it out."

His hand hung in the air, his fingers twitching, his eyes unblinking. Now up close, it occurred to her that he could be high. If that was the case, then reasoning with him might be fruitless. Her finger caressed the trigger as she waited for his decision.

He blinked. It was a small gesture but she knew what it meant. In his own mind, he'd conceded. It was confirmed when he moved his hand away from his waistband and sighed deeply.

"Good choice, Boss," Keri said. "Now lie down on the floor so my gal pal can take your gun."

He did as he was told. Mags took the gun from his waistband and stepped over next to Keri.

"Now the rest of you boys come on over here where I can see you and lie down next to your boss."

They followed her instructions. When they were all prone, she walked over, grabbed one of the nightsticks, and leaned down next to Laker Cap. His head was down so he couldn't see her.

"You're getting off easy, Boss," she whispered. "This could have gone much worse for you. Don't try to find me. I've killed tougher guys than you. You understand, bitch?"

He started to respond but Keri didn't wait to hear it. She brought down the nightstick on his head. There was loud crack and then a second one when his head hit the warehouse floor. His body slumped. He was unconscious.

Things moved quickly after that. Keri had the younger guys drag Laker Cap and Sammo into the bathroom, then hand over all their phones and get in themselves. She smashed off the inside door handle and then locked it from the outside.

She wanted to arrest the johns, whom she assembled in a far corner of the warehouse. But that meant she'd be breaking her cover. Right now they thought she was a female version of them—an adult hoping to take advantage of underage girls. But arrest them and they'd know that was a lie. Even locking them in the bathroom with the others and calling 911 was unwise.

Arrests, even by others, meant paperwork and loose talk about the hardcore chick who'd taken them all down. It was just one more way word might get back to Cave. It also increased the chances that everyone she busted would want retribution. She didn't need more enemies. Right now, it was only Laker Cap, and maybe Sammo, who wanted her dead. They'd feel even more strongly after what she was about to do.

'Boys," she said to the three johns. "This is your lucky day. You can leave."

It took everything she had not to call them perverts as they walked to the exit door. The man in front, a forty-something guy in a polo shirt and retro black Members Only jacket, gave her a half sneer as he walked by. Something in her snapped.

She stepped forward quickly and kicked him in the shin. Wincing in pain, he took a swing at her. She avoided it easily, grabbed his arm, and pinned it behind his back. Stopping just a fraction of an inch before breaking it, she held his arm there, letting him wonder if she'd give that last little push.

"You gonna sneer at me anymore, tough guy?" she muttered as she frog marched him to the door.

Whether it was from stubbornness or pain, he didn't respond. Keri slammed him against the metal door before bringing her knee up to his groin, making direct contact. She let go of his arm as he doubled over, slamming his forehead against the door. The loud clang reverberated throughout the warehouse. As he sank to the floor, she turned to the remaining johns.

"Anyone else want to give me a dirty look?" she asked. "Maybe share a few thoughts?"

The men stood silent, frozen in place.

"I didn't think so. Leave. Don't come back. Or I'll use my gun. Not that I need it."

They rushed out, followed closely by Sneer Guy, who crawled more than walked. She slammed the door behind him, trying to pour all her rage into that act so she could set it aside for what she knew came next.

When they were gone, she turned her attention to the girls. There were eight of them in total. Keri wanted to ask them if they'd seen Evie. But she knew that might blow her cover. Any of these girls might tell their pimps about the suspiciously curious woman at the warehouse.

Besides, none of them were in any condition to answer questions. Half looked scared. The other half were too drugged up to express any emotion. Mags was sitting on a mattress next to one who was in particularly bad shape, helping her sip some water.

Still, this might be the only chance she would get to ask them about Evie. If she didn't at least try, then all that effort to reach out to the Black Widower, not to mention the $10,000 she'd sent him, would be wasted. She decided to give it one last, very delicate shot.

"Listen, girls," Keri said to the ones who could hear her. "My friend and I aren't interested in hurting you or making you do anything you don't want to. In fact, we'd like to help you, if you'll let us. I know a woman who runs a home for girls in your situation. I don't know if she can house all of you but I'm sure that if she can't, she'll find other places that will. We'll even get you rides."

"I don't want to go to some home," one of the druggy girls slurred. "I just want out of here."

"That's fine too," Keri said, even though every part of her screamed that it was not fine. "If you just want a ride to the bus station or a shelter or wherever, we can coordinate that too. But I doubt any of you want to stay here, right?"

Everyone who could shook their head.

"Okay, then we'll make it happen. I just have one question. That guy who came in earlier asking about that girl, I know you couldn't say anything to him before. But you can speak openly now. Did any of you see her here?"

At first, Keri didn't think anyone would answer. But finally a waifish blonde-haired girl spoke up.

"I only got here this morning," she said. "But they didn't take or add anyone since then."

Two others, both Hispanic, both around twelve years old, shook their heads sadly. The last one, a pale brunette who looked like she feared Laker Cap might bust out of the bathroom at any second, barely even acknowledged her, looking away without responding.

"It's really important," Keri insisted, trying to keep her voice even. "If you could just think back…"

Mags, sitting next to the barely responsive girl on the mattress, caught her eye and almost imperceptibly shook her head. Keri knew what she was trying to say. Hell, she was thinking it herself.

It's no good. These girls don't know anything. And they're in bad shape. Pummeling them with questions will only make them worse. Let them be. You'll find another way. There's always another way.

Reluctantly, Keri pushed her own pain into the ever-growing pit in her stomach and tried to focus on these girls, all desperately in need of her help.

She ordered cabs to take the four drugged-up girls directly to the hospital. Of the remaining four, the two Hispanic girls asked to go to shelters. Only two, the waifish blonde and the pale brunette, were interested in the group home.

They got in the backseat and Mags drove since Keri felt, despite everything, like she might drift off at the wheel. She had to make a call but before she did, she turned to her friend and asked the question that had been eating at her for a half hour.

"What the hell were you thinking?" she demanded.

"What?"

"I'm talking to Uriel and you decide to just sneak off to check out a brothel run by armed thugs?"

"I didn't know they were armed," Mags replied, far too casually for Keri's taste.

"This isn't funny. Things could have gone much worse in there."

"They didn't even know I was there until you texted me."

"That's your defense?" Keri asked, disbelieving.

"I don't need a defense…Mary," she said sharply, apparently not sure if she still needed to keep up the fake name ruse in front of the two girls in back, although both looked oblivious. "The truth is, I saw a blonde female near the back of the warehouse and I thought it might be the person we were looking for, so I went to check it out. I didn't want to get your hopes up in case I was wrong."

"And?"

"And it was a good thing I didn't say anything because it ended up just being a very short elderly woman wearing an inappropriate wig."

"Are you telling me the truth?" Keri demanded skeptically.

"I am. Although I admit that once I was there I thought taking a peek inside wouldn't do any harm. And it wouldn't have if I hadn't gotten a really loud text while I was trying to spy on them."

"So you put your safety on the line for a potential story?" Keri asked, incredulous.

"It started because I thought I might have seen Evie! And then as long as I was back there anyway…" She sighed. "Listen, you know what I do for a living. But you don't know why I do it. And I'm not going to apologize for pursuing a story I believe is important."

"What do you mean I don't know why you do it?"

"We all have our demons," Mags said. "Not everybody's end up on the news. But we still have them. Anyway, I saw an opportunity to get up close to a situation that might be worth investigating, so I took it. In retrospect, maybe it wasn't the wisest move. But darling, I'm not always the wisest girl. Ask my ex-husband about that."

Keri could tell that her friend wasn't going to back down. They were equals in the stubbornness department. She decided to let it go for the time being, especially since she still had to find a place for the girls.

She called up Rita Skraeling, who ran the South Bay Shared Home in Redondo Beach. She was housing a fourteen-year-old girl named Susan Granger, whom Keri had rescued from her pimp last year.

In recent months, Susan had really blossomed at the home. Keri tried to visit her weekly. Susan seemed interested in becoming a cop and peppered Keri with questions about law enforcement on every visit.

"I have room for one girl right now," Rita told her, her gravelly, nicotine-stained voice rasping over the phone. "Give me whichever one looks worse off. I'll text you the address of another good place in Long Beach for the other girl. I know they have an open slot right now."

"Thanks, Rita, and one more thing. This needs to be unofficial. On the paperwork, just say a good Samaritan brought them in. I can't have it traced back to me."

"Normally, I'd say screw off to that," Rita replied. "But since it's you, I'll look the other way."

"I appreciate it."

She had just hung up when another call came in. It was Ray.

"You get some sleep?" he asked.

"Yeah," she lied, suddenly remembering again how exhausted she was. "What's up?"

"CSU found a partial fingerprint in Jessica Rainey's stuff, one they missed before. Castillo and I are on our way to check it out now. Can you meet us?"

"Sure," she said. "Where?"

"The school. The print belongs to one of her teachers."

CHAPTER EIGHTEEN

Keri pulled up in front of the school at 10:45 a.m. She sat there quietly for a moment, wondering whether the clearly deranged person who'd taken Jessica was in one of the classrooms on the seemingly pristine campus.

Mags had agreed to drive the two girls to the group homes so Keri could head straight here. Neither said much for the rest of the drive back but the hug they shared before parting ways was intense. Keri could feel her friend thanking her with the tightness of her squeeze.

"Drinks are on you next time," Keri had said when they pulled apart. Mags nodded but said nothing. It was a rare occasion when Margaret Merrywether was left speechless.

Keri shook the pleasant memory from her head and focused on the task at hand. There was a potential kidnapper in the school and it was her job to find out the facts.

She walked to the main office, zipping up her jacket against the chill in the air. Ray and Jamie Castillo were waiting. When she stepped inside, they filled her in.

"Our suspect is Justin Hensarling," Ray said. "Thirty-one years old. He teaches 6th grade history. Jessica is in his third-period class. CSU found a partial print on the iron-on school logo on her gym shirt. They didn't think to check the clothes at first because they don't usually maintain prints. But Edgerton noticed the logo and had them try."

"Why are we so suspicious about a print on her shirt?" Keri asked. "Couldn't it be inadvertent?"

"It's possible," Ray said. "But the girls only wear gym uniforms during gym class. And he doesn't teach gym. His classroom is clear across campus. There's no reason his print should ever have come in contact with her shirt."

"Fair enough," Keri said. "Let's meet Mr. Hensarling."

"Okay, so how do we want to handle this?" Castillo asked. "If he's our guy, he might get suspicious if the principal asks him to come to the office. We don't want him losing it in a classroom full of kids."

"Good point," Keri said. "Is he married?"

"Yes," Castillo said, looking at his file. "For three years."

"Okay," Keri said, pausing for a moment to think before launching into her plan. "We have an office assistant go to his classroom and ask him into the hall because he has an urgent message from his wife. When he steps out, we'll be there waiting to escort him to a secure area."

Ray and Jamie nodded, and moments later, the principal agreed to the plan on the condition that they stay out of sight. She didn't want to freak out the kids. And if it turned out there was an innocent explanation, she didn't want her teacher's reputation injured because he was seen being interrogated by uniformed police officers.

They agreed and the assistant led them to the classroom. Castillo waited in an exterior hallway while Keri and Ray positioned themselves on either side of the classroom door, out of sight.

The assistant, clearly nervous, knocked on the door and opened it.

"You have a message, Mr. Hensarling," she said, her voice shaking.

Ray looked at Keri and she knew he was thinking the same thing she was—this woman was going to blow the whole thing.

"Well, bring it on in, Nicole," they heard Justin Hensarling say casually.

"Um, you may want to look at it out here," she replied. "It's from your wife."

They heard a scrape as Hensarling quickly pushed his chair back.

"Keep reading, students," he said, his voice now far less casual. "I'll be right back."

It occurred to Keri that the assistant's quaky voice might actually be a benefit. Hensarling might attribute it to her having bad news from his wife that she was hesitant to share. A second later, he stepped into the hallway.

"What is it, Nicole?" he asked as he took the paper. "You've got me worried here."

He unfolded the paper, saw that it was blank, and looked up, confused. It was only then that he noticed Keri standing a few feet away.

"What's going on?"

"You can go now, Nicole," Ray said from behind Hensarling, startling him. "We need to have a chat with you, Mr. Hensarling."

Nicole scurried off and the teacher involuntarily backed away from Ray. Keri moved in close behind him and spoke quietly in his ear.

"Your wife is fine, sir. But we're with the LAPD and we need to speak to you. We'd like you to step outside so we can talk without making a scene. Do you understand?"

Hensarling was shaken but he nodded and followed Keri out the door to where Jamie was waiting. Ray followed close behind. Jamie led them to an out-of-the-way alcove out of sight of any classrooms.

"Mr. Hensarling," Ray said when they finally stopped, "do you know why we're here?"

"No?" Hensarling answered although it sounded more like a question.

"Is there anything you'd like to tell us regarding your interactions with your students?" Keri asked. She didn't want to be too accusatory to start. Maybe he'd hang himself without their help.

"I don't know what you're talking about," he insisted unconvincingly.

"Mr. Hensarling," Ray said. "Do you know Jessica Rainey?"

"Of course I know her," he said, sounding annoyed at the question. "She's in my class. Is that what this is about? You think I had something to do with her disappearance?"

Keri glanced over and nodded at Jamie, who stepped forward.

"At this point I'm going to read you your rights, Mr. Hensarling," she said, looking intimidating in her uniform. "If you're still willing to answer our questions after that, I'm sure we can clear all this up."

She proceeded to Mirandize him. When she was done, Keri stepped forward and spoke in a quiet voice.

"Understanding these rights, are you willing to talk with us, Mr. Hensarling?"

"Yes. I have nothing to hide," he said confidently

"Then why was your fingerprint found on Jessica Rainey's gym shirt?" Ray asked.

Hensarling's face went white and he stood dumbly for a full five seconds before answering.

"That's not what you think," he finally said, sounding suddenly far less confident.

"What is it then?" Ray asked.

"Oh Jesus. I can't believe this. I never thought that anyone would care."

"Mr. Hensarling," Keri said, stepping even closer so that she was only inches away from him. "I'm losing patience with you. There's a missing girl out there. If you're not responsible, explain yourself. Whatever you did, if it wasn't kidnapping a child, you'll be in less trouble if you're forthcoming about it."

"Oh god," he said, starting to whimper. "I have this thing. I like to…smell their clothes."

"What?" Castillo blurted out disgustedly, getting a look of rebuke from both Keri and Ray. Once a suspect starts talking, you don't do anything that will make them stop.

"I like to smell the girls' clothes," he repeated. "There's just something about the scent after they've been sweating. I know it sounds strange but…I like it."

"Go on," Keri said, making sure to keep any judgment out of her voice.

"When the girls are at lunch or a break, I'll sometimes take their clothes out of their backpacks and…smell them. I swear that's all. It's not the panties or anything—just the used gym clothes. I don't even look to see whose they are. It doesn't matter. I must have smelled Jessica's at some point. I don't really know."

The three cops stood silently. No one really knew what to say. Keri had never heard anything like this before. She was sure it was illegal but didn't even know exactly what law he had broken. Eventually she forced herself to speak.

"Where were you yesterday afternoon between two thirty and three p.m.?" she asked.

"What?" he asked, still rattled by the prior topic.

"Where were you—" Keri started to repeat when Hensarling interrupted.

"I had academic decathlon," he answered excitedly. "I'm the coach. School ends at two thirty-five. The team starts practice at two forty-five and it runs until four p.m. I was in my classroom the whole time. There are ten students who can attest to it."

Keri, Ray, and Jamie all looked at each other. No one could hide their disappointment. The bell rang and kids started to pour out into the courtyard.

"Do you have a class this period, Mr. Hensarling?" Ray asked.

"Yes," he answered.

"Well, we're going to have to call in a substitute. You'll need to come down to the station to discuss this further. Please wait here with Officer Castillo."

He stepped further into the alcove and motioned for Keri to join him.

"What do you think?" he asked.

"I think he's probably telling the truth. Who would admit to something like that if it wasn't true? Besides, he doesn't give off the vibe I get from those ransom letters. I doubt he could muster that kind of fervor."

"Well, vibe or not, he's guilty of something, although I'm not sure what," Ray said. "We can have Castillo check with the decathlon kids about his alibi. Meantime, let's get him to the station so we can hand him off to someone else and pursue some leads that might actually go somewhere."

"Sounds good to me," Keri agreed. "I don't want to spend any more time with this guy than I have to."

"Hey guys," Castillo called out to them, "Edgerton didn't want to interrupt you so he texted me."

"What's up?" Ray asked.

"You should head back to the station. He just got a call from a sheriff in Missouri. He recognized the MO. It looks like our guy has done this before."

CHAPTER NINETEEN

Keri, Ray, and the team were all in Lieutenant Hillman's office with the door closed. It was quieter than the bullpen, so they could better conduct the conference call with Sheriff Mitch Calvert of Boone County, Missouri, which according to a quick map search, included the city of Columbia.

"Our entire team is on with you, Sheriff Calvert," said Kevin Edgerton, who had spoken briefly with the sheriff earlier. "Can you please tell everyone what you told me before?"

"Sure. Where should I begin?" Calvert asked. From his voice, Keri guessed he was in his fifties or sixties.

"Sheriff, this is Lieutenant Cole Hillman. I run the Missing Persons Unit for our West LA Division. We appreciate you reaching out. Maybe you could start by telling us what made you think there might be a connection between our case and yours."

"Sure. The first thing was the notes—the ransom notes. They've got the same kind of language that we got in some notes from a case here about seven years ago."

"Hi, Sheriff, this is Detective Keri Locke. How were they similar?" Keri asked.

"They had the same religious overtones, like the guy was a zealot. Also, our guy never showed up at the first ransom drop here either. And in the second note we got, there was no request to meet up, just like with the second one you got. Also, our girl was about the same age—eleven, name was Noreen Appleton. From a small town called Elkhurst just outside Columbia."

"This is Ray Sands, Sheriff. How come we never heard about your case when we were looking for similar ones?" Ray asked.

"I'm embarrassed to say it. But we got a confession from a vagrant and we closed the case. The guy was new to town and had been arrested a few times for petty stuff so there was already some animosity toward him from locals."

"But you had doubts?" Keri asked.

"I did. It never quite sat right with me. I didn't know how the guy would access a typewriter to write those notes. And he didn't talk in the flowery way they were written. I doubt he even knew most of the words in them. And we never found a body. But we had the confession, so it wasn't an unsolved case and there was no reason to post the letters in the database."

"You say you never found a body?" Keri asked.

"Nope. We scoured the county, even used cadaver dogs, which was a real expense for us. Had to bring them in from St. Louis. But it didn't make any difference in the end. And our suspect refused to say anything. At the time, we thought he was protecting himself—no body, hard to make a case. But looking back, I think he might just not have known anything."

"Detective Manny Suarez here. How many notes did you ultimately get?" Suarez asked.

"Just the two. We never heard from him after that. I don't know if he lost interest or moved on or what. Of course, if it was the vagrant, that makes sense because we arrested him so maybe he never had time to write a third one. But I don't really buy that."

"Was he convicted?" Hillman asked.

"He was. Jury took less than thirty minutes. First degree murder—even without the body, he got thirty years to life. Didn't last long though—wasn't a fan of confinement. We found him in his cell the morning he was supposed to be transported to the state prison. He'd shaved off a piece of his metal meal tray and used it to slice up his wrists."

"I'm sorry, Sheriff," Hillman said.

"Yeah, me too. It's one of those I wish I could have back, you know? Especially if my corner-cutting has put another girl at risk."

"Why do you think he confessed if he didn't do it?" Keri wondered.

"I've asked myself that many times. Part of me thinks he just did it for the attention. I could tell he liked having all the cameras around. But once he saw the girl's family in court, he seemed to lose his enthusiasm. I think he knew he was adding to their suffering. His apology at sentencing was really heartfelt, which was odd considering he wasn't guilty. Maybe he was atoning for other sins."

The room was quiet after that as everyone let the thought sink in.

"Thank you, Sheriff," Hillman said eventually. "I think that answers everything. Maybe you could send us copies of your ransom letters. There might be something useful in them."

"Will do. I wish y'all the best of luck. And that little girl too," he said before hanging up.

"Well, you know what this means?" Brody said. He'd been silent through the entire conference call so Keri was surprised that he had input now.

"What's that, Frank?" Hillman asked.

"It means this guy has committed crimes in multiple states. It's federal now. We can hand this thing over to the FBI and let them deal with this dog of a case."

"Jeez, Brody," Keri said, repulsed and unable to conceal it. "Aren't you retired yet? Please tell me you're gone soon because you've already basically checked out."

"What? Because I know a loser case when I see one? At least we can get it off our ledger. One less unsolved case for West LA Division. I'm actually being a team player here."

"I'm not sure about the team player part," Hillman said, picking up the phone and dialing. "But he's right. I do need to call the FBI. There's no guarantee that this is the same suspect but we have to alert them in case. They'll probably want to send a team to Elkhurst too."

"But the second we do that, they'll shut us out," Keri warned.

"Not necessarily," Hillman said. "They'll want to take point for sure. But they'll need us to fill them in and I suspect they'll want us for tactical support and to establish a rapport with the family."

"Like the one Locke established with Tim Rainey?" Brody asked sarcastically.

Ray stood up and stared down at Brody, who was lounging sloppily on a couch.

"Shut up, Frank," he said in a quiet, terse voice. "Know your limits or I'll help you find them."

Ray Sands was the only detective in the unit whose balls Frank Brody was reluctant to bust. Aware that he'd gone too far, he got up and hurried out, mumbling something about having to take a piss.

"Thanks," Keri said. "But I had that."

"I know you did but I worried that your version of 'had that' was going to be to kick him in the throat. I just wanted to save you a suspension."

Before she could reply, Hillman hung up.

"The feds say they've been waiting for us to call," he said. "They'll be here in ten minutes."

FBI agents Winchester and Crowley sat in the conference room, listening as the Missing Persons Unit updated them on everything they knew about the case so far. Winchester was the younger of the two, likely under thirty-five. Attractive in a blocky kind of way, he clearly spent a lot of his time working out. He wore a tight dress shirt that accentuated his bulging chest and arms. Keri wasn't impressed. He kept interrupting to ask things they were about to tell him anyway.

Crowley seemed to have more potential. He was older, likely in his late forties, and had enough stubble growth to suggest he sometimes forgot appearances when work became all-consuming. His shirt and jacket were wrinkled, almost as if he'd slept in them the night before. He stayed mostly quiet and the comments he did make were on point.

"This is an odd one," he acknowledged when they were done with their presentation. "I have to say, we've gotten our fair share of ransom notes and lots of letters from religious fanatics. But I don't think they've ever overlapped before."

"And they're not overlapping here either," Winchester said with unjustified certainty. "What I think we've got here is a guy faking being a nut job to keep us off the scent."

Even though she'd only just met him, Keri had had enough of this guy, especially if he was just going to regurgitate the stale theories of her colleagues.

"Then why didn't he take the money the first night in the park, when he had the tactical advantage?" she asked, trying to keep the disdain out of her voice.

The rest of the unit, even Brody, nodded in agreement.

"Maybe something wasn't right," Winchester said defensively, "something only he knew about."

"Okay," Keri countered. "Then what about the second note? He didn't even offer a drop location. How was he going to get his money?"

"He was probably going to do it via the phone number he gave the Raineys. But something went wrong with it."

"So according you," Keri said, her blood rising, "the same guy who kidnapped Jessica without anyone seeing, who managed to avoid surveillance at the FedEx store, who didn't leave a single clue to his identity also forgot to buy a working cell phone?"

Ray stared at her hard, a warning that she was in dangerous territory. Alienating an FBI agent was never a smart move.

"It's possible," Winchester grumbled.

"Possible," Crowley said, trying to lower the temperature in the room. "But not likely."

"Okay," said Winchester. "So maybe it's not about the money. Maybe he's just some pervy sex freak. You read those letters. This guy is seriously into discussing sin."

Keri grunted despite herself. Now Hillman shot her a look. She was amazed he hadn't shut her down yet. Part of her suspected he felt the same way about Winchester and enjoyed seeing him get taken down a peg.

"Detective Locke," Crowley said with just a hint of amusement, "I gather you feel differently?"

"I do. He may be a freak but I doubt it's of the pervy sex kind."

"How could you possibly know that?" Winchester demanded.

"Just look at the letters, Agent. Yes, they're about sin—but hers, not his. He doesn't want to rape this girl. That would be a violation of his warped faith."

"What does he want then?" Crowley asked.

"Just what he says he wants—to purify her through blood."

"You really believe that?" Winchester asked, skeptical.

"Why wouldn't I? What's that famous line—when someone shows you who they are, believe them. He's showing us who he is, even if he's trying to fight it."

"What makes you think he's trying to fight it?" Crowley asked.

"It's like I said to the unit that first night—if he was totally committed to this, he wouldn't have offered to return her to let Tim Rainey purify her. He has to know her father won't kill her. But if he can convince himself that it's possible, then he's not violating his beliefs by letting her go. That means there's still some vestige of his humanity fighting against his murderous impulses."

"If that's true," Crowley said, "maybe we can use that. Maybe we can appeal to what's left of that humanity."

"Maybe," said Keri skeptically. "But I see some problems with that."

"What?" Winchester demanded, almost belligerently.

"We have no idea how to get in touch with him," Keri said, refusing to be baited by the guy's tone. "All his interactions have been one way. He sends letters. He sends texts and dumps the phone. There's no way to connect with him if we can't communicate with him."

"Good point," Crowley agreed. "What's the other?"

"The other what?"

"You said you saw 'problems,'" he reminded her. "Was there another one?"

"Yeah. Even if we knew how to get in touch with this guy it might not do any good."

"Why do you say that?" he asked.

"Because if what that Missouri sheriff told us is right, we may not be getting any more letters. They only got two. Then they never heard from him again. It was like he could only hold the darkness at bay for so long before he gave in. If that's the case, we may already be too late."

*

Jessica knew it was daytime. She could see minuscule slivers of light between the cracks in the concrete room. She was tempted to yell for help again but she knew it was a waste of time. Those tiny cracks weren't enough for her voice to penetrate. Besides, she was too tired to try.

Most of her energy the last few hours had been focused on finding a way to loosen her left hand, still handcuffed to the pole in the middle of the room. She had tried pounding at it with the bucket that had held the stew. She had visions of freeing herself and then hitting the guy over the head with the bucket when he came in the room.

But all she had done was bruise her wrist. And she was reluctant to try again, because in the hours since then, she'd had to use the bucket as a toilet. So instead, she'd managed to tear off a shard of plastic from her water bottle and fashion it into a thin pin. For over an hour now, she'd been poking it into the handcuff keyhole, trying to somehow unlock it.

So far it hadn't worked. All she had to show for her efforts was a burlap dress drenched in sweat and some cut up fingers. She was just debating whether to give up when she heard a noise. It took a moment for her to realize it was a voice—the man's voice.

He was somewhere just outside the door and it sounded like he was talking with someone. It didn't take long for her to grasp that he was in a heated argument with himself. She couldn't

114

make out full sentences but she could hear phrases like "rotting essence," "purification ritual," and "mercy for the lamb."

It dawned on her that he was arguing about her, debating with himself about whether he should kill her or not. One voice, calmer and quieter, seemed to be making the case for sparing her life. The other voice, louder and more frenzied, believed that the time had come to "release her from the prison of her bodily wretchedness." That voice seemed to be winning.

Jessica stopped trying to free her hand and scrambled back to the other side of the metal pole, as far from the door as possible. She eyed it warily, waiting to see if he would open it. But after a few more seconds, the voices receded, as if he were walking down a hall. She took a deep gulp of air, only now aware that she'd been holding her breath the whole time.

As she took a second breath, she sensed something off in the air. There was a putrid scent that reminded her of the time her family had gone on a trip to the mountains. When they'd stepped into their rented cabin, they were immediately overwhelmed with a similar rancid smell.

It turned out that a raccoon had somehow gotten into the cabin but couldn't find his way back out. Her father had discovered the rotting body curled up under the bed in the master bedroom.

A wave of simultaneous realization and horror washed over Jessica. She turned to the darkened corner of the room and saw that she was now at least five feet closer to the body of the dead girl than she had been before. Just that small difference in distance was enough for the stench of the girl's rotting body to overwhelm her nostrils.

Jessica scurried back to the other side of the pole and reached for the bucket. Oblivious to what was already inside it, she leaned over and threw up.

CHAPTER TWENTY

Keri needed a break. Her back ached and her eyes were starting to blur involuntarily.

For the last five hours she and the rest of the team had been poring over FBI and local police reports from all over the country. They had been going through every case that had even one similar hallmark to the Jessica Rainey one, looking for a break. So far, they'd come up empty.

Agents Crowley and Winchester, now officially in charge of the case, had given the unit access to the FBI case files. It may have sounded like a form of cooperation and goodwill. But in truth, it was just a way for them to dump the grunt work on the local cops while they went out in the field to look at locations the LAPD had already vetted.

According to Hillman, they had already been to the school and to the Rainey house to interview the family and were now on their way to Chace Park. Keri doubted they'd find anything new but she was glad to have them out of her hair.

She stood up, stretched, and went to the break room to grab some coffee. Looking out the window for the first time in hours, she saw that it was now dark. The clock read 5:57 p.m.

Seeing the time jogged her memory. There was an uncomfortable call she needed to make and if she didn't do it before 6 p.m., it would be even more awkward.

Because she'd used a big chunk of the money from the sale of her houseboat to pay the Black Widower for the tip about the warehouse brothel, she didn't have enough left for the private investigator she'd wanted to hire to surveil Jackson Cave. But there was one person with nearly unlimited resources and, in theory, the desire to use them: her ex-husband, Stephen.

With all her own leads exhausted, Keri's plan was for the PI to track Cave's movements and calls to see if they might reveal something about Evie. She already knew the lawyer was involved.

Thinking back, she recalled all his connections to the case. He had been the attorney for the Collector, who had originally kidnapped her daughter almost six years ago. Just this last fall, he had tipped off the older man who was holding Evie that Keri was on to him. And he'd almost certainly hired the Black Widower to kill the older man and return Evie to the shadows. Somehow, Jackson Cave was the key to all of it. And she needed to know what he knew.

The PI she wanted to hire was a guy named Curt Wadlow. Keri knew him because their work had overlapped on several cases. She liked and respected him. He and his small team were meticulous and careful, which was essential when going after someone as wily and powerful as Cave. But that talent didn't come cheap.

She could pay Wadlow's $5,000 deposit. But he'd warned her that the kind of surveillance that would be required to go after someone like Jackson Cave would quickly add up, potentially going as high as $20,000 in the first month. And that was after the discounted rate she knew he was giving her. She just didn't have it.

That where her ex came in. She and Stephen Locke had divorced nearly five years ago. While Keri's life fell apart for a while after that, his only seemed to improve. He'd been made a partner at his Beverly Hills talent agency. He had married one of his clients, a perky but talentless starlet named Shalene. They had a child, a little boy named Sammy who was about three now.

Keri resented him but not so much due to his new life as because of how easily he had seemed to shed his old one. He had moved on without ever looking back and didn't seem even slightly weighed down by the dissolution of their marriage or even the loss of his own daughter.

Sometimes Keri thought she was being uncharitable. But then she'd remember how less than a year ago, she'd gone to him pleading for his assistance to hire an investigator. Not only had he rejected the request, he'd told her she needed to move on, that he was worried about her mental health.

The meeting had ended in shouting, mostly from her. She said some things she wished she could take back. Of course, that was before Keri had seen Evie with her own eyes, coming within fifty feet of her before her daughter was ripped away a second time.

So Keri stepped outside into the unusually cold early evening Los Angeles air and prepared to call a man she despised and beg him for the money to find his own daughter. She knew he usually got home around 6 p.m. and if he was home when she called, he likely wouldn't pick up. Better to get him when he was alone.

She dialed his number and waited as the phone rang, trying to ignore the uneasy feeling growing in her chest. After three rings, he picked up.

"Hi, Keri," he said, his voice already sounding wary.

"Hi, Stephen. Did I get you at an okay time?"

"I'm almost home so I only have a few minutes," he said. "Is everything okay?"

"Yeah. I'm sorry to bother you. I won't beat around the bush. I need your help."

"What is it this time?" he asked tersely.

Keri felt the irritation rise in her throat and reminded herself to keep it in check. This was to be expected. She knew he was going to push her buttons, even if he didn't realize he was doing it.

Stay calm. Keep focused on your goal. Do whatever it takes. Evie is more important than your pride.

"I'm not sure if you're aware of this but we had a break in Evie's case in November."

"Go on," he said, revealing nothing.

"Just after Thanksgiving, I found a clue that led me to the address where she was being kept. I saw a man shoving her into a gray van. They got away but I saw her, Stephen. It was our little girl. She even called out "mommy" to me. I'm sending you a video clip now. It's from a Walmart parking lot later that night. It shows the man who took her getting shot and the shooter carrying her to the trunk of his car and driving off."

"I see the clip," Stephen said, noncommittal.

"Okay, well, unfortunately, that's where all the leads run dry. The man who put her in the trunk is a professional assassin. He knows how to cover his tracks. I've tried to track him down but it has only led to dead ends. But I have another idea."

"What's that?" he asked.

This is the time he usually gets dismissive. Why is he holding back?

"I know we discussed this before but I want to hire a private investigator. There's another lead worth following, one I know has potential. But following it up is going to be expensive, more expensive than I can handle on my own. I need your help, Stephen."

There was a long silence on the other end of the line. She could almost picture her ex-husband screwing up the courage to say what he'd clearly been holding back this whole time. She imagined him brushing his wavy hair out of his eyes and adjusting the hip, thin-framed glasses he didn't really need.

"Keri, I have a confession to make," he said quietly.

"What?" she asked, attempting to keep her voice level, even as her stomach did a flip.

"I've already seen the video."

"How?"

"Your partner, Detective Sands, showed it to me," he said.

"What?" she asked, bewildered. "When?"

"Last month. He came by the office and showed it to me. He asked me the same thing you are, for money to hire the investigator you want."

"Why is this the first I'm hearing of this?" she demanded.

"Probably because he didn't want to tell you what I said, what I'm going to repeat to you. I don't see anything in that video that proves that the girl in it is Evie."

"What?" Keri said, disbelieving. "But it's her. She's wearing the same clothes from earlier in the night. That's the same van. It's all smashed up."

"You're not going to like what I have to say, Keri. That's why I didn't reach out—because I was worried about how you'd react."

"Just tell me, Stephen," she said, forcing herself to keep the bitterness out of her voice. There was still a chance she could convince him, but only if she stayed cool.

"You can't see her face in that footage, Keri. And no one was with you when you claim to have seen her earlier in the night. When I pressed him, even your partner admitted that he was taking your word that the girl was Evie."

"Why would I lie?"

"I don't think you're lying, Keri. I believe you saw a girl that night who was being forced into a van and that you got into a crash chasing it. The video does show a girl. But it's been almost six years since we lost her. And you're telling me that in the middle of the night, from a significant distance, you recognized a girl you haven't seen since she was eight and knew it was our daughter. Isn't it possible that you saw a blonde-haired girl and you willed it to be Evie?"

"She called out to me when I shouted her name, Stephen," she said, knowing her voice was getting hard and unsure how to stop it. "It was her."

"Please put yourself in my shoes, Keri. My daughter, our daughter, has been missing for over half a decade. And my former wife, who by any fair assessment has devoted her life to finding her, says she saw her. But no one else saw her. And the video footage she claims shows her is inconclusive. Am I supposed to upend my whole world based on that, allow myself to hope again based solely on…your word?"

Keri knew her word meant nothing to him anymore so she didn't even bother to appeal to him on that basis. But Stephen was a practical guy. Maybe that was the way to win him over.

"Even if you have doubts, what harm is there?" she asked. "The worst that happens is you spend a little money and it doesn't pan out. The possible benefits far outweigh the cost."

"Not the emotional cost, Keri. It's like I have this wound and over time it's scabbed over and healed. But what you're proposing wouldn't just rip off a scab. It would take a knife and cut a brand new hole in the wound. Why would I do that to myself?"

"Because you might get your daughter back," Keri insisted slowly, knowing she was near the limits of her self-control.

"But here's the thing, and I hate to say this. I just don't believe you, Keri. I don't think you're lying. But I don't trust that you saw what you think you saw. And I'm not willing to tear my life apart based on your word. I can't keep reopening the wound. I have to move on with my life. Can you understand that?"

Keri, nearly overwhelmed with frustration bordering on rage, opened her mouth. She was about to respond when something inside of her made her stop. It was like a light had been switched on, not just in her head but in her very being. It was an epiphany, perhaps the saddest one she'd ever experienced. He just didn't care anymore.

What he said was reasonable on the surface. The pain of trying to find Evie and failing was too much for him. But she could sense that it wasn't true. She could tell in his voice that he was paying lip service to emotions that weren't really there any longer.

There was a time where he'd loved Evie, and Keri too. He had been a good father and a decent husband. But he didn't love them anymore. He'd shut that part of himself down a long time ago. Maybe he felt he had to in order to survive. And Keri hadn't made it easy on him. Her drinking and cheating and permanent aura of grief had pushed him away.

But she refused to believe that any parent who still cared would ever reject a chance, however small, to find their missing child. Even now, years later, the parents of missing children she couldn't find would come into the station to ask if there were any new leads. Ray once told her about a father who, for the last decade, still came in every year on the day his daughter disappeared to check in with him in the hope that he might have uncovered some new clue.

But not Stephen. He was done. He had chosen his new life, his new wife, and the living son he could still hug and kiss and read to at night. Part of her understood that. She wasn't as angry as she expected. He wasn't a bad person. But some part of his soul had atrophied because of what happened. And it was gone forever.

He would never agree to give her the money or to help in any way. Doing so wouldn't just be pursuing a lead that might not pan out. It meant upending his whole, reconstructed world. And that wasn't something he was willing or able to do. It just wasn't in him. So she stopped asking.

"I understand," she said.

"I'm sorry, Keri."

"Okay."

"I hope you find some peace."

"Thanks," she said and hung up.

She was on her own.

Or maybe not completely.

As she looked up, letting the chilly air dry the tears running down her cheeks, she saw Ray walking out the door, looking around. As he peered out into the dark, she studied him, the man who had secretly asked her ex-husband to help because he knew that it would be too difficult for her.

He was the man who had put himself on the line, risking his pride and his independence by asking her to be more than just a partner and friend. Despite the conversation she'd just had, Keri felt a smile start to form at the corners of her mouth.

"You looking for me?" she called out, realizing as she said it that the question had more than one meaning.

He turned in her direction.

"Yeah, you're going to want to come back inside. Tim Rainey is about to do a press conference on live TV."

CHAPTER TWENTY ONE

When Keri arrived in the conference room, heart pounding and out of breath from running, everyone was already crowded around the monitor. She pushed her way through so she could see.

Rainey was just stepping up to the microphone. His face was strained and exhausted from lack of sleep. He was clearly nervous but his expression was determined.

"This message is for the person who has my daughter. I will meet any of your terms. I will go wherever I need to and pay whatever amount you demand. I just want my daughter back. Please. I will do anything. I beg of you. Let my little Jess go. That's all I have to say."

With that, he turned and returned to the house, ignoring the flashing lights and cacophony of shouted questions from the assembled reporters.

"Ugh," she heard Lieutenant Hillman say and turned to see him slump into a chair in the corner of the room.

"This is not good," Manny Suarez muttered.

"What was that idiot thinking?" Brody demanded, gruffly voicing the question everyone was silently asking.

"He's desperate," Ray said. "Cut him some slack. Still, this is a nightmare. I can only imagine all the calls he's already getting from the crazies and the con artists. I can't believe he thought this was a good idea."

"Neither can I," Keri agreed.

"You sound suspicious," Ray noted.

"It just doesn't make any sense. I know he's desperate. But what good did he think this would do? He's not stupid. He had to know that a big public appeal wasn't going to have any impact on the guy who did this. You read the letters. Did they sound like the work of a guy who would be swayed by a devoted dad?"

"They don't sound like the work of someone who could be swayed by anything," Ray pointed out.

"Exactly. Something's not right here," Keri said as she walked out to her desk to grab her coat.

"What are you planning to do?" Ray asked, following her.

"I'm going to go over there and ask him what the hell is really going on."

"But it's not our case anymore, Keri," he whispered. "We can't just go barging in. The feds will have our heads."

"Not ours," Keri insisted. "Just mine. And maybe not. Winchester's a jerk but I think I can charm Agent Crowley into letting me have a go at Rainey. You stay here and keep Hillman occupied while I sneak out."

"Is that an order?" Ray asked, more amused than angry.

"Sorry, would you please cover for me so I can violate orders?"

"It would be my pleasure," he said. "Just keep me posted."

"Is *that* an order?" she asked snarkily as she headed for the door quickly, not letting him get in a comeback. She imagined him behind her, fighting the urge to make a crack, knowing it would draw attention. Once again she felt a smile sneaking across her lips.

*

There were no smiles to be had at the Rainey house when she arrived forty-five minutes later. It was hard enough to navigate the gauntlet of wooden barriers, officers, and TV trucks in the surrounding neighborhood just to get to the front door. But when she stepped inside, she was met almost immediately by the frowning Agent Winchester.

"What the hell are you doing here?" he demanded roughly.

"I just wanted to update you and Agent Crowley on the status of that case file research you had us doing," she answered sweetly. "There have been some interesting developments. Where's Crowley? I can fill you both in together."

She could see he wanted to tell her off but the phrase "interesting developments" held him at bay. It was a load of bull. There were no developments. But if she could just get to Crowley, she was pretty sure she could convince him to let her talk to Tim Rainey and determine what was going on.

"Follow me," Winchester growled and led the way into the kitchen, where a half dozen agents, including Crowley, were crowded around the kitchen island, studying what appeared to be a map of the area. Carolyn Rainey and Nate were seated at the breakfast table, putting together a jigsaw puzzle. Tim Rainey was nowhere to be seen.

Crowley looked up and seeing her, walked over.

"This is a bit of a surprise, Detective Locke. To what do we owe the honor?"

"She says the case files we gave them had something interesting," Winchester said before Keri could reply.

"Really?" Crowley asked, looking mildly surprised.

"Yeah," Keri said. "What I found interesting was that there was virtually nothing relevant in any of them. It was almost like they were given to us as busy work so we would stay out of the FBI's way. But I know you guys would never do that."

Crowley and Winchester exchanged uncomfortable looks but neither spoke so she continued.

"Anyway, I just wanted to report that not a single file had anything of value. But as long as I'm here, how are things going?"

Winchester looked annoyed that they'd been played but Crowley, apparently amused, answered.

"I'm sure you saw that nightmare of a statement Rainey gave."

"I did."

"Then you can imagine the reaction we've gotten. We've been fielding calls from every crackpot in the greater Los Angeles area. It's been awful."

"Why do you think he did that?" Keri asked. "He had to know it wouldn't do any good."

"We'd love to ask him," Winchester said. "But the second he walked in the house, he went straight up to his bedroom, closed the door, and locked it."

"He muttered something about needing to rest and said to let him know if we got any worthwhile responses," Crowley added.

"So he made this impassioned plea for his daughter, then just went upstairs to take a nap?" Keri asked, incredulous.

"He's not really in tip-top form," Winchester said.

"You mind if I go up and try to talk to him?" she asked.

Winchester looked stunned at the idea.

"He'll rip your head off," he said, not entirely unhappily.

"That's okay. He already hates me. One more vitriolic tongue-lashing isn't going to make that much difference to me. I just didn't want to step on anyone's toes. After all, it is your case now."

"You know," Crowley mused, "it's not a terrible idea. If he says anything worthwhile, that's great. If he shuts you down or blows up at you, our relationship with him hasn't been harmed. I say have at it."

Winchester, unable to think of a good reason to oppose the idea and likely intrigued by the idea of Keri getting yelled at, nodded.

"Okay, I'll let you know how it goes," she said. "That is, if you can't already guess from the screams and shouts."

As she turned to leave, she caught Carolyn Rainey looking at her furtively, almost guiltily. The woman averted her eyes the second Keri made eye contact.

That was weird.

But saying nothing, Keri left the room and made her way up the stairs. The Raineys' bedroom was at the end of the hall. She got there and paused for half a second before knocking.

Is this really a good idea? Maybe I should just let the man rest. He clearly needs it.

But she couldn't let go of the feeling that something wasn't right. And so she knocked, softly at first, then louder.

"Mr. Rainey. It's Detective Locke. I know you're unhappy with me but I need to speak to you. It's important."

She waited a few seconds and then knocked again, this time banging loudly. There was no way he couldn't hear that.

"Mr. Rainey, I really need you to open the door."

She glanced back down the stairs and saw a couple of the agents poke their heads out the kitchen door and stare up at her.

I'm committed now.

She slammed the door hard with her fist, making the whole thing rattle. When that got no response, she checked the handle. It was indeed locked. Now she was genuinely worried. An image of Tim Rainey lying on the bed with an open bottle of sleeping pills in his hand flashed through her head.

"Mr. Rainey," she shouted. "I'm concerned for your safety. If you don't open the door right now, I'm going to have to break it down. You have five seconds."

She started counting down. When she reached zero, she braced herself to slam her shoulder into the door. She was just starting to move forward when she felt a hand on her forearm. It was Winchester.

"As much as I'd love to watch you throw yourself at that door, maybe you better let me give it a go."

"You don't think I can do it?" she demanded.

"I'm sure you can but I also know you broke your collarbone less than a year ago. If someone else is willing to use his body as a battering ram, maybe let him."

"How do know about my collarbone?" Keri demanded.

"We're the FBI, Detective Locke. You'd be amazed at what we know."

Before she could respond he launched himself at the door, hitting it with a force she hadn't thought possible. There was loud crack as the thing came off its hinges and crashed to the floor. Winchester stumbled in, almost falling before gathering himself. Keri stepped in after him. Rainey wasn't on the bed or anywhere in the room for that matter.

"Where the hell is he?" Winchester asked.

"Good question," Keri said. "You check under the bed and the closet. I'll take the bathroom."

Without waiting for a response, she headed in the direction of what she assumed was the bathroom. She undid the clasp on her gun holster and rested her fingers on the grip, ready to pull it out if necessary.

The bathroom, including the shower and walk-in closet, was empty too. When she stepped back into the bedroom, she saw Winchester checking the bedroom window. She noticed he was holding his weapon loosely in his right hand.

"Locked from the inside," he said when he saw her. "He's not in the closet or under the bed."

"Bathroom's clean too," Keri said just as Crowley and two other agents burst into the room.

"What the hell?" he asked of no one in particular.

"He's not here," Winchester said.

"Where the hell did he go?"

Winchester looked helplessly at Keri.

"I have absolutely no idea," she admitted.

CHAPTER TWENTY TWO

Keri ignored the chaos around her. As the FBI agents scoured the bedroom, she leaned against the hallway banister, allowing her thoughts to travel wherever they wished, waiting for them to form into something coherent and useful.

Ever since she'd watched Tim Rainey give his press statement, something had felt off. There was no point to it and he surely knew it. But he had done it anyway. She recalled his face as he spoke. He didn't look desperate. He looked determined, as if he had a specific purpose in mind.

After about five minutes, the agents filed out of the room, disheartened. They hadn't found anything that suggested how Rainey had gotten out or where he might have gone. She stepped back into the room and sat down on the bed, trying to put herself in the mindset of Timothy Rainey.

It was clear to her that the press statement was a ruse of some sort. Maybe it was intended to make the FBI think he'd lost it so they'd just leave him alone long enough for him to get out. She suspected that while that may have been part of it, there was more to his performance than just that. He had some deeper purpose.

What was it?

Two other crucial questions ate at her. How had he gotten out and more importantly, where had he gone?

She set aside the second question for now, choosing to focus on the first one, which seemed more solvable for the time being. Getting up, she wandered around the bedroom for a few minutes, peeking in the closet and turning on the light. She felt along the walls for any hollow space but found none.

She got down on her stomach and shined her flashlight under the bed, looking for any disturbed carpeting that might reveal a trap door. She knew the FBI agents had already checked for one but wanted to set her mind at ease.

She walked over to the still-locked window. How could he have gotten out and left it locked? And even if he had, it was a twenty-foot drop to the ground below. It was hard to imagine he could have just walked away from a jump like that.

She made her way into the bathroom and looked more closely at the walk-in closet, checking it for hollow spots as well. There were none but she did notice something unusual.

The closet had one wall that was inset, cutting into the otherwise rectangular room. She returned to the bathroom, assuming that she would find that the inset was because the shower or bathtub needed the extra space. But neither did.

In fact, that section of wall jutted into the space of the shower as well, making it slightly smaller than one would expect. She tapped it but it was solid. Puzzled, she went into the adjoining bedroom, Nate's, and found the same purposeless section of wall jutting out into the room slightly. She rapped on it and found no hollow spots there either.

Like the other sections she had checked, the wall felt somehow firmer *and* spongier than just regular drywall. On a hunch, she grabbed Nate's aluminum bat, which was lying on the floor beside his bed, got into a batter's crouch, and swung at the unusual section of wall with all her might.

The force of the impact knocked the bat from her hands and rattled her whole body. She checked the spot where she'd hit the wall and found no indentation, only a slight rip in the Batman wallpaper. She dug her fingernails in and peeled it back.

Behind the wallpaper, there was a layer of thick foam. She took out her Swiss army knife and cut into it. The foam was at least half an inch thick. She managed to pull back a chunk and feel what was underneath. It was some kind of metal. When she tapped it with her flashlight, it didn't echo. Whatever it was, it was thick.

Just then, Crowley walked into the room and turned on the light.

"What's going on, Locke? It sounded like you collapsed on the ground or something."

"Agent Crowley. I think I found out how Rainey got out," she said, tapping on the metal again. "Unfortunately, we're going to need a little help to get in there."

"What is that?" he asked.

"If my hunch is right, it's a panic room. And I'm guessing it has its own exit from the house."

"A panic room? Those things are impregnable."

"They are. Unless you know how to get in," she said as she walked past him and headed for the stairwell. "And there's someone here I think can help us with that."

She hurried down the stairs and turned into the kitchen, where she wasn't surprised to find Carolyn Rainey staring right at her. Now Keri understood why the woman had given her that odd look earlier.

"Mrs. Rainey," Keri said, "you're going to have to let one of the agents take over helping Nate with that jigsaw puzzle. We need to talk."

Carolyn Rainey whispered something in her son's ear, gave him a kiss on the cheek, and motioned for the closest agent to take her seat. Then she got up wordlessly and followed Keri into the living room.

"I need the access code to the panic room," Keri said without any preamble.

"I don't know what your talki—"

"Don't waste my time, Mrs. Rainey. I want the location of the access panel and the code. Then you're going to tell us where your husband went."

Carolyn Rainey stood there, her legs seemingly locked in place. She opened her mouth, then closed it, then opened it again. Clearly she was going through some internal struggle.

"You may think you're protecting Tim," Keri said, forcing her tone several degrees softer, "but you're not. You're putting him at greater risk. Unless he's had some sort of Special Forces training I'm unaware of, wherever he went, he's at a distinct disadvantage."

"He has a gun," Carolyn said. Winchester, who had just joined them, groaned. Carolyn Rainey looked at him with confusion on her face.

"That's not any more reassuring," Keri said, answering her unasked question. "I guarantee you the person he's after has one too and is more adept at using it. Let me help your husband. Whatever he's doing is not going to get Jessica back. I hate to be blunt but this guy isn't giving her back at any price. The only way we're going to find her is through diligent investigative work. Your husband is putting your daughter and himself in greater danger with this stunt. Now tell me what I want to know."

Keri could see the dam break in Carolyn Rainey's eyes before she spoke. A second later, it all came tumbling out.

"The access panel is under a tile behind the towel rack in our bathroom. Just push it in and it will pop out and slide over to reveal the keypad. The code is 93#1576#."

Winchester, who had written down the code, leapt up the stairs three at a time. A swarm of agents followed him. Keri and Carolyn Rainey were left alone at the bottom of the stairs.

"It won't do you any good," Rainey continued. "He's long gone."

"That's why you're going to tell me everything," Keri insisted. "The press statement—was it just a trick so the FBI would think he'd lost it and leave him alone in the room?"

"That was just a side benefit. The truth is, when we got the last FedEx package, it also included a small phone with a note. It said to hide the phone and not mention it to the police. It said we'd receive a text message at some point and if we followed the instructions exactly, we could still get Jessica back for Tim to 'purify' her himself."

"You got the text tonight?"

"Yes. It said to call a press conference and plead for her life. It wasn't important what Tim said. He just had to make sure it was televised. Then the guy would know we'd gotten the message and were willing to meet. He said to meet exactly twenty minutes after the press conference ended."

"He's gone," Crowley shouted, emerging from the bedroom. "There's a fireman's pole in there that leads down to a hidden door at the back of the house. Winchester just slid down. He says there are fresh footprints in the grass outside."

Keri nodded and turned back to Carolyn.

"Where did he go?" she whispered. "Tell me quickly so I can get a head start. It's better if not everyone shows up at once with sirens blaring. It could set the guy off. I can go in quick and quiet."

Carolyn Rainey didn't need convincing.

"He said to meet at the basketball courts in Del Rey Lagoon Park, down at the corner of Pacific and Convoy."

"That's less than a mile from here," Keri said. It was also less than half a mile from her own apartment, and only a block from the beach. She had walked past the lagoon dozens of time in recent months.

"Yes, but he had to get there on foot so twenty minutes wasn't much time. That's why he was in such a rush to get to the bedroom."

Okay, listen. I'm going to head out now. Give me a five-minute head start, and then tell Crowley what you told me. Got it?"

"Please make sure he's okay," Carolyn Rainey pleaded.

“I’ll do my best,” Keri said, making no promises.

She headed for the front door and noticed Crowley eyeballing her quizzically.

“I’m going to call the station and fill them in,” she called up to him. “Maybe there’s been a sighting.”

He nodded, though he looked less than convinced. She wouldn’t have been either if another law enforcement officer had suddenly gone from aggressively interrogating someone to casually ambling off.

When she got out the door, she walked to her car as quickly as she could without drawing suspicion. She doubted Carolyn Rainey would hold out long in the face of FBI questioning. The only advantages Keri had were her familiarity with the area and this brief head start.

She’d be lucky to get there two minutes before the feds.

CHAPTER TWENTY THREE

It took every ounce of restraint Keri had not to floor it once she was on the road. But that would have drawn suspicion from the FBI, local cops, and the media alike, so she cruised out of the neighborhood at the posted twenty-five miles per hour. It only took her three minutes to get to Del Rey Lagoon Park but every second felt like an hour.

When she pulled up a block away from the dark, deserted park, she could tell that she was too late. Whatever had happened, it was over now.

She could see a shadowy figure hunched over next to a rented white U-Haul van with its sliding door open, his silhouette visible in the van's dim interior light. It looked like Tim Rainey. Somewhere near him she heard an awful mewing sound.

She broke into a run, ignoring the icy burn in her throat as she sucked in the frigid night air. As she got closer she saw movement and realized he was alive. She slowed a bit, enough to pull out her weapon. When she reached him, she saw that he was on all fours and realized that the mewing was actually him wailing softly with what was left of his hoarse voice.

She could see a blue duffel bag underneath his torso. It looked full and unopened. Next to his right hand, lying on the ground, was a handgun. She looked up, peering into the van. It was completely empty. She moved closer to Rainey and kicked the gun out of his reach.

"Mr. Rainey," she said, her eyes still searching the entire area, "it's Detective Locke. Tell me what happened."

In the distance but growing louder she could hear the sound of multiple sirens. She glanced at her watch. She had only parked sixty seconds ago and guessed they'd be here in another sixty. Agent Crowley was impressive.

"Tim," she said, hoping the personal touch might reach him, "we've got a real situation on our hands. You snuck out under the FBI's nose. You came here by yourself. And you have a gun. This could go very badly for you. I want to help. But we only have about forty-five seconds before this place is crawling with cops. So tell me what happened. Now!"

That seemed to shake him out of his reverie. He looked up at her. His eyes were swollen from non-stop crying.

"He said he'd give her to me. Just bring the money and we'd trade. He was so specific. He said she'd be in the U-Haul waiting for me. I was going to shoot him if he was there but I was worried I might hit her so I didn't. And then, when I opened the door, I thought I was going to see her dead body. If I had, I would have used the gun on myself."

"But she wasn't there?" Keri asked, choosing to skip over his last comment. "The van was empty?"

"Except for this," he said, holding out a plastic baggie with some kind of clothing inside. "It's another piece of her shirt. It was just lying on the floor of the van."

He dropped the bag on the ground. Keri noticed writing on it. She took a step closer and saw, in thick, blocked lettering, one word: SINNER.

She looked up. The sirens were much closer now and she thought she could see flashing lights breaking through the darkness only blocks away.

"Did you see anyone at all?" she pleaded.

"A few cars drove by. A few people came through the area. Most were walking dogs. There weren't any guys by themselves. I've been here over an hour. After a while I realized he's just been toying with me. He doesn't want the money. He just wants to torture us. I'm never going to see my little girl again."

He put his head back down and resumed his hoarse mewing.

Keri wanted to say something reassuring but feared he might be right. Instead, she focused on the job at hand.

"Tim, listen closely. We've only got a few seconds. I need you to stand up."

He stayed where he was, on his hands and knees, his body protecting the duffel bag of money like it was his child. The sirens were deafening now and she could tell the vehicles would round the corner any moment.

This guy's gone. You've got to save him from himself.

She moved quickly to Tim Rainey, put her hands under his armpits, and lifted him to his feet. He seemed oblivious. Then she pulled a tissue out of her pocket and used it pick up Tim's gun. After checking the safety, she shoved it in the back of his waistband.

The cars and their relentless flashing lights had rounded the corner. Everything around them was bathed in a wash of blue, red, and white, like they were in some outdoor disco. She could tell Tim wasn't aware of any of it and, without stopping to think about it, she gave him a hard slap across the cheek.

He stumbled for a moment but her action seemed to bring him back to the world. His puffy eyes cleared a bit and he looked directly at her. She could hear vehicles screeching to a halt and car doors being opened.

"Listen to me, Tim. This is important. Don't tell anyone else you pulled your gun. You could get in trouble for that. Just tell them what happened, minus the gun. It stayed in your waistband. You only brought it for protection. Do you understand?"

He nodded vaguely. She reiterated the point.

"These guys will forgive a lot for a guy in your situation: not mentioning the phone, sneaking out—they're bad, but understandable. But if they think you're an unhinged vigilante, they may have to take you into custody. And Carolyn and Nate need you right now, just like you need them. So no gun talk, okay?"

"Okay," he said, seeming to get it. There were shouted voices, getting closer. She couldn't make out the words but the tone didn't sound friendly.

"Okay, Tim," she said calmly, ignoring the voices and focusing all her attention on Rainey, "we both need to raise our hands above our heads now so they know we're not a threat. I'm going to tell them you have a gun so they're not surprised. Just let them take it and follow their orders. You got it?"

"I got it," he answered, raising his hands in unison with her. Her back was to the people running their way but she could hear them approaching and could tell they would be in earshot very soon.

"Tim, I know things seem hopeless," she said, loud enough for only him to hear. Their eyes were fixed on each other. "But I give you my word. I'm not done with this. I haven't given up on finding Jessica."

He looked at her and opened his mouth as if to speak, then closed it again. She knew she was making promises she might not be able to keep. But if it helped keep Timothy Rainey from killing himself, it was worth it.

"I'm going to have to deal with these guys first," she continued, referencing the agents whose footsteps were only yards away. "But I will keep looking for your daughter. Don't give up. Don't hurt yourself. Be a husband to Carolyn and a father to Nate. That's your job. Promise me you'll do your job."

The feds were on them now, swarming. But just before they forced Timothy Rainey to the ground and cuffed his hands behind his back, Keri was sure she saw him nod.

CHAPTER TWENTY FOUR

An hour later, Keri sat on the stained loveseat in Lieutenant Hillman's office, waiting, pretending everything was fine even though it most definitely was not. The door was closed so she couldn't hear much. But she knew everyone in the bullpen was stealing glances at her so she kept her face impassive, hiding the churning anxiety she felt inside.

A lot of what happened after the FBI arrived at the lagoon was a blur. She informed the agents that Rainey was armed and despite her protestations that he wasn't a threat, they took him into custody. Crowley briefly had her handcuffed as well. She suspected it was mostly out of a sense of frustration and didn't complain.

He and Winchester interrogated her on the way to the station. She answered their questions mostly honestly, saying she thought that having the cavalry all arrive at once would put Tim Rainey at risk, and Jessica too if she'd been there.

They railed at her that it wasn't her call to make, that this was a federal case, that she'd deliberately withheld relevant information and potentially obstructed justice. She wanted to scoff at that last charge but held back, knowing it would be counterproductive.

Instead, she repeatedly apologized, saying she thought she was doing the right thing to help keep Tim Rainey safe and realized now that it had been a mistake. By the time they got to the station, the fury inside both men seemed to have subsided.

But that didn't mean they wouldn't still pursue some kind of disciplinary action. The very fact that she'd been stuck in Hillman's office this long while he met with them in the soundproof conference room suggested things were far from peachy.

In the bullpen, she could see the entire team standing around uncomfortably, watching the action through the conference room windows like it was a silent film. Every now and then, Ray would glance in her direction and shrug or shake his head. She knew him well but didn't have a clue what any of his body language meant.

Finally, the meeting broke up. Keri craned her neck to see what was happening. To her horror, she saw that it wasn't just Hillman, Crowley, and Winchester who'd been in the meeting. It was also the two Internal Affairs detectives who'd been investigating the death of the Collector at her hands.

And there had been one more person in the room, LAPD Chief Reena Beecher. Beecher stepped out into the hall and Keri marveled at how the veteran cop with thirty years on the force could look so regal. In her mid-fifties with blackish-gray hair tied back in a professional bun, she was tall, with a lean frame and angular facial features marked by deep worry lines. She looked like a mildly attractive hawk.

Beecher had been captain of West LA Division when Keri joined it. Even though Keri barely knew the woman, she was aware that Beecher had been an advocate for her. Keri's rescue of multiple children in high-profile cases had allowed Beecher to save her from disciplinary action and even suspension on more than one occasion.

But a few months ago, Reena Beecher had been promoted to police chief of the entire Los Angeles Police Department. And while her greater authority might have seemed good for Keri on the surface, she worried that it could actually be counterproductive.

Beecher was no longer just an advocate for officers in her division. She was responsible for the reputation of the entire force. Keri worried her actions tonight might not stand her in good stead with her guardian angel.

Beecher left the bullpen without glancing back at Keri. That wasn't a great sign. The look on Hillman's face as he walked toward her reinforced her concern. He was frowning and his entire face seemed pinched, like he was in physical pain.

He opened the door, stepped in, and closed it again quickly. Then he walked over to his desk and sat down, his eyes on the floor the whole time.

This isn't good. He likes to stare people into submission. But he won't even make eye contact.

"What's the story, boss?" she asked in a forced, casual tone she knew wasn't convincing.

Finally he looked up at her and she braced for what she sensed was coming. He sighed deeply.

"I'll start with the good news," he said, "because there isn't much of it and it won't take long. The FBI has decided not to pursue any formal action against you. Crowley likes you, despite what you did. And even that asshole Winchester seems to respect you. They know that without you, they might still be waiting for Tim Rainey to come out of his bedroom."

"So far, so good," Keri said, more to buck herself up than anything else.

"I also think they decided they didn't need to pile on, what with everything else."

"Everything else?" she asked.

"Internal Affairs is reevaluating the case involving you and the Collector, Brian Wickwire."

"I thought I was on the verge of being cleared," Keri said.

"That was the preliminary determination. And that's why you were allowed to remain on active duty. But IA got a tip earlier today from a source claiming you went to Wickwire's apartment after your confrontation with him and tampered with evidence."

"Lieutenant, I—" Keri began.

"Don't say anything, Locke," Hillman interrupted. "I don't want to know and I most certainly don't want to be a witness. Just keep your trap shut and get in touch with your union rep. Don't share anything with anyone besides him. And that includes your partner. He can be called to testify too."

"Did they say who this source is? Don't I get to confront my accuser?" Keri knew damn well who the source was—Jackson Cave. But the question was: how had he gotten his tip to IA? Had he revealed himself? Did he contact them directly or go through an intermediary?

"They didn't say," Hillman answered. "But that's definitely something to bring up with your representative. It could be a compelling line of defense."

"What did Chief Beecher have to say?" Keri asked.

"Not much she could say. You know she's gone to bat for you more than once. She even overruled me when I wanted to suspend you after the Ashley Penn case. But this is out of her hands. If it looks like she's covering for a vigilante cop, even one going after the guy who kidnapped her daughter…well, it's just not politically feasible."

"So what does this mean?"

"It means you're suspended indefinitely, Keri," Hillman said, telling her what she had already suspected. "It'll be with pay but you won't be able to come in until this is resolved."

"Can't I just work a desk?"

"Can't do it—regulations. Besides, there's no telling how long this could last."

"Can I at least finish out the Rainey case? I promised Tim Rainey I'd keep looking for his daughter."

"I'm afraid not," Hillman said. "The suspension is effective immediately. And Keri, you know as well as I do that you shouldn't have made that promise, suspension or not."

Keri wanted to tell him that it was to talk a suicidal father off a ledge but that would have required revealing that Rainey had pulled his gun, making his life even more complicated. She kept quiet.

"And one more thing," Hillman said, a pained expression on his face. "I'm going to need your badge and gun."

Without argument or delay, Keri undid her belt holster and placed it on Hillman's desk, with the gun attached. Then she pulled out her badge and placed it beside her weapon.

"What do I do now?"

"Go home," he said gently. "It's late. Contact your union rep and set up a meeting for as soon as possible. Then go to sleep. Things will look a little better in the morning. Just view it as a much-needed vacation."

"So I should just kick back and have some margaritas while a girl is being held captive by a child-killing religious zealot?"

"Keri," he said, "just because you're gone doesn't mean the case is over. The FBI is on it. We're on it. There are other skilled investigators in the world, you know."

"I know, but…" she started to say, but he held up his hand to stop her.

"Besides," he continued, "you've got more to focus on than just one case. This is your career at stake. It's in real jeopardy and that's where your attention should be for the foreseeable future. Now go home and see if you can sleep for twelve hours or so. You're looking pretty ragged."

She was about to get offended at that last line when she saw Hillman crack a rare smile. He was just playfully teasing her, giving her a hard time to shake her out of her funk. That wasn't his style. She felt a wave of emotion hit her. If Cole Hillman, the human gray cloud, was trying to make her feel better, things must be pretty bad.

"Okay, boss," she said quietly and turned for the door.

"Hey, Locke," he said as she started to leave, "if you tell anyone this I'll deny it. But even with your baggage and your terrible attitude and your disregard for authority and your inability to play nice with others, you're just about the best Missing Persons detective I've ever had. I hope to get you back. It'd be a shame not having you around, driving me to an early retirement."

"Thanks, Lieutenant," she said, because she knew she couldn't say more without losing it.

She went to her desk, prepared to put all her essentials in a box before heading out. But she found that Ray had already done it for her. He was leaning against it, waiting for her.

"I figured you wouldn't want everybody watching while you went through all your stuff, so I packed it up for you. If I forgot anything important, let me know and I can grab it for you tomorrow."

"Thanks," she said. "You knew I was being suspended?"

"Not officially. But it wasn't hard to read the body language in there. You want me to drive you to the lagoon to get your car?"

"Sure," she said. "Let's get out of here. I can feel about a hundred eyes on me right now."

He nodded and grabbed the box of stuff. When Keri turned to leave, she found a small crowd had gathered behind her. Everybody from the unit—Kevin Edgerton, Manny Suarez, Jamie Castillo, Garrett Patterson, even Frank Brody—was standing there.

"Not so fast," Edgerton said. "You think you're getting out of here without saying goodbye?"

"It's not permanent," Keri insisted. "I'm just on suspension."

"We know," he replied. "But we don't give a damn. We're sending you off right, even if it's just for a few weeks."

Before she could stop him, he was wrapping his arms around her. Patterson followed. Manny Suarez shook his head with a rueful smile on his face.

"It's gonna be so boring without you around," he said, pulling her in for a hug. "I guess I'm going to have to be the troublemaker now."

"Good luck with that," Keri said. "Have you ever gotten a bad report? Besides, I know someone else who's more of a frontrunner for problem child."

She nodded at Officer Jamie Castillo, who was standing a bit apart, her eyes tinged with wetness that she tried vainly to blink away. Keri waved her over and Jamie moved in quick to embrace her, hiding her tears by wiping her cheek on Keri's shirt.

"You going to pick up the mantle while I'm gone?" Keri whispered in her ear.

Castillo nodded and pulled back a little, looking Keri square in the eye.

"You know you're the reason I became a cop, right? I don't think I ever told you that."

Keri shook her head, dumbfounded.

"About three years ago, a little boy went missing in my neighborhood late at night. He was four years old. His mom called nine-one-one but the cops didn't show up for over an hour. When they finally arrived, they did cursory interviews and took a few notes. They called in backup and did a search of the area.

"But after about a half hour without finding anything, they gave up. They told his mom that he had probably wandered off to a friend's and would be back later. She got mad. It was after midnight, she told them. Her little boy didn't go visiting friends in the middle of the night. But the cops didn't want to deal with this woman who was losing her mind. They just said they'd be in touch and left. All except for one, that is."

Keri felt a surge of recognition, realizing she knew this story already. Her face began to turn red. Castillo ignored it and continued speaking.

"One female uniformed officer, blonde, perky-looking but with a hard edge to her, obviously pretty junior, told her partner to go ahead, that she wanted to look around a bit more. So her partner left her there. They all did.

"She went over to the mom and asked her for some tea. They went into the house and she talked to the mom for twenty minutes, asking questions about her son. Not just stuff like what he looked like and what he was wearing but what he liked to do, what were his favorite foods. The mom said he loved building things; that he was always pretending to create buildings with his Legos and his Tonka trucks. I know this because the window was open and I was hiding outside listening in.

"After a while, the mom calms down and the officer said she was going to look around a bit just in case anything was missed before. She left the house and proceeded to walk the entire neighborhood for hours. I followed around behind her, making sure to keep my distance. I heard her partner on the radio. He sounded pissed that she was still out there, saying he was getting crap from the other officers and would she please let him pick her up? She told him to come help her or screw off. He didn't come.

"I went home after that because it was late and I was tired so I missed the rest of what happened. But from what I read later, just before dawn, she came across a construction site about a mile away. She broke through the fence lock and searched the whole area. In one half-finished building, she found a refrigerator that had toppled over on its front so that the door was facedown. There was a sound coming from inside. She rolled it over by herself and opened the fridge door.

"The little boy was inside. He was whimpering but alive. He'd gone to the site because his mom had driven by earlier that day and he saw the construction equipment and the exposed beams and wanted to check it out. He'd climbed into the fridge for fun but it was on an uneven surface and when he closed the door, it had fallen forward, trapping him inside.

"He'd gone missing on a Friday night. The construction crew wasn't scheduled to return to work until Monday morning. By then, he would have suffocated for sure. But he didn't because one cop with a hunch wouldn't give up, even when everyone else did.

"I thought to myself that maybe that cop could use a little more help from people who were as stubborn as she was. So I decided that day to finish getting my GED, so I could join the police academy and maybe one day help her out. And now, here I am, getting to work with her every day."

"How come you never told me that story?" Keri asked, not even trying to hide the tears streaming down her face.

"I wanted to save it for when it would be the most embarrassing for you," Jamie said, wiping her own wet cheek with the back of her hand.

"Well, mission accomplished."

"I know we'll be seeing you again real soon, Keri," she said, giving her one last squeeze on the arm.

Keri turned to find only one more person left to navigate. Frank Brody stood in front of her, his sauce-stained shirt untucked as usual.

"I guess I should say something," he muttered, "or else everyone will think I'm a real asshole."

"That ship has already sailed," Ray said, grinning.

"Shut up, Sands. I'm trying to be nice here!"

"Yeah, shut up, Sands," Keri agreed. "I want to hear this."

"Okay, Locke, let's make this brief. I guess you're not the worst detective I've ever worked with. And even though you are a massive pain in my rear who gives me a permanent headache, you have done some good around here. And even though I'll probably be long retired before you get back, assuming you ever do, which I kind of doubt, I hope you crush those IA scumbags. Also, you have a pretty solid ass."

"Thank you, Franklin," Keri said.

And with that, she and Ray left the West Los Angeles Pacific Division police station. Keri couldn't help but wonder if, for her, it would be the last time.

CHAPTER TWENTY FIVE

They were almost to her place when a wave of exhaustion hit Keri.

"Do you think you could just drop me at home?" she asked Ray. "I'm really tired. I'll just walk over to the lagoon and get my car in the morning."

"Sure," he said and pulled into the small alley behind the building that housed Keri's apartment and the Chinese restaurant below it. It was almost 9 p.m. and the place was pretty empty although the strong smell of Kung Pao chicken still hung heavy in the air.

Keri trudged up the stairs to her place, with Ray, carrying her box from work, right behind.

"You can just put it on the breakfast table," she told him. "I'll deal with it in the morning. It's not like I have anything else to do."

"You want some water?" he asked, apparently refusing to go there.

"Sure," she said and plopped down on the couch. Ray poured two glasses, then handed her one and sat down beside her.

"Quite a day," he said.

"Quite a week," she countered.

"And it's not over yet."

"For me it is," she pointed out.

"No it's not. You've still got work to do. You've got to call your union rep for one thing."

"I'll do it tomorrow, Ray. I just want to give my brain a break for one night, you know?"

"I do," he said.

Keri realized that he must be completely wiped out too. She looked over at him. His eyes were closed. He looked nice that way, relaxed, as if the brutality of the world couldn't quite touch him. She wondered how long it had been before he got used to closing his eyelid over that glass eye, how long it was before he made peace with losing a part of himself.

"What?" he asked, somehow sensing her eyes on him.

"Nothing," she said, though she didn't stop looking at him. "You're an interesting guy, Ray Sands."

"How so?" he asked, opening his eyes and looking back at her.

"Well, if I'd never met you and I saw some huge bald black guy and heard he was a former professional boxer, I don't know that my first thought would be 'He's probably a finder of lost children. He reunites families. He fixes the places that are broken in the world.' I wouldn't have made that leap, I don't think."

He sat up and looked at her, half embarrassed, half confused.

"I think that's the nicest thing you've ever said to me."

"Really?" she asked. "That's pretty sad. It shouldn't be. I've never told you that you're kind?"

"I don't think so," he said.

"Or unfathomably brave?"

"I'd remember that," he assured her.

"Or dangerously attractive?"

There was a long silence as she saw him process her words. She watched him, acutely aware of the Kung Pao scent wafting through the room. She breathed it in, suddenly cognizant of all her surroundings.

She noticed how her floor lamp in the corner cast shadows across the room. She noticed that the dust on her coffee table was disturbingly thick. And she noticed that despite the cold weather, a bead of sweat was rolling down Ray's forehead at the same speed as a drop of condensation on the glass of water he was holding.

"What are you doing, Keri?" he finally asked.

"I'm sorry for the other day," she said. "In the car. I was scared."

"You're not scared now?" he asked.

"No," she said. And somehow she wasn't. She could sense his taut, wired body pulsating with nervous energy. And yet she felt calm, completely, almost lazily at ease.

"What's changed?" he asked, still hesitant despite himself.

"Maybe it's because I've been suspended," she murmured, leaning in close to him, feeling as confident as she ever had in her life. "We're not co-workers anymore."

"What happens when you get your badge back?" he asked, but with less hesitancy than before.

"I'll cross that bridge," she said, pausing to brush his lips lightly with her own, "when I come to it."

They sat there, inches apart, frozen in space and time, for the longest second of Keri's life. And then, without another thought, she kissed him again, this time firmly and deeply. He didn't hesitate anymore, and pulled her toward him, pausing only to brush the hair out her eyes so he could get a better look at her.

Something about that made the blood rise in her and before she knew it, she had pushed him down onto the couch and climbed on top of him, never allowing their lips to part for more than a moment. Ray tried to put his glass of water on the coffee table but missed completely. Keri heard it topple down on the floor and shatter. She didn't care.

*

When Keri woke up the next morning, she discovered that she was in her bed. Then she remembered that after the couch, and the kitchen table, the bed was where she and Ray had eventually ended up.

She glanced at her bedside clock. It was after 8 a.m. She couldn't remember the last time she'd gotten up so late. She rolled over in bed to find that she was alone. Sitting up, she listened for any noise from the bathroom.

"Ray?" she called out. There was no response. She got up, put on her robe, and walked out into the living room. She couldn't tell if the goose bumps she felt all over were due to nervousness or the chill in the morning air.

"Ray, where are you?" she asked even though there were really only two rooms he could be in and if he wasn't in one of them, he wasn't here.

A hint of worry crept into the back of her brain, even though she knew it was ridiculous. Had he bailed? She noticed that the broken glass by the couch had been cleaned up.

Did he clean up the glass and then leave?

She was just shaking the thought from her head when the front door opened and Ray walked in. He was holding a tray with two coffees from the place down the street.

"Good morning, sleepyhead," he said, a broad smile on his face. "I would have left a note, but I couldn't find a pen. Or any paper."

"I figured," she lied, taking the coffee. Feeling shyer than last night she asked, "How are you?"

"I'm very, very good," he said goofily. "I haven't been this good in a long time. How are you?"

"I'm also quite good," she said. "You've performed a valuable service to a lady in need. You're free to go now."

His face dropped and she knew she couldn't continue messing with him.

"Are you always going to be this easy to tease?" she asked.

His smile returned immediately.

"I think you owe me for that," he said playfully.

"Owe? What do I owe you?"

"I can think of something," he replied, moving toward her.

He was leaning to kiss her when her cell phone rang. She recognized the ringtone. It was Susan Granger, the fourteen-year-old teenage prostitute she'd rescued from her pimp and gotten placed in Rita Skraeling's group girls' home.

Ray must have seen something in her eyes because he pulled back.

"I don't know who that is, but I can tell you need to answer it."

"Are you sure?" she asked. "It can probably wait."

"No. It will be eating at you. Answer it."

She didn't need to be told twice.

"Hi, Susan. It's Keri Locke. Is everything okay?"

"Hi, Detective Locke. I'm sorry to call you but it's kind of important," she said. Keri could hear the tension in her voice.

"What is it, sweetie?"

"You know that girl your friend, Ms. Merrywether, brought over yesterday, the one who you found in that warehouse brothel?"

"Yes, of course," Keri said.

"She wants you to come over here. She says she has information about your daughter."

CHAPTER TWENTY SIX

When Keri pulled up in front of the group home, it was almost 9 a.m. After she'd gotten the call from Susan, Ray had immediately dropped her off at her car next to the lagoon and she'd headed straight to the home, taking the back way by the beach along Vista del Mar to avoid the rush hour traffic. Rita Skraeling was waiting for her at the front door when she arrived.

"Her name is Darla—she's thirteen," Rita rasped, as they walked down the long hallway to the bedroom area. "She was hesitant to say anything at first. But Susan got her to open up. She mentioned how a man had come in just before you asking about a girl named Evie. When Susan heard that, she pressed and…well, I'll just let her tell you. She knows more details than I do anyway."

They came to a closed bedroom door at the end of the hall. Rita knocked.

"This is Ms. Skraeling," she said. "May I please come in?"

Keri looked at her, surprised at the normally guff woman's formal demeanor.

"We're trying to reestablish boundaries for them; let them know they are entitled to personal space, both with their bodies and their surroundings."

After a moment, a familiar voice responded.

"Please come in," Susan said.

Rita opened the door and they stepped inside. The room had two full beds. Susan was sprawled casually on one of them, next to another girl, who was hunched over, sitting cross-legged and hugging herself. It was the girl from the warehouse, Darla. She'd been so unresponsive before that Keri hadn't even learned her name. She decided to focus on Susan to try to set the other girl at ease.

"Hey, Susan. How's it going? Read any new Nancy Drew lately?" she asked, referring to the book series. Susan had become obsessed with them and loved discussing each one after she finished. Keri found it a challenge to finish them in time for their weekly get-togethers.

"Hi, Detective. I actually finished the latest the day before yesterday. I'm ready to talk about it whenever you are, although maybe not today."

Keri once again marveled at how the terrified girl she found on the street in the middle of the night only months ago was now brimming with such confidence, totally comfortable in her surroundings. Her blonde hair hung in curly ringlets around her shoulders and she wore a powder blue T-shirt that said "Grrrl Power" in big, bold letters.

"Yeah, let's hold off," she agreed. "I'm a little behind anyway. I see you've got company."

"Yeah, I'm sure you remember Darla. You got her placed here after you helped her get away from the situation yesterday."

Keri was impressed with how Susan did her best to avoid triggering any bad memories for Darla by keeping her language non-specific. She had said on multiple occasions that she wanted to be a cop and Keri could almost imagine her in a blue uniform even now. She stifled the urge to smile.

"Of course I remember Darla. Good to see you again."

Darla glanced up briefly to acknowledge Keri before returning her focus to her lap. The girl was unfathomably pale, as if she hadn't been exposed to sunlight in months. Her black hair had clearly been washed last night but it hung in long, stringy ropes that dangled down, covering the black sweatpants she wore.

"Well, anyway," Susan began, "Darla and I got to talking this morning and she mentioned that a man came in yesterday just before you did and he was asking about a blonde girl named Evie. Do you know that guy?"

"Yes, he's a friend of mine named Uriel. I asked him to go in there and check around because I'd heard that my daughter might be inside and I hoped he could find out."

"Well, Darla heard what he said. And then when you came in later and asked about her too, she recognized you from TV and realized that the Evie he was asking about was your daughter."

"Is that right, Darla?" Keri asked, trying to engage the reticent girl.

Darla nodded without looking up. Then in a quiet voice, almost a whisper, she spoke.

"I'm sorry I didn't say anything yesterday. I was too scared to talk in front of the others. But I felt bad later. So I knew I had to tell you. I saw her."

Keri felt the blood drain from her face. Susan saw it too and held up a hand, as if to say, "stay cool." Keri took a deep breath and forced herself to speak calmly, as if her question was no big deal.

"Darla, did you say you saw my daughter, Evie, in the warehouse?"

Darla nodded again and added in another near-whisper, "Not that day; the day before. They took her away the day before."

"Did they say where they were taking her?" Keri asked in as measured a voice as she could muster.

"I don't want to say," Darla muttered.

Keri opened her mouth and was about to speak when she felt Rita Skraeling's hand gently touch her forearm.

"Easy," she mouthed silently.

Keri swallowed hard, trying not to let the strain she felt leak into her voice. But before she could say anything else, Susan rescued her again.

"Detective Locke, I think what Darla's worried about is, she doesn't want to hurt your feelings. What she has to tell you is sad and she doesn't want the person who saved her to be sad. Is that right, Darla?"

Darla nodded and Susan pressed on.

"But what I told her was that you deal with sad stuff every day. You find girls like me and her every day. And even if it makes you sad, it doesn't stop you from doing it again the next day. Sad is part of the job."

"That's true," Keri agreed, feeling a gut punch as she remembered that sad wasn't part of her job anymore because she didn't have a job.

"I told Darla," Susan continued, "that what makes the sad worthwhile are the happy moments, when you are able to get a kid back to a family that loves them, like that girl Sarah, the one you found in Mexico."

"Yes," Keri said, following along because Susan seemed to know what she was doing and because she was worried the rawness of losing the chance to help girls like this might overwhelm her. "That was a happy moment."

"So I told Darla that anything she can tell you that might give you a chance to find your daughter would be good, even if part of it made you sad."

"Susan's right, Darla," Keri agreed. "If there's anything you can tell me, I'd really appreciate it. I won't be angry that you told me something sad. You didn't cause any of this. It's not your fault. Please don't be afraid to tell me."

Darla seemed to stop breathing. Keri worried that she'd pushed too hard even though she felt she'd barely pushed at all. But just when she was about to give up, Darla raised her head and stared directly at her with her devastated, dark eyes.

"The main man who took her said she was a good catch, because she was feisty and because she was the lady cop's daughter. It makes her more of a prize, like anyone who gets her is actually punishing you. So she's really expensive. They were going to upgrade her to a Hill House Party."

"What does that mean, a Hill House Party?" Keri asked.

Susan jumped in. "They're like the warehouses, lots of girls for sale, but high-end. They use a fancy house in the Hollywood Hills and bring in rich guys, who will pay way more than the warehouse prices."

"How do you know about these?" Keri asked her, trying to keep the horror out of her voice.

"I was taken to one when I was younger," Susan answered. "I think I was eleven. They said I was fresh so I was valuable. But I guess I wasn't so fresh after that because I was never taken back."

"Have you ever been to one of these?" Keri asked Darla, who shook her head. "Do you know how to find them?"

Darla didn't answer so Keri looked at Susan.

"They're pop-ups, also like the warehouses, so not even the clients know where they are until they get a text a few hours beforehand. Sometimes they have a few in a week. Sometimes they go months between parties if they think Vice is onto them."

"So there's no way to know where she'll be or when," Keri said, frustrated.

Susan looked at her, then at Darla. Finally she spoke.

"Tell her, Darla."

Keri bit her tongue, fighting the urge to shake the girl. Darla seemed to be screwing up her courage. Appearing to find it, she lifted her head again.

"I heard them say they were taking her to the Vista and that your daughter was the Blood Prize."

Keri's blood went cold and her fingers began to tingle.

"What does that mean? What do you mean, Blood Prize?"

Darla's head was back down again and she seemed to be shaking. Keri looked at Susan, who had tears in her eyes as she spoke.

"The Vista is the name for the biggest Hill House Party there is. They only do it once a year. They never announce when. It could be tomorrow. It could be in six months. And the Blood Prize is the biggest prize of the night. They auction her off. Whoever pays the most gets to be with her and then..." She trailed off.

"What?" Keri demanded.

"He gets to kill her afterward. He slices her throat, at the stroke of midnight, right there in front of everyone."

A heavy silence filled the room. Susan lowered her head. Not even Rita Skraeling could make eye contact.

Keri suddenly felt dizzy and weak. Her skin was clammy. Her eyes fluttered and then closed involuntarily. Her legs buckled and she sensed that she was falling. She reached out for the wall but felt only empty air.

As she started to go down, she felt arms, four of them, all strong, grab her and keep her upright. She managed to open her eyes slightly and saw that the arms had dragged her over to the other bed in the room and that she was lying on her back. Both Susan and Rita Skraeling hovered over her, worried looks on their faces.

"I'm going to get you some water," Rita said, and then turned to Susan. "Sit with her and hold her hand until I get back."

A moment later Rita was gone and all Keri could see was Susan's face. She felt the girl gently stroking her arm with one hand and squeezing her hand with the other. There was a look in her eyes that Keri couldn't quite place. It wasn't kindness or even sympathy really. And then she identified what it was: determination.

As if to confirm it, Susan leaned and whispered quietly in Keri's ear.

"I have a plan."

Keri's eyes widened with surprise. She still felt dizzy and out of it and wasn't sure she'd heard the girl correctly.

"Wha...?"

"Just listen. I'm going to find out where and when Vista is. And when I do, I'll let you know."

"How?" she asked, the words sounding funny on her numb lips.

"I'm going to go undercover. I'm going to get back into hooking and find a way to get invited to Vista. It's the only way. Otherwise, by the time you find out about it, it will be too late."

"Nooo…"

"Shhh. Rest. Ms. Skraeling's bringing the water. You'll feel better in a minute."

It took several minutes but after some water and a few cookies, Keri did feel better. When she was able to stand up, she thanked Darla for the information and walked with Susan and Ms. Skraeling back down the hall.

"Rita, do you mind if I have a word privately with Susan?" she asked.

"Of course not, if that's all right with her."

"Sure," Susan said, seeming to have expected this. "Why don't we go to the library?"

The library was really just a sun room with a couple of shelves filled with books, a loveseat, and two beanbags. They sat down together on the loveseat. Before Keri could say anything, Susan launched in.

"Don't worry, Detective. I'm not *really* going to do what I said. I'm not crazy."

"Then why did you say it?" Keri asked, unconvinced.

"I saw how hurt you were and the idea just popped into my head. But I know now that it's not something that could really happen. I mean, even if I was serious, what are the chances I'd actually get in? Pretty much zero. I may have read one Nancy Drew book too many."

Keri studied the girl's face. She seemed sincere. But girls who'd learned to survive on the streets were skilled at making people believe what they wanted. Keri was usually pretty good at seeing through such facades. But she wasn't usually this emotionally compromised.

"But," Susan continued, "I would like to reach out to some girls I used to know to find out if they've heard anything. I know it's a long shot but if anyone has a lead, it's worth following, don't you think?"

"I guess you can do that," Keri said reluctantly, feeling as if even that might be too much, "if Ms. Skraeling says it's okay. But nothing beyond that, okay?"

"Okay."

"I need you to promise me, Susan. I don't know what's going to happen with my daughter. But I can't bear to lose you too. You've become very special to me. You have so much potential and I see you fulfilling more and more of it every day. Promise me you won't put any of that at risk."

"I promise, Detective," Susan said, smiling. "It was just a wild thought. I would never do anything that interfered with our book club meetings. I was actually hoping I could get Darla to join the next one. What do you think? Nancy Drew mystery therapy?"

"I'm in," Keri said, as they got up and hugged goodbye.

"See you soon, I hope," Susan said as Keri headed for the door.

"Everything okay?" Rita asked as she met Keri at the front door.

"I think so, just keep an eye on that one," she said, looking back at Susan, who was immersed in a book, her legs curled up under her, her blonde hair gently swaying, the morning sunshine highlighting her untroubled face.

"Why?" Rita asked.

"Because she reminds me of me and that usually means trouble."

*

Keri was on the 405 freeway about halfway home when it happened. She was focusing on the mental image of Susan's curly blonde hair brushing her shoulders, letting it soothe her, anything to keep the bubbling pit of panic in her gut from boiling over.

Susan's hair was like a visual mantra, keeping her from completely falling apart. It was weird how something as small as that could have such a powerful emotional impact on a person.

Suddenly, she had a flash of recognition that almost made her swerve into the next lane of traffic. She could feel herself hyperventilating and reminded herself to breath slower. She looked at the time. It was almost 10 a.m. If she hurried, she could be at the Rainey house by 10:15.

CHAPTER TWENTY SEVEN

Jessica wasn't sure how long she'd been asleep when she was suddenly awoken by the sound of loud music. It was some kind of organ music with men chanting, but they just repeated the same word over and over again: koyaanisqatsi

The door opened and the beekeeper stepped into view again. He raised his hand up in the air as if ordering Jessica to rise. She tried to but had trouble. She'd been lying on the concrete floor for so long and in such an uncomfortable position that both her legs were asleep.

Using the metal pole for support, she finally got up. A second later, she was being hosed down again with water so cold, it took her breath away. After about thirty seconds, the man turned off the hose, walked over, and undid the handcuff attached to the pole. He then attached it to his own arm.

He began walking at a brisk pace. It took Jessica a second to process that she was supposed to go with him. She slipped on the slick floor, stumbled, and fell to her knees, but the man seemed oblivious and kept walking, dragging her for several seconds until she regained her footing.

They were moving down a cold, dimly lit tunnel toward a wooden staircase. When they got there, he immediately began ascending them quickly, even skipping one entirely. It required everything Jessica had to keep up. At the top of the stairs was another metal door just like the one to the room she'd been kept in.

He unlocked it and pulled her through a thick, tunnel-like mass of jungle-style vines, littered with sharp thorns. He seemed undaunted but the sharp points cut into her arms and face and she winced involuntarily. That seemed to make him mad and he tugged hard on the handcuff, yanking her forward forcefully.

And then suddenly there was sunlight, at least some version of it. The roof of whatever place they were in was made of some sort of gauzy canvas and the room was stiflingly hot. There were plants of varying sizes throughout the entire cavernous space. They were in a greenhouse.

Suddenly, Jessica realized that she was no longer in a soundproof room and opened her mouth to scream. The hoarse beginning of the word "help" had just started to escape her lips when the man stuffed a thick rag in her mouth.

She looked at him and though she couldn't see his expression, she knew he must have been anticipating her reaction, wondering whether the rag would be necessary. He tugged at her arm again, even harder this time, and she saw where he was taking her. In the middle of the greenhouse was a long stone slab propped up on two additional stone blocks.

It looked familiar but Jessica couldn't quite place why. She knew she'd seen this sort of thing before somewhere, maybe in a textbook or at a museum. The man took the handcuffs off both their wrists and shoved her roughly onto the slab so that she was lying flat.

He grabbed her right arm and attached it to something dangling from the side of the slab. It was some kind of manacle. As he did the same to her other limbs, she heard him muttering something softly to himself. His voice was low and it took her a few seconds to get it. But after enough repetitions, she understood. He was saying "purify the sinner."

And that's when she realized what she was lying on. It was an altar.

*

Keri was arguing with the FBI agent stationed at the Raineys' front door. She demanded to see the family but the agent, young and square-jawed, simply repeated the phrase he was apparently ordered to say: "You do not have authorization to enter, ma'am. Any requests to talk to the family must go through appropriate channels."

After three times going around with him, she was tempted to get physical. It was only the knowledge that assaulting a federal officer could get her in more trouble than an Internal Affairs investigation that held her back.

They both stood there, staring at each other in awkward, tense silence, when Keri heard the door being unlocked. It opened to reveal Tim Rainey. He was wearing a T-shirt and athletic shorts. The circles under his eyes were so dark from lack of sleep that it looked like he'd been punched in each.

But she noticed that his hair was brushed and his eyes didn't have that wild, panicky look she'd grown accustomed to.

He had the appearance of a man who was resigned to the events around him.

"Let her in," he said quietly but firmly to the agent.

"Sir, she doesn't have auth—" the man started to say before Rainey interrupted him.

"I say who has authorization to enter my home, Agent Buxton. Step aside."

After briefly hesitating, Buxton did so and Keri entered. Rainey closed the door behind her.

"Coffee?" he asked.

"Sure." She wanted to jump in and immediately ask him her questions but sensed that he wanted to address something else. She gritted her teeth and forced herself not to say anything else until she got a better sense of his headspace.

"I'm surprised to see you," he said as he led the way toward the kitchen. "I thought you were kicked off the case."

"Not just the case but the entire force," she answered and seeing his raised eyebrows, continued. "I've been suspended, but not for this. I've had a...controversial last year. I don't always follow protocol to the letter."

"You mean, like secretly helping a guy half out of his mind not get arrested for pulling a gun in a public place and threatening to shoot up a van?"

He was smiling slightly. Keri took it as a good sign and decided to respond in kind.

"That's nothing. I've done stuff way more against the rules than that. Following orders isn't really my thing."

"Well, I wanted to thank you for violating them last night. You were right. Whatever happens with Jess, Carrie and Nate need me. If we're going to survive this, I need to be here for them."

He poured her a cup and then one for himself.

"Where are they, by the way?" she asked.

"They're both sleeping in Nate's room. They need it."

"So do you," Keri pointed out.

"Believe me, I've tried. Not even medication has helped. But I'm pretty sure you're not here to check on my sleeping habits, Detective. I can tell there's something you want discuss. Go ahead."

"You're right," she admitted. "But before I say anything, I need to be clear about a few things. I am no longer on this case and am officially on suspension from the LAPD. So anything I ask is just as a concerned private citizen, you understand?"

"I get it."

"And the questions I have won't necessarily improve the outcome for Jessica," she said. "I don't want you to get your hopes up."

"Understood," he said, sounding as if he really might.

"Okay, let's go back to the first FedEx package you received. The timestamp was one fifty-eight p.m., right?"

"That sounds right," he agreed.

"And we thought that was pretty brazen because Jessica didn't even get out of school until two thirty-five. So he sent it before he had even abducted her. We were all amazed that he would take such a risk because if something went wrong with the abduction and you got the letter, you'd take precautions and he'd likely never get another chance."

"Yeah, we definitely would have. He was taking a big risk."

"But there was something else weird about it, something I didn't really think about until now," Keri said.

"What?"

"That package also had strands of Jessica's hair. But how could he have strands of her hair to send to you at one fifty-eight if he didn't kidnap her until around two forty-five?"

Rainey's mouth dropped open. "How?" he asked, genuinely perplexed.

"He had to have access to your house before the abduction. He's been in your home."

Rainey was quiet for several seconds.

"You think this man broke in and stole some of her hair?" he asked, stunned.

"I doubt that. Your wife works at home. There's not much time when the house is unoccupied and I don't think he'd try it at night. You have a security system and there are too many variables. I think you or your wife let this man into your home. I think he's an acquaintance or someone who worked for you."

"But we already gave you a list of everyone we know and who does work for us," he reminded her. "I thought you didn't find anyone suspicious. And I heard that guy who worked on our neighbor's place, the peeping Tom, was a dead end."

"He was," Keri admitted. "But I think we missed something. I hate to ask you to wake your wife, but I want to go over everyone who's had access to this house with both of you. Can you get her and the list you put together?"

Rainey hesitated for a second. She could tell that he didn't want to wrest his wife from her slumber, especially to confront the possibility that they may have invited a threat into their own home. But he nodded.

"Give me a couple of minutes," he said and left the kitchen.

Keri sipped the coffee but was too anxious to sit still. She got up and wandered around the kitchen, then made her way through some of the other first-floor rooms. Out of the corner of her eye, she saw movement in front of the house and walked over.

She wandered over to the dining room and pulled back the curtain to see what the commotion was. One of the photographers from a local paper had apparently gotten inside the perimeter and had been taking close-up shots of the house. Two officers were forcefully returning him behind the police tape.

Keri looked out at the scene. There were still multiple law enforcement vehicles on the street, and yellow police tape created a wide oval around not just the house but parts of the neighbors' property too.

She glanced at the front yard and saw it was getting torn up by all the foot traffic. A small Nerf football lay in the grass. With everything going on, no one had thought to collect the toy and it rested forlornly, almost hidden by the long blades.

A thought popped into Keri's head and she almost dropped her coffee as she turned and headed toward the stairs. She was about to go up when she saw Tim and Carolyn Rainey leaving Nate's room and tiptoeing toward her. They must have seen the look in her eyes because they immediately picked up the pace. They were only halfway down the stairs when Keri, unable to wait any longer, blurted out her question.

"Do you do your own yard work or do you use someone?"

"We use someone," Carolyn said, taken aback. "George McHugh Tree and Lawn Service. He was on the list. I thought everyone we gave you checked out."

"When was the last time he came out here? Your grass looks a little overgrown."

"It's been several weeks, now that I think about it. He only comes every couple of weeks in the winter, and he had to postpone the last time because one of his guys had quit and he was backed up with other clients. He finally called and said he's supposed to come in a few days. Why?"

"So it's not just him then?" Keri asked. "He has employees?"

"Yes," Carolyn answered, suddenly understanding.

"But they're not on the list," Keri noted.

"No. To be honest, I don't even know their names, and since it's been a while since they were here I never even thought about it. He rotates two or three guys."

"You ever let them in the house, say to use the bathroom?"

"I did it all the time," Carolyn said, her voice faltering.

"I need George McHugh's number," Keri ordered.

Carolyn rushed into the kitchen. Tim stared at Keri, his eyes wide.

"Remember, don't get your hopes up," Keri told him.

A second later, Carolyn returned with McHugh's number. Keri called and got him directly. Until a few weeks before he'd had three employees; he gave her all their names and information. The guy who had quit was Johnny Peters.

"One last thing," Keri asked him. "Why did he quit?"

"He didn't really have a big reason," McHugh said. "Just said he was tired of LA and it was time to move on."

"What was he like?" Keri asked.

"Quiet. Polite. Kept to himself. Mostly just did his job and went home. He seemed to especially enjoy tending the plants; had a real green thumb. I never had a problem with him; was sad to see him go."

Keri hung up and immediately called Jamie Castillo on her cell phone.

"Stir crazy already?" Jamie asked when she picked up.

"I need your help, Jamie," Keri replied brusquely, dispensing with the pleasantries.

"Always," Jamie answered without hesitation.

"But I need you to do it quietly so no one knows it's for me. I don't want you to get in trouble."

"Not a problem. What is it?"

"Just to be clear," Keri reminded her, "it *could* be a problem for you if the wrong people find out that you're helping me. You don't have to."

"Have you forgotten who you're taking to?" Jamie asked, borderline insulted.

"Fair enough. Here's what I need. I'm going to send you the names and social security numbers for three guys who worked for the Raineys' yard service. Put them all in the database and get their driver's license photos. But I want you to focus particular attention on Johnny Peters. See if he has a record. Check for any aliases. And send his photo to Sheriff

Calvert in Missouri to see if he recognizes him. Then let me know what you got, okay? This is time sensitive."

"On it," Jamie said and hung up before Keri could add anything.

The Raineys were looking at her with a mix of anxiety and optimism that was unsettling.

"Please don't start getting too excited," she insisted. "Even if this is the guy, you should prepare yourself for the possibility that it's too late. Tim, you've been a witness to what a cruel bastard he is. The chances that he's already done something horrible are pretty strong. Don't forget that."

They both nodded but she could tell they were allowing a flicker of hope to rekindle itself inside them. And despite her misgivings, she couldn't really blame them.

It only took ten minutes for Castillo to call back. The second she started speaking, Keri could tell they were on to something.

"Keri?"

"Yes."

"I've got Sheriff Calvert on the line with me," she said. "He wants to talk to you. Go ahead, Sheriff."

Keri held her breath, waiting for the older man to speak.

"Detective Locke?"

"Yes, Sheriff, I'm here."

"The Peters guy—I recognize him."

CHAPTER TWENTY EIGHT

Keri hurried to her car as she listened to Calvert. She had just said goodbye to the Raineys, telling them she had a lead she needed to follow up and would get back to them as soon as she knew more.

As she spoke she punched the address listed on Peters's driver's license into her GPS and headed off. It was in Mar Vista, near the Santa Monica Airport. Allowing for a brief stop at her apartment to get her personal non-department-issued weapons, it would take about twenty minutes to get there. She put Sheriff Calvert on speaker.

"So this guy Peters went by another name when I encountered him," he said. "It was also something with a 'J.' It'll come to me in a minute. Anyway, he was part of a religious group. You know those caravans that go from town to town and set up revival tents for services? It was one of those types of things."

"Do you remember anything about the group?" Keri asked. "Were they some kind of cult?"

"They were pretty devout. But I wouldn't call them cult-like. Folks around here are pretty religious as it is. These people were maybe a shade more intense, but not so much that it was a concern, if I recall."

"So what made Peters so memorable?"

"Well, he used to mow my lawn sometimes for one thing. He did it for several folks in town. I think that's how he made his pocket money. But that alone wouldn't stick with me. It's that I had to arrest him once for proselytizing on the street."

"That's not allowed?" Keri asked, surprised.

"No, it is. But he was literally in the street, blocking traffic. And he was a little more aggressive than most. Put his hands on a few people; made them uncomfortable. I got a few complaints so I went down to talk to him. He was very polite and stepped onto the sidewalk but he refused to stop getting in people's space. I politely insisted. He politely declined. So I politely put him in cuffs and took him down to the station for the night."

"What happened after that?"

"Nothing much," he said. "I let him go in the morning. We never had any more trouble from him. I've got so say, he never struck me as the type who might be capable of anything like this."

"So how long did he stay in town?" Keri asked, ignoring the last comment. In her experience, almost no one ever seemed like they were capable of the crimes they committed. That meant nothing.

"I can't recall exactly. I believe the caravan left the county a couple of weeks later and I assume he went with them. I don't remember seeing him after that."

"I'm sorry to interrupt," Jamie piped in. "But I've been checking into Johnny Peters's history, Keri. And it looks like he doesn't exist."

"What?" Keri asked as she looped from Culver onto Lincoln and headed north to Mar Vista.

"He applied for the driver's license three years ago but there's no record of him prior to that. No electric bills, no bank account, no social media presence. Everything starts after that. But there's still not much. He gets paid in cash. Other than the license and the rental agreement at his apartment, there's no paper or digital record of the guy. He doesn't use any city services or if he does, he pays for them in cash. No cell phone bill. And of course, nothing online."

Keri was quiet for a moment. Jamie and Sheriff Calvert both seemed at a loss as well.

"Sheriff," Keri said, hoping against hope. "Any chance you officially booked Peters when you arrested him? Get a mug shot? Take fingerprints?"

"Sure," he answered, sounding a little piqued. "We follow procedure here too, Detective, even for minor misdemeanors."

"I'm sorry," she replied. "I didn't mean to imply you didn't. I was just hoping you might check your records to see if you still have the stuff on file?"

"Of course. But it's been a while. If I had the approximate date, I'm sure I could hunt it down."

"Check the two weeks before and after the date that Noreen Appleton went missing."

Calvert went silent for a moment and she knew the gears were turning in his head.

"Give me a minute," he said.

While they waited, Castillo spoke up.

"Keri?"

"Yeah, Jamie?"

"I didn't want to say it earlier while the sheriff was talking but Ray's standing over me right now. I came into the conference for some privacy and he followed me. Now he's hovering over me, holding out his hand for the phone. He looks pretty pissed."

"Is there anyone else in there with you?" Keri asked.

"No."

"Then put your phone on speaker."

"It's on," Jamie said a moment later.

"How's it going this fine morning, Raymond?" she asked sweetly, trying to short-circuit what she knew was coming.

"I know you're not investigating this case the day after you were suspended from the force," he said angrily, not sounding sure at all, "because no sane person would do that."

"I'm just a regular gal exploring a hunch," she said unconvincingly. "I was about to read you in as soon as I finished talking to Sheriff Calvert."

"Read me in now!"

Before she could respond, Calvert spoke up.

"Hey, folks. I'm just going to pretend I had you on hold and didn't hear any of the conversation just now, if that's all right with you. Having established that, I have some information for you."

"Go ahead, Sheriff," Keri said, glad for the interruption.

"The man's real name is Jason Petrossian. He'd be thirty now. I'm looking at his mug shot and it's definitely the same guy. He was arrested one week before Noreen disappeared. I took the liberty of putting his fingerprints in the federal database just now. It's something I should have done back then, but the thought never even occurred to me at the time."

"What did you find, Sheriff?" Keri asked, certain from his tone that it wasn't anything good.

"Well, about four years before he came through here, he was arrested in Pennsylvania in connection with the disappearance of a twelve-year-old girl named Bethany Jeffers. But the investigators there couldn't definitively tie him to it. They eventually had to release him. He dropped off the grid soon thereafter. The girl was never found."

No one spoke for a several seconds. Finally Keri cleared her throat.

"Thank you, Sheriff."

"Yep," he said softly. "Sorry I can't be of more help."

"You've been a huge help," Ray insisted.

"Yeah," Calvert replied bitterly, "I can't help feeling that if I'd have done a little more due diligence at the time, Noreen Appleton might have been found and your girl wouldn't be missing."

"You couldn't have known," Keri said.

"We all know that's not true," Sheriff Calvert said, his voice thick with regret. "If y'all don't mind I'm going to say goodbye for now. I want to follow up a few threads I should have looked into back in the day."

"Of course," Keri said.

"Please let me know how things shake out there?"

"Will do," Ray promised. He waited for the click indicating Calvert had hung up before saying anything else.

"Keri, you still there?"

"I am," she said, clutching the steering wheel as she braced for more verbal finger-wagging. But his voice stayed level.

"Okay," he said. "Castillo and I are going to my car now to head to Petrossian's apartment. Once we're on the road, I'm calling Agent Crowley to give him the heads-up so he can meet us. Then I'm calling Hillman to update him."

"That all sounds good," Keri said, fully aware that he wasn't finished.

"So far, no one who would say anything knows about your involvement in this. You haven't yet done anything today to completely compromise your career. We can simply say you discovered this lead and passed it on to us. You can turn your car around, go back to your apartment, and no one will be the wiser. Sound good?"

"You know I can't do that," Keri said flatly.

"Of course you can. You're telling me you *won't*."

"I'm less than ten minutes from his place. The extra time it would take you to get there could be the difference between Jessica Rainey living and dying. That's not an option. So I'm telling you I *can't*."

"Will you please at least wait until we get there?" he pleaded. She was impressed. He knew her well enough to change tactics when he realized he was fighting a losing battle.

"If I don't see any signs of imminent threat and you can get there in fifteen minutes, I'll think about it."

"We'll be there," Ray said.

Keri hung up, feeling a little guilty. After all, she had no intention of waiting.

CHAPTER TWENTY NINE

Keri reconsidered her decision when she arrived at the address. Something about the place just didn't feel right.

As she sat in her car down the street, she pulled out her binoculars and studied the apartment. It was in a small complex, the end unit of a building with six studio apartments. They were all on the second floor, directly above their garages.

What troubled her was that the units were so bunched together. There was no way he could carry a girl from his garage up to that apartment without getting noticed. And they were all so small that, if she was alive, there was no way he could keep her quiet enough to avoid detection.

Even if she was dead, the neighbors would smell something. Keri allowed herself half a second to wonder what had become of her that she could note that detail so matter-of-factly and without emotion.

Worry about your fading sense of empathy later. Figure this out.

So if he wasn't keeping her in the apartment, where else could she be? If he had a rented storage unit somewhere, there should be a record of it. Even places that took cash payments usually required an application be filled out with some kind of security deposit held on a credit card.

She glanced around to see if there were any storage places in the immediate area. The apartment was on a hill just off Rose Avenue near Centinela Avenue. It overlooked Santa Monica College. Tiny Santa Monica Airport was also visible in the distance. She could even see a Little League field and a nursery with multiple greenhouses. But there were no storage complexes in sight.

Her phone rang. It was Ray.

"How close are you?" she asked.

"Three minutes out," he said. "Crowley and Winchester are en route too. They may get there first, actually, since the FBI building on Wilshire is closer. They insisted we not enter. They're being very proprietary."

"Yeah, well. I don't think it's the place anyway."

"Why not?" he asked.

"Too small, too exposed. It just doesn't feel right."

"We'll be there to check it out soon," he replied. "Stay out of sight. You don't need the feds seeing you."

"Hurry," Keri insisted. "If this isn't the place, we need to start looking for the right one soon. Got to go—they're here."

Keri hung up and ducked her head as the sedan carrying Crowley and Winchester drove by. They parked a half block from the apartment complex and walked confidently toward it. They gave no indication that they planned to wait for Ray and Castillo.

When they reached the building, Winchester tugged on the bottom of the garage door but nothing happened. It must have been locked. They proceeded up the exterior stairwell and reached the top, in front of Unit 1. Petrossian lived in Unit 6 so they had to pass all the other apartments to get there.

Keri quickly texted Ray to say: *they're here - approaching apt. door.*

When they got close, Crowley peeked through the window. Using her binoculars, it looked to Keri like the curtains were drawn. Both men got on their knees anyway and crawled on all fours until they were in front of the door to Unit 6.

A text came through and Keri looked at it. It was from Ray saying: *pulling up now.*

Keri looked up to see his car pass hers and park a few feet in front of her. He and Castillo got out and looked her way. She pointed at the apartment door and they both glanced up in time to see the FBI agents draw their guns.

The men stood on either side of the door. Keri saw Crowley knock and heard his voice in the distance.

"FBI—we have a warrant. Open up."

They waited about five seconds. Then Crowley spoke again, louder this time.

"FBI—open the door now!"

There was still no response. Crowley nodded at Winchester, who stepped back from the door and kicked it in. He rushed in, followed closely by his partner.

"Let's go," Ray said to Castillo, and then pointed at Keri. "You stay here."

Keri nodded, fighting the urge to sprint to the apartment. She watched Ray and Jamie do exactly that before turning her attention back to the door. No shots had been fired. She could hear voices, although she couldn't understand what they were saying.

Ray had just reached the top of the stairs, with Jamie about midway up, when an explosion suddenly rocked the apartment. A ball of fire shot out the door followed closely by Agent Winchester, who stumbled out covered in flames. She could hear his screams clearly. He dropped onto the narrow hallway floor and tried to roll back and forth.

Keri leapt out of her car and began running toward the complex, her eyes fixed on Winchester. Within seconds, Ray had reached him and was using his own jacket to pat the flames down. Crowley still hadn't come out.

When she got to the foot of the stairs, she found Jamie Castillo lying flat on her back on the ground. She rushed over and bent down close to the young officer. She was conscious and her eyes were open, but she seemed disoriented.

Keri ran her hands along Jamie's body and through her hair, feeling for open wounds or gushing blood. Her face and hands, both exposed, had several small cuts but nothing too bad. Keri felt Jamie's head again, checking for bleeding that might have resulted from landing on it.

"I'm okay," Jamie suddenly shouted. "I used my arms to break my fall. I didn't hit my head."

"Can you hear me?" Keri asked.

"I can't really hear you," Jamie shouted, even louder this time. "My ears are ringing pretty bad."

Keri nodded, took off her own jacket, and rested it under Jamie's head.

"Stay here," she yelled. "Don't try to move."

Jamie nodded her understanding and Keri sprinted up the stairs. Winchester was still on the floor of the hallway. He was no longer on fire but he was writhing around, moaning loudly. Ray was nowhere to be found.

She pulled her gun and slowly approached the charred door of Unit 6. Only then did she realize that she hadn't put on her bulletproof vest. She took a long, deep breath, then pivoted and spun into the room. It took her a second to gather her bearings. Everything was smoking and sections of the room were still burning.

"Over here," she heard a voice call out and followed it.

Ray was in the breakfast nook, kneeling over Crowley, giving him CPR. The FBI agent was unidentifiable, the entire front of his body burned beyond recognition. Ray glanced up at her and shook his head.

"Let's get him out of here," she said.

Ray nodded and put his hands under Crowley's armpits. Keri grabbed the underside of his knees and they carried him outside and laid him down next to Winchester.

"How is he?" someone yelled from the stairwell. It was Jamie, trying to stand and clinging to the railing for support.

"He's dead," Ray shouted back.

"What?"

"She can't hear anything," Keri said. "Her ears are ringing from the blast. How are you able to hear me?"

"I barely can. It feels like church bells ringing in my ears. Maybe being close to a wall helped a little?"

Keri remembered that Ray had reached the top of the stairs as the blast hit. It made sense that not being so exposed might have offered him some minimal protection.

She looked him over and he seemed to be generally okay, although his jeans were bloody on his right upper leg. She bent down closer and saw that there was a chunk of glass embedded in it. Blood was seeping out on either side of it.

"I've got to call this in," Ray said. "Winchester needs an ambulance bad."

"Ray, you've got a big piece of glass in your leg. Look."

He glanced down as he dialed his phone.

"I'll survive," he said, then added, "Is that my ears ringing or do I hear sirens in the distance?"

"Sirens," Keri said, noticing them too.

"Then you should get out of here. There's nothing you can do to help these guys and if you're found here, it will only make it harder for you to get your job back."

Keri looked down at the two men on the ground, one dead and the other not much better. Then she looked over at Jamie, who had slumped down onto the top step of the stairwell.

"I can't just leave," she insisted. "Petrossian set this up. He killed an FBI agent. I have to help."

"I understand, Keri," Ray said, putting the ringing phone to his ear. "But there's nothing you can do right here, right now. Go."

Then he pointed to his phone to indicate someone had picked up.

"Yes," he yelled into the receiver. "This is Detective Raymond Sands, badge number 22391. I need immediate emergency medical assistance at…"

Keri turned her attention away from Ray and back to the two FBI agents on the floor at her feet. He was right, of course. There wasn't anything she could do to help. And if she was found at a crime scene while suspended she could guarantee she'd never get back on the force. She had to go.

The sirens were getting louder but she took a moment to grab Ray's jacket, the one he'd used to douse the flames engulfing Winchester, and delicately placed it over Crowley's mangled face.

He was a good guy. He didn't deserve this.

She looked out across the expanse of homes in the distance. Off to the west, she could faintly see where the land met the Pacific Ocean. Much closer, she could now better see the Little League field she'd noticed before. She could also see the nursery and its greenhouses. The sign appropriately read "Ocean View Nursery."

She also noticed something she hadn't been able to see from her car down below, another greenhouse set apart from the others. It was blocked off by a wooden fence, as if it were on separate property. And it appeared to be in worse shape than all the others. Something in her brain clicked.

"Keri, go!" Ray hissed, shaking her out of her reverie.

She looked up. He was pointing at an ambulance and two police cars speeding down Centinela, just below them. They would be here in less than a minute.

"Be careful with that leg," she yelled as she ran past him and started down the stairs. As she passed Castillo, she patted her on the shoulder. The officer looked up at her with a pleasant but fuzzy expression.

She sprinted back to her car and was just pulling out and heading down the street when she saw the ambulance arrive in her rearview mirror.

She turned right, out of sight of the approaching police vehicles. But she didn't make another right and go down the hill that would start her back on the path to Playa del Rey. Instead, she turned left and headed up the hill, toward that one isolated greenhouse.

CHAPTER THIRTY

Keri sat across the street from the nursery, lost in thought. She ignored the employees who had come out into the street to stare at the burning apartment building several hundred yards away.

She was putting puzzle pieces together in her head, making sure they all fit. Petrossian lived nearby but his apartment wasn't equipped to hide an abducted girl. He would want to keep her someplace close by for easy access, somewhere he felt comfortable.

His boss, George McHugh, had said he really liked caring for plants; that he had a green thumb. Even years ago, back in Elkhurst, he had mowed lawns.

Then she recalled the language of the letters. They were littered with terms like "pruned," "grow," "uprooted," "soil," "weeds," and "fertilizing." She even recalled a reference to a "hothouse" which now seemed obvious in retrospect.

He loved gardening and plants. What better place to keep Jessica than an isolated, out-of-the-way greenhouse within walking distance of his apartment? It wasn't soundproof, but somehow she suspected Petrossian had found a way around that.

She got out of the car and approached a middle-aged woman who looked like the manager of the nursery. She had a tight perm and eyeglasses that hung from a chain on her neck.

"What's up with that one greenhouse behind the fence?" Keri asked.

"What?" the woman said distractedly as she stared at the smoke rising in the air. "This isn't really a good time."

"Ma'am," Keri in her most authoritative voice, "I need your full attention. I'm with the Los Angeles Police Department and I'm asking you about the small greenhouse that abuts this property. Is it part of your business?"

The woman turned to her. She was still irritated but one look at Keri's flashing eyes and she decided not make a fuss.

"It still belongs to the owner of the nursery," she said. "But it had some leaks and water damage so he stopped using it. A local man offered cash to use it, said he'd fix it up and pay monthly rent. He only asked if he could put up a privacy fence so customers wouldn't mistakenly walk in there."

"Have you ever been inside?"

"Once or twice to collect the rent," the woman answered, becoming more interested with each passing question, "why?"

"What's it like in there?" Keri demanded, answering the question with one of her own. "You see anything unusual?"

"No. He did a nice job. It's just a greenhouse with a lot of plants. He's more into tropical vines than I would be. But I think he likes to experiment. Can you tell me what this is about?"

"Just one more question. Is his name Johnny Peters?"

"Yes," the woman said. "You're starting to scare me."

"Listen. I need you to close the nursery. You and all your employees and customers should leave the property. Do it quickly and quietly. Go down to the local coffee shop or something."

"Is this on the level?" the woman asked suspiciously.

"It's on the level," Keri said, taking her gun out of her holster, knowing it would have the desired effect. "Johnny Peters is very dangerous and you don't want to be anywhere near here when I talk to him."

That seemed to make an impact, as the woman stepped away from her, turned, and shooed everyone to their cars. She started to lock the nursery's front door but Keri stopped her.

"Is there any way back there other than through the fence door?" she asked.

"I guess you could go around the back of the property and climb one of the hedges. They're high though."

"Thank you," Keri said. "Now lock up and get out of here."

As the woman closed the main office and scurried to her car, Keri returned to her own vehicle and opened the trunk. She attached the small pistol inside to her ankle holster and put on the department-issued bulletproof vest Hillman had forgotten to collect from her yesterday. She had forgotten it at Petrossian's apartment and been lucky she hadn't needed it. She wasn't going to make the same mistake twice.

Then she walked along the fence line to the back of the nursery property. She saw the hedges the woman was talking about. They were high but had thick branches that she was pretty sure she could negotiate to climb over the wall.

Before she did, she took out her phone and typed a text. It read:

Found abductor's location. Small greenhouse adjacent to Ocean View Nursery at Centinela & Rose. Not far from his apartment. Suspect name is Johnny Peters aka Jason Petrossian. Concerned he knows he's been made and may take drastic action. Evacuated employees. Going in. Silencing phone. Need backup.

She sent it to Ray, Jamie, Hillman, Edgerton, Suarez, Patterson, and even Frank Brody. There was no way to hide her involvement now. She was committed, no matter the fallout. She might go down for insubordination but if it meant saving Jessica Rainey, it was a small price to pay.

Keri silenced her phone, holstered her gun, and began to scale the most sturdy-looking hedge. The branches held up and she was able to peek over the fence. The greenhouse was only fifteen feet away. No one was in sight and she couldn't hear anything unusual.

As quickly and quietly as she could, she climbed over the wall and made the six-foot drop to the ground. The earth was hard because of the cold and her knees rattled. She thought they might buckle and she'd collapse. But despite the ache, they held steady.

She pulled out her gun again and carefully made her away around to the front of the greenhouse, taking care not to step on any of the crinkly dead leaves on the ground. When she got around to the front she saw that the door was slightly open. She knelt down as low as she could get and approached slowly.

When she was right outside the door, she held still for a moment, straining to hear anything other than the wind, the chimes from the nearby nursery, and the distant sound of sirens, hopefully from an ambulance rushing Winchester, Ray, and Jamie to the nearest hospital.

She slowed her breathing and noticed that when she did, her exhales were visible in the chilly air. With her left index finger, she pulled the door open slightly, listening for any creak. There was the slightest dull whine, barely audible even to her.

She was in a vulnerable position now and knew she had to move fast. Without waiting to think, she pushed the door open hard with her left hand and rolled into the greenhouse at what she hoped was an unconventional angle. She immediately scurried behind a huge pot and surveyed the space.

No one was immediately visible and she still heard nothing. As expected, the greenhouse was filled with plants of various sizes and colors. She had no idea what any of them were and didn't really care. She was just looking for movement from behind any of them.

She made her way around the edge of the place, staying near the larger plants, looking for anyone hiding behind others. At one point, she bumped into a small stool, almost knocking over a can of wasp and bee spray. She managed to right it before it toppled to the ground. After covering the entire length of the space, she felt fairly confident that he wasn't in here.

She delicately stepped out into the center of the greenhouse, fully aware that this place was even more likely to be booby-trapped than his apartment. Now that she finally had a clear line of sight, Keri noticed something she'd overlooked before.

What had initially appeared to be a stone work table in the middle of the room was actually something else. She stepped closer and saw manacles attached near the four corners of the rectangular table.

There were dark bloodstains at one end, about where Keri imagined a prone person's neck might rest. The realization of what was in front of her hit her in a wave and she fought back the urge to retch. This was a sacrificial altar.

As she looked away, she noticed something out of the corner of her eye. Peering in closer, she saw what appeared to be small droplets of fairly fresh blood on the edges of the altar and more, just above the dark bloodstains, where a person's head might be positioned. They were only just starting to dry. Keri guessed they were less than ten minutes old.

The amount of blood was too small to be from a knife slitting or even poking into skin. And then she saw more of them. They were on the ground next to the altar with even more along a line that led toward a thick clump of vines, apparently the ones the nursery manager had mentioned.

They did seem unusual compared with everything else in the greenhouse, thick and curled, like green snakes. And they had sharp thorns, clearly the source of the blood droplets. They must have been difficult to cultivate and maintain. They were so lush that it was hard to see through them into the shadows beyond.

As that thought passed through her mind, she involuntarily lifted her gun and pointed it toward the vines. They were dense enough that someone could easily have hidden in them and come out behind her when she had been studying the altar. She silently chastised herself for not noticing that earlier.

But no one had come out. And now she was aiming a gun into the darkness. If he was in there, he'd given up his tactical advantage.

Or has he? Is this part of his trap?

"Come out with your hands up," she ordered in a voice barely louder than a whisper. There was no movement or sound in front of her.

She took out her pen flashlight and shined it into the darkness, looking for any tripwires or indications of a false floor. Seeing none, she stepped carefully into the thick, ropy foliage, squinting her eyes almost shut to avoid them being poked by the thorns. It was only when she felt the thorns ripping into her skin as she moved forward that she realized they might have been poisoned. It wouldn't have been difficult to dab some of them with a chemical that could incapacitate or even kill her.

Too late to worry about that now.

She moved forward another step to discover she had reached the end of the vine tunnel. She was at the back wall of the greenhouse. But something seemed off. The wall in front of her was too thick to be the polyethylene sheeting that covered the rest of the greenhouse.

She reached out with her flashlight and gently tapped the wall. It was metal, something very thick, maybe even soundproof. She shined the flashlight over the middle area of the wall and saw what she was looking for—a small lever that was clearly some kind of handle. The huge piece of metal was a door, one that almost certainly led underground, which explained how Petrossian was able to create a soundproof environment in a cheap greenhouse.

Pleased with herself, Keri put away the flashlight, got a better grip on her gun, and reached for the handle. She took a deep a deep, calming breath and allowed the stillness and silence to envelop her. Only it wasn't completely silent.

She was just about to open the door when she noticed the faintest noise coming from somewhere above her. It almost sounded like a dull buzzing. She took out the penlight again and pointed it up. Above her was some sort of wooden roof, well hidden among the vines. She moved the light along the wood until the point where it met the door. That's when she saw it.

Protruding from the wooden roof was a tiny nail head, no longer than a centimeter. But it was close to the door and would surely catch on the top of it when opened. And that would force down the door of what was apparently a trap roof, releasing whatever was quietly buzzing inside. Remembering the spray she almost knocked over, she needed only one guess as to what it might be.

Keri briefly considered trying to pull out the nail head. But she worried that doing so might open the trap roof. Besides, there was no guarantee that he hadn't created backups in case she found that one. Frustrated, she stepped out of the short tunnel and back into the main section of the greenhouse.

I don't have time for this. He must know about the raid on his apartment and the explosion. He has to assume that we'll canvass the area and discover that he rents this place. There's not enough time to be so careful. I could already be too late to help Jessica.

Keri walked over to the wasp spray and shook it. It was about half full. She looked around, desperate for some solution, when her eyes fell on a roll of string. Glancing around, she noticed pieces of it all over the greenhouse, being used to pull some plant branches away from each other so they'd grow straight.

If it's strong enough for that, maybe I can use it for something else.

She rolled out a ribbon of the string about ten feet long, cut it with some shears, and returned to the vine tunnel. She placed the spray on the floor near the entrance and stepped back into the thorny cave.

Using her penlight to guide her, she gently twisted the middle section of the string around the nail head several times. Then, holding the two ends of the string carefully, she backed up to the mouth of the tunnel, holstered her gun, and picked up the spray can again.

She got a good grip on the string, wrapping it around her fingers. Then, refusing to think too much about the consequences, she yanked hard. Almost immediately she heard a click and a squeal as the hinged roof trapdoor opened. A moment later there was thud, followed by loud, angry-sounding buzzing.

Keri took a step and waited, knowing what was coming and yet, still terrified.

CHAPTER THIRTY ONE

Keri wanted to run for it but stood her ground, knowing she'd have more success if all her tiny enemies were in one concentrated area. It was taking longer than she expected, as if the little bastards were lost in the vines and couldn't find their way out. And then suddenly, they did.

A massive swarm of bees emerged from the tunnel seemingly all at once, so thick in the air that they created their own dark cloud. They converged toward Keri as she lifted the can and sprayed them in a long arc from front to back.

She saw dozens of the little monsters fall immediately, but the others temporarily dispersed and, seemingly even more livid, swarmed about, trying to regroup. Keri took advantage of their confusion to run for the door. She grabbed a heavy, empty pot along the way. Once the door was halfway open, she propped it with the pot and took a few steps back, waiting for the next inevitable onslaught.

It only took a few seconds before they began flying outside. But because the door was only partially open, she was once again able to hit them in one tight pack. They poured out for a good ten seconds and she sprayed them the whole time.

Finally the horde diminished to a trickle. Keri stopped spraying, stepped back into the greenhouse, kicked the pot away, and closed the door. Looking around, she saw that there were still some bees inside but only a few were still flying with any sense of purpose and they seemed more focused on escaping than attacking.

She was tempted to douse each of them individually but knew she needed the remaining spray for the hive, which she assumed had thudded to the ground in the vine tunnel and would still be housing some additional soldiers.

Stepping over to the vine entrance, she flashed the light inside. The hive was indeed there, lying smashed like honeycombed watermelon. There were bees buzzing desperately around but not as many as she'd expected. She stepped forward, and, holding the crook of her other elbow up to her mouth, nose, and eyes, she sprayed the hive until the can was empty. Then she kicked it into the corner and stepped forward again.

She felt more stings but this time wasn't sure if they were from thorns or bees. She didn't care anymore. She put the penlight away, took out her gun, and pulled on the lever of the metal door. It opened easily and, to her surprise, silently.

She stepped to the side of the entrance where she was out still out of sight and peeked in. The doorway did indeed lead down. There was a steep flight of wooden stairs, lit only by single naked light bulb hanging from an overhead string. She could see just beyond the bottom of the stairs, where what appeared to be a tunnel extended out into the darkness.

Keri was about to step down when she had a thought. As quickly as she could, she took the string she'd used to yank the nail head and wrapped it around the metal hinge of the roof trapdoor. Then she took the other end and tied it to the handle lever so the metal door stayed propped open. That way, she and Jessica would be able to make a quicker escape. It would also allow any law enforcement who found the greenhouse to locate the underground entrance without searching forever.

Satisfied that it was strong enough to hold, she started down the stairs with her eyes focused on the bottom and the tunnel beyond. Even stepping carefully, she found the fourth step to be a little rickety and quickly stepped down to the next one to regain her balance.

The hinge of the fifth step flexed, then popped straight, turning into a vertical slab of wood. The step itself disappeared. Keri realized she had fallen for another one of Petrossian's traps. But there was nothing she could do about it as she lost her balance and careened forward. She hurtled the final ten feet to the ground, her fall broken intermittently by the remaining wooden steps.

Sprawled out on her stomach at the foot of the steps, Keri waited a beat, preparing to deal with the pain of whatever injuries she might have just suffered. Her knee throbbed where it had slammed a step on the way down and her palms felt raw where she'd extended them to take the brunt of her landing. But other than that, she seemed functional. Apparently the soft dirt floor had protected her from anything worse.

She looked around in the dull light, searching for the gun she'd dropped when she'd needed both hands free to brace for the fall. But most of the tunnel was in shadow. It could be anywhere.

Acutely aware of how defenseless she was, Keri reached down for the small pistol in her ankle holster. As she was removing it, she heard movement in the darkness ahead of her. As quickly as she could, she freed the gun and twisted to point it in the direction of the sound.

But she wasn't quick enough. Just as she was extending her arm forward, but before she could pull the trigger, a body rushed forward and a foot kicked her hand hard, sending the pistol flying off somewhere behind her.

She tried to roll away from the figure so she could buy enough time to get to her feet. But her back jammed up against the bottom step, giving her nowhere to go. The figure was coming at her again. While she couldn't see his face, she was able to see that his hands were empty. They were balled up into tight fists headed straight for her face.

Keri was in an awkward position, lying on her side, trapped by the stairs at her back. Still, she managed to raise her right arm to deflect the first punch. She wasn't as fortunate with the second one, which slammed down hard on her right cheekbone.

The force was startling; enough to smash her entire body back against the bottom step. The pain in her cheek made her gasp involuntarily. For a second, her vision was a constellation of flickering dots of color.

As a result, she didn't see the second strike coming. It landed on her right temple, making her lose whatever reserves of coiled tension she'd maintained until then. She slumped back, unable to move or even focus on anything but the screaming pain in her head.

She was dimly aware that someone was dragging her by her feet along the dirt floor. She felt the back of her head bump on a few rocks, but that pain paled in comparison to the pulsating anguish that ran up and down the right side of her face.

Ignore the pain or you will die. Find a way out of this.

Keri forced herself to think. She should be dead. If her attacker had wanted to slit her throat, he could have done it by now. That meant he wanted her alive for a reason, even if only briefly. She had to use that window of time.

She opened her eyes. Despite the blurriness, she saw that she was being pulled toward a lighted room at the end of the tunnel. The man dragging her was hard to see clearly because he was backlit but she could tell he was wearing some kind of mask.

A few moments later they were in the room and she realized what it was—a beekeeper's mask. The sheer weirdness of it made it scarier than she would have expected. Even in so much pain, she felt a fearful tightening in her chest.

His face wasn't fully visible behind the netting but it sure looked like the DMV photo of Johnny Peters. As she was squinting to get a clearer view, she felt her feet hit the ground. He had dropped them. The surface felt harder than before, like asphalt or concrete. As she processed that detail, she saw that he was coming at her.

She tried to lift her hands in defense but they were only mildly responsive and never got higher than a few inches off the ground. His fist crashed into her chest and she felt all the air leave her body.

She coughed and gasped, trying desperately to breathe. After what felt like an eternity, she was finally able to inhale. Slowly, she opened her watery eyes again to discover that she was curled up in the fetal position.

She glanced around and took in the room for the first time. It too was lit by a single bulb above her head. The whole room was encased in concrete, which was surely soundproof. She was lying next to a metal pole that extended from the floor to the ceiling.

On the floor near the pole was a metal bucket lying on its side. Even in her diminished physical state, she smelled something gag-inducing and could guess what the pool of liquid near the bucket was comprised of.

Gently turning her head, she saw legs, four of them, about six feet away. She craned her neck up and saw something that filled her with both relief and horror. Jessica Rainey was standing directly in front of her, alive and conscious.

But Johnny Peters was right behind her. His left arm was gripped tightly around her chest. His right hand held a hunting knife with a six-inch blade at the girl's throat.

Keri tried to speak but found that words were not yet available to her. Breathing was still a challenge. He saw that she was trying and apparently decided that he would beat her to it. And so, for the first time since she'd encountered him, Johnny Peters spoke.

"You have interrupted the purification ritual. So now you will get to observe it. And then you will have the honor of being part of it."

Aware that he could act at any time, Keri made herself speak.

"Your ritual is unclean," she rasped. She wasn't sure where she was headed with this, but anything that might confuse or delay him was worth a shot.

"What?" he demanded, sounding both surprised and angry.

"Johnny," she mumbled as she rolled over onto all fours, "this isn't how you planned it, is it? There's no altar down here. Do you think the Creator would be satisfied with how you're conducting this sacrifice?"

"What do you mean?" he asked, his voice still edgy but more filled with bewilderment than fury now.

"We're beneath the earth, Johnny," Keri said in a stronger voice, grabbing the pole and pulling herself to her feet. "This is no place to honor the Lord, where worms crawl and rats scurry about. I thought you wanted to purify Jessica. But doing it down here is shameful. She should be up there, on the altar, in the full light of the Lord. To do it in this hole would be a transgression against him. Is that what you want?"

As he thought about it, Keri took stock of the situation. She was in pain but she was functional. She knew she could move if she had too. She had no weapon but Johnny Peters didn't seem to have anything but the knife. Jessica looked filthy and terrified. But other than what looked like thorn pricks, she didn't appear to be physically injured.

"You've given me no choice," Peters snarled, snapping her focus back onto him. "You've interfered with the sacrament. It's no longer safe to do it up there. The creator will understand that my motives were true. He will forgive me."

Keri saw his grip tighten on the knife and spoke quickly.

"Will he?" she asked. "Have you really shown pure motives, Johnny?"

"What are you saying?"

"Would someone who is proud of what he's doing hide his face behind a mask? Or would he let the Lord look down upon his servant without hindrance?"

"I took it off before, when I was about to consummate the purification," he insisted.

"Then do it again now, if you have nothing be ashamed of."

He did exactly that, keeping the knife at Jessica's throat as he let go of her with his other hand, ripped the mask off, and tossed it in the corner. The face underneath it didn't evoke any sense of pure evil. Johnny Peters was just a thirty-year-old man with dark blond hair, cut short. His skin was tan, a result of working outside all day. His blue eyes would have been pretty if they weren't so frenzied.

"Satisfied?" he asked petulantly.

"You shouldn't be asking if I'm satisfied. You should be asking if he is, the Creator. I, for one, don't think he is."

"Why not?" he asked, regripping the knife. Keri noticed that he had inadvertently nicked Jessica's neck and a thin line of blood was trickling down toward the burlap dress she wore.

It's now or never. He's confused. I have him on his heels. Go for it.

"Because if he was, why would he have sent me, Jason?"

"What did you call me?"

"I know who you are, Jason Petrossian, because the Creator sent me. He ordered me to stop you. I am his angel of vengeance."

"You're lying! You're just trying to trick me!" He was shouting now.

"Then why would he tell me that I am the guardian angel for them?"

"For who?" he screamed.

"For the girls you tried to kill, Jason. I have been sent to bring them back to you."

"What are you talking about? Tried to kill?"

"You know who I'm talking about, Jason. You tried to kill Bethany Jeffers in Pennsylvania. You tried to kill Noreen Appleton in Missouri. But the Lord resurrected them."

"Resurrected?" he whispered as his eyes widened. Keri saw his grip on the knife loosen slightly.

"He made me their guide," she continued, not wanting to lose the momentum. "I've brought them to you, Jason. I've brought them here, at the Lord's behest, to show you the truth."

"What truth?"

"Ask them yourself," she said, nodding at the tunnel behind him.

Jason turned to look behind him. As he did, Keri reached down, grabbed the bucket on the floor, and silently stepped toward him. He started to turn back to her.

"I don't see—"

But before he could complete the sentence, she was there, swinging the bucket down onto the knife with one hand as she pushed him away from Jessica with the other. Off balance, he stumbled back against the wall of the room.

Everything seemed to slow down. Keri saw Jason looked down at the knife. She hadn't knocked it out of his hand but it had speared the bucket, which now covered the blade. He stared at it as if he couldn't quite understand how such a thing was possible.

"Run, Jessica," Keri yelled at the girl, who looked equally dumbfound. "Down the tunnel and up the stairs."

Jessica Rainey didn't need to be told twice. She turned and sprinted for the door. Jason lunged at her but Keri leapt at him at the same time, knocking him against the open metal door. He crumpled to his knees as the force of the collision bounced her back into the center of the room.

The metal door, which had banged hard against the wall, rebounded and swung back. As they both watched from the ground, helpless to stop it, it slammed shut. Keri heard a clicking sound as it locked in place.

Jason stared at the door in disbelief. Then he turned back to her, his expression turning to a mix of both rage and something close to pleasure. He grabbed the rim of the bucket and yanked the knife free from it. A cruel smile came over his face.

"Now," he said as he got back up, "you're trapped in here with me."

CHAPTER THIRTY TWO

Keri got to her feet as well. An unexpected calm came over her. Jessica was safe. Even if Jason had a key to the door, there was no way he would get to her before she escaped and found help. The police would be here any second, if they weren't already.

Of course, they wouldn't make it in time to help Keri, stuck down in this dungeon with a madman. But something occurred to her in that moment.

I don't need their help.

"No, Jason," she said slowly. "You're trapped in here with me."

A flicker of hesitation passed across his eyes. That was all she needed.

All her training kicked in as she rushed at him. He turned to face her, the hunting knife firmly in his right hand. He started to swing it sideways at her. At the last second, she dropped to the ground, feeling a ripple in the air just above her head as the knife passed over her.

She rolled into him, letting her momentum slam into his legs. He was already off balance from his swing and miss. Keri knocked his feet out from under him, making him topple forward onto his front.

Keri, who had never stopped moving, popped up out of her roll and moved back toward him. He was still holding the knife. Even though he was in an awkward position, he swung it back toward her, just as she'd been expecting.

She stayed barely out of reach and let it pass just in front of her before slamming her foot down on his forearm, pinning it against the ground. The blade was facing away from her so she smashed her other foot down on the back of his hand. His grip failed and the knife fell from his fingers. She kicked it into a dark corner of the room, next to a dark lump she hadn't noticed before, one that looked suspiciously like a body.

Jason was still wincing from having his hand crushed but tried to get up using his other one. Keri kicked his arm out from under him and his left side thudded down hard onto the concrete floor. Now he was lying on his back, gasping for breath.

She didn't wait for him to recover. Instead, she dropped on top of him, her knees using his stomach to break her fall. That forced his chest and head to lurch up and forward like one end of a see-saw, just as she knew they would. She punched his face as it rose to meet her fist. They connected cleanly and his head dropped back down. His skull hit the ground with a satisfying thump.

He groaned in agony but she didn't care. She punched him relentlessly about the chest and face, over and over again. She didn't stop until her knuckles were raw and she could no longer feel her arms.

Finally, she reared back and looked down at him. He was still, other than the slight movement of his chest rising and falling. He didn't appear to be conscious.

In the silence, Keri felt a sudden pounding in her ears. It startled her so much that she lost her balance and fell off Jason Petrossian. After a moment, she realized the sound wasn't actually coming from her own head but from the door. Someone was banging on it.

She thought she heard another noise as well. It sounded like a dull murmuring. Eventually, it hit her. People were on the other side of the door, shouting.

She got onto her hands and knees and patted Jason down. In his right front pants pocket, she found a long metal key. She crawled over to the wall and used it to brace herself as she got to her feet. Then she stumbled over to the door, put the key in, and turned. There was a click. She saw the handle lever move and stepped back as the door opened.

Standing in front of her was Ray. His right thigh was heavily bandaged. Along with him stood the entire Missing Persons Unit. Hillman and Suarez were on either side of Ray, each holding onto him to keep him from losing his balance. Edgerton and Castillo were next. She was leaning heavily on him. Patterson followed and bringing up the rear was Frank Brody. He was bent over, breathing heavily with his hands on his knees.

"You okay?" Ray asked.

"Uh-huh," she said, though she wasn't sure of it. "Petrossian's on the floor in there. He's unconscious for now."

Suarez left Ray to Hillman's care and stepped into the room. Patterson quickly followed. Apparently he was embracing more fieldwork. Keri started to walk out of the room but suddenly became aware that all the pain she had ignored until now was rushing back at her.

The whole right side of her head ached. Her chest burned. And as she stepped forward, the knee that had hit the stairs seemed to lock up on her. She felt herself starting to fall forward.

Keri reached out for the wall but it was too far. She was halfway to the floor when she felt a pair of arms catch her and ease her down gently. She looked up to see Brody's worried face.

"Frank," she said, smiling up into his bloodshot eyes, "I didn't know you cared."

And then she passed out.

CHAPTER THIRTY THREE

Unlike some of Keri's many hospital visits, this one only lasted twenty-four hours. The doctors determined that none of her injuries required more than an overnight precautionary stay. She had bruising on her chest from the punch there. Her knee was swollen but there was no structural damage. Despite being hit twice in the head, she didn't have a concussion.

They had worried that she had an orbital bone fracture near her right eye. She'd gotten that same injury to her left orbital bone in a prior confrontation with another abductor last year. But she'd gotten off lucky this time—only a puffy, purple face.

As she lay on her apartment couch recuperating, multiple well-wishers came by. She did her best to be friendly and conversational. But deep down she was already itching to get back on the hunt for Evie. The doctors had insisted she stay off her feet for at least twenty-four hours and she was already going stir-crazy.

As a result, she found herself getting impatient, despite her best efforts not to. Ray, who was staying with her to help out, clearly sensed her frustration and tried to keep the visits short.

First the Raineys stopped by. Little Nate was excited that a policewoman lived so close and asked if she wanted to come over for a play date.

"Maybe when I feel a little better," Keri suggested, managing to keep the edge out of her voice for the little guy.

Tim Rainey couldn't stop thanking her. He used up all the tissues he'd brought and went through some of Keri's with all his nose-blowing and tear-dabbing. But otherwise he kept it together. Jessica wasn't very talkative but she did hold Keri's hand the whole time they were there. Carolyn lingered a bit as Tim took the kids downstairs.

"The psychologist says she's still in shock," she said when they'd all left. "Recovery is going to take a long time. But she sent her home anyway. She thinks it's better for Jess to be in a familiar environment. We're going to have someone visit daily for a while. But I wanted you to know that physically at least, she's okay. Only some cuts, scrapes, and dehydration."

"I'm glad," Keri said.

"That's because of you. We won't ever forget it. And I won't forget that you saved my husband too. I know you're going through a rough time with your department right now. But you should know—I'm going to be very vocal and visible in the press. If you lose your job, it's not going to be because my voice wasn't heard."

"Thank you, Mrs. Rainey," Keri said quietly.

"It's Carolyn. And by the way, I'm bringing you cookies tomorrow, so be on the lookout."

Other team members came by throughout the day, although Frank Brody didn't make it. According to Edgerton, he claimed to be under the weather. But everyone suspected the guy just couldn't handle any more warm fuzzies.

Castillo called in from the hospital. She was being kept under observation because of the concussion she'd suffered in the bomb blast. She said they expected to let her go the next day and that she'd stop by in person then.

Sheriff Calvert called to check on her as well. He said the department was setting up a team to retrace Petrossian's whereabouts during his time in Elkhurst. Now that they had something to go on, he hoped to find Noreen Appleton's body.

Keri drifted in and out of sleep for much of the late afternoon. When she finally sat up, Ray told her that Mags had called while she was taking a nap earlier and would check back in with her after she'd had a few days to rest. Hillman came by in the early evening and his visit ended up being longer by necessity.

"Are you recovered enough for some updates?" he asked, pulling a kitchen chair into the living room and plopping it down in front of Keri's couch.

"I get the feeling they're coming whether I'm ready or not."

"I'm afraid so," he admitted. "Where do you want to start?"

"How's Winchester?"

"He's in the burn unit with first-degree burns over forty percent of his body. They have him in a medically induced coma so it's too early to know what other damage he might have suffered. I'll keep you posted. Also, I don't know if you want to attend, but Crowley's funeral is the day after tomorrow."

"I'll be there," Keri assured him before quickly moving on. She just couldn't think about that right now. "What's the situation with Petrossian?"

"He's conscious now, under armed guard at the hospital. He was read his rights but he won't stop talking, mostly about purification rituals. He claims that you're an agent of Satan."

"He's hardly the first," Keri muttered sarcastically.

"Yeah, well, it looks like his lawyer is already prepping an insanity defense. And this is one of those rare times when it might work. He's never walking free again but I could see him spending the rest of his days in a pysch ward."

"Did he admit to anything?" Keri asked.

"Not in so many words, but he has made passing references to other towns in his ramblings. The FBI is tracking down every place he's lived and checking for missing persons cases that match his pattern. I hate to say it, but I think they'll find quite a few. And that's not including the other bodies we found in the room beneath the greenhouse."

"Have they been identified yet?" Keri asked.

"One of them has. Carlotta Cantu was the more recent victim, probably killed in the last seventy-two hours. She worked the streets in East LA."

"How old was she?" Keri asked, knowing the answer would gut her.

"She was twelve."

"I wonder why he picked her," Ray said. "She doesn't seem to fit the profile."

"Who knows?" Hillman said. "Maybe there was a connection we don't know about."

"Or maybe," Ray mused, "she was just for practice."

"And the other body?" Keri asked quickly, processing what Ray said but refusing to let it truly sink in.

"It was just a skeleton so no ID yet. We're waiting on dental records. But the medical examiner says she was female, between the ages of twelve and fourteen. She's been dead about three months."

Keri nodded but didn't respond. Ray came over and handed her a cup of tea.

"Tell her the rest," he said to Hillman.

"The rest?" Keri asked quizzically.

"I wasn't going to hit you with everything at once," Hillman said, glowering at Ray. "But I guess I don't have a choice now."

"I guess not," she agreed. "So spill it."

"There's definitive bad news and a less definitive kind of good news."

"Bad news first," Keri ordered. "Always."

"The bad news is that the Internal Affairs investigation is still ongoing. Someone powerful wants to take you down and despite recent events that would work in your favor, they're refusing to close it."

Keri glanced at Ray, who nodded back. They both knew who the "someone powerful" was.

"And the less definitive kind of good news?" she asked, pulling herself into a more upright position.

"You're very popular right now. You just saved a little girl and caught what appears to be a serial child killer. We'll set aside for now the fact that you weren't technically a cop when you did it. The media is on your side. And while Chief Beecher has had to navigate some tricky politics when it comes to you, you know she's always been on your side too. She sees this as a chance to close the door on the whole thing."

"How would the door get closed?" Keri asked suspiciously.

"If she has her way," Hillman said, "with a formal reprimand for your actions in regard to the Collector. After all, he did abduct your daughter. Most people can understand how you might have bent the rules a bit on that one. She wants to move on from this. And in my experience, when Reena Beecher wants something, she gets it, no matter how powerful the forces on the other side are."

Keri was more skeptical but she kept her doubts to herself for now.

"Thanks, Lieutenant," she said.

After he left, she felt a wave of exhaustion wash over her.

"What time is it?" she asked Ray, yawning despite her best efforts.

"Almost seven p.m."

"I don't know how much longer I can last."

"Yeah, it's been a big day for you, what with lying on the couch and all," he said, scooping her up and carrying her into the bedroom.

"Hey! Don't tease me. I'm convalescing."

"I know," he said as he placed her gently on the bed and pulled the covers up for her.

"What about a shower? I haven't showered all day."

"You can shower in the morning," he whispered as he kissed her on the cheek and turned off the lamp by the bed.

"Is that all I get?" Keri demanded, trying to sound put out even as she felt her eyelids getting heavy. "Don't you want to have some sexy time?"

"Soon," he said as he closed the door.

But Keri didn't hear him. She was already asleep.

CHAPTER THIRTY FOUR

When she woke up the next morning it was 7:08. She couldn't remember the last time she slept twelve straight hours. She and Ray were having a leisurely breakfast of the coffee and bagels he'd picked up when Keri's cell phone rang.

"Can you hand that to me?" she asked, as she was on the couch again and the phone was over on the kitchen table.

"Your days of convalescing are coming to a close," he growled playfully as he tossed it to her.

She looked at the screen. It was the number for Susan Granger's group home. She answered, and Susan herself was on the other end.

"What's up, Susan?" she asked.

"Are you sitting down?" the girl asked in a tone of voice Keri had never heard from her. She sounded unnerved, almost panicked.

"I'm lying on the couch. Why? What's wrong?"

"I did what we talked about and reached out to some girls I still keep in touch with on the street. One of them got back to me in an email late last night but I was asleep so I didn't see it until just now."

"Okay," Keri said, the dread in the teenage girl's voice starting to rattle her.

"She said that word around town is that the Vista event that happens once a year, the one with the Blood Prize, is happening tomorrow night."

"Tomorrow night?" Keri repeated, uncertain that she had fully comprehended the words she'd just heard.

"Yes," Susan confirmed. "She said that word is that things are too hot and if they don't do it soon, they might lose out on this year's Blood Prize."

"Why?" Keri asked, noticing that her voice sounded very distant. Ray was looking at her with a concerned expression.

"Because the cops are getting too close. They're calling this year's prize the mini-pig, because they say she's the daughter of a cop."

"Mini-pig?" Keri whispered, barely able to get the word out.

"I'm so sorry, Detective Locke. But Darla was right. They've chosen Evie. She's the Blood Prize."

Keri could barely hear her anymore. She looked up at Ray but he was blurry. Everything was a swirl of sounds and images. She felt the phone slip from her fingers.

She recognized the feeling. This was a panic attack, like the ones she used to get, the ones she thought she'd conquered. But now she knew she hadn't.

And as she began to slip into the familiar, clammy darkness, one last thought passed through her head:

I have thirty-six hours to save her.

And I will.

By God, I will.

A TRACE OF HOPE
(A Keri Locke Mystery—Book 5)

"A dynamic story line that grips from the first chapter and doesn't let go."
--Midwest Book Review, Diane Donovan (regarding Once Gone)

From #1 bestselling mystery author Blake Pierce comes a new masterpiece of psychological suspense. A TRACE OF HOPE is the final book in the Keri Locke series, bringing the series to a dramatic conclusion.

In A TRACE OF HOPE (Book #5 in the Keri Locke mystery series), Keri Locke, Missing Persons Detective in the Homicide division of the LAPD, is closer than she's ever been to finding her daughter. Finally, she gets a fresh lead—and this time, she will do whatever it takes to bring her home alive.

At the same time, a new, urgent case is assigned to Keri: an 18 year old girl has gone missing after being hazed by her sorority. As the race is on to find her, Keri plunges deep into the world of pristine college campuses, and comes to realize that all is not what it seems.

A dark psychological thriller with heart-pounding suspense, A TRACE OF HOPE is book #5 in a riveting new series—and a beloved new character—that will leave you turning pages late into the night.

"A masterpiece of thriller and mystery! The author did a magnificent job developing characters with a psychological side that is so well described that we feel inside their minds, follow their fears and cheer for their success. The plot is very intelligent and will keep you entertained throughout the book. Full of twists, this book will keep you awake until the turn of the last page."
--Books and Movie Reviews, Roberto Mattos (re Once Gone)

Blake Pierce

Blake Pierce is author of the bestselling RILEY PAGE mystery series, which includes eleven books (and counting). Blake Pierce is also the author of the MACKENZIE WHITE mystery series, comprising eight books (and counting); of the AVERY BLACK mystery series, comprising five books; and of the new KERI LOCKE mystery series, comprising five books (and counting).

An avid reader and lifelong fan of the mystery and thriller genres, Blake loves to hear from you, so please feel free to visit www.blakepierceauthor.com to learn more and stay in touch.

www.ingramcontent.com/pod-product-compliance
Lightning Source LLC
Chambersburg PA
CBHW070948120726
47910CB00004B/1159